CW00498282

The LAST of the BAILEYS

꧁꧂

PAULA PAUL

a novel

THE LAST OF THE BAILEYS

Copyright © 2022 Paula Paul. All rights reserved.

ISBN 978-1-66787-532-3 (Print)
ISBN 978-1-66787-533-0 (eBook)

No part of this publication may be reproduced, distributed, or transmitted
in any form or by any means, including photocopying, recording, or other
electronic or mechanical methods, without the prior written permission of
the author, except in the case of brief quotations embodied in critical reviews
and certain other noncommercial uses permitted by copyright law.

This is a work of fiction. Names, characters, businesses, places,
events, and incidents are either the products of the author's imagination
or used in a fictitious manner. Any resemblance to actual persons,
living or dead, or actual events is purely coincidental.

Chapter 1

It had occurred to Trudy that her house might be haunted.

She dismissed that as a foolish thought. She'd always prided herself on being a woman of good sense and practicality, and now, after close to seventy years of living, she was pretty sure that the only thing that haunts is truth.

She wasn't so sure, though, that truth could make rattling sounds in her basement or the sound of glass breaking like someone had dropped one of the Mason jars of canned peas that had been resting on a dark, dusty, cobweb-encrusted shelf for God knows how long. When she went down to look, carrying a flashlight with her, since there was no electricity down there, she found no sign of anything having been broken. Trudy wasn't sure whether any of the Mason jars were unaccounted for because she'd never counted them. She avoided the basement for good reason—it was dark and full of dust and cobwebs, and it always made her sneeze.

When Josephine came walking over from the next block to borrow Trudy's angel food cake pan, the first thing she said was, "What's that rattling I hear? Something under your house?"

"I haven't seen anything," Trudy said. She wasn't giving Josephine any more information than was necessary since she was sure to find a way to turn it into gossip.

"Well, you ought to get an exterminator out here from Littlefield or maybe Lubbock. Could be rats, you know?" Josephine said.

"Oh, I don't think so," Trudy said. The truth was she hadn't considered that it *could* be rats. She hoped that wasn't the case. Rats were worse than ghosts.

"We don't want them infesting the whole town, do we?" Josephine said. "You ought to at least get a cat."

"I'll give that some thought, Josephine."

"By the way, what's going on with Clara?"

"Clara? Nothing that I know of." Trudy handed the cake pan to Josephine, who promptly set it on the kitchen table and sat down.

"I heard she's fixing to quit her job," Josephine said.

"She's no spring chicken. Maybe she just wants to retire," Trudy said as she sat down across from her. "Want some ice tea?" Trudy would never admit she and Clara were the same age, just as she would never say which side of seventy she was. She would only say she was close.

"No, thanks. Tea makes me need to pee, but listen, when I called the sheriff, I tried to get him to tell me what's going on, but he didn't take my hint."

"You called the sheriff to ask him about gossip?"

"Who said it's gossip? And anyway, that's not why I called him. I couldn't get that front burner on my stove to turn on, so I called to see if he could fix it."

"Uh huh." Trudy was losing interest.

"He did, too. Fixed it good as new. He's a nice young man. He grew up in Littlefield, and I heard he's got a girlfriend that lives there. Hope he don't marry her and move back."

Josephine went on for several minutes. Trudy poured herself some tea, dropped four ice cubes in, and sat down across from Josephine again. Trudy was only half listening, but she responded with nods of her head and occasional little murmurs. She wasn't interested in the gossip of the town she'd been away from for decades until recently. She'd never actually lived in Anton, Texas, but her great-grandmother, Julia Bailey, had owned the house Trudy now lived in, and all the family gathered there to visit frequently, so Trudy got to know most of the old-timers in town. The house was still a boarding house when Trudy used to visit there as a child. She had gone down into the basement with her sister and cousins a time or two back then, but they didn't stay long. It was dark and smelled musty. Instead, they would sneak up the stairs to the forbidden rooms on the second floor.

That was back when there were still a few lodgers in the old house that was built back in the 1920s to cater to the railroad men. The tracks were two blocks away. When the trains, now down to two a day, came rumbling though the town, no longer stopping, the old Bailey House trembled with longing for the old days.

"I happen to know she drinks wine every day," Josephine said.

"Oh," said Trudy.

Since Julia didn't want her guests disturbed, the cousins were forbidden to go up to the rooms. Julia never called it a boarding house, despite the three meals a day she served to the boarders. It was a hotel to her, The Bailey Hotel. It was later called the Bailey House by locals. There was a rumor that one of the rooms was haunted because a woman had died in it under mysterious circumstances, which, of course, made it compelling for all the cousins who never obeyed Julia's command to stay out of the rooms.

After Great-grandma Julia died, Great-aunt Maxie took over the place. That was maybe forty years ago. Then Aunt Maxie died, and the house was left vacant for ten years. Now the house was Trudy's. She'd bought it by paying the back taxes. That was three years ago, just after her husband, George Walters, died. He left her with a huge debt due to his bad investments. That was something she hadn't expected. She had to sell her home in an upscale Dallas neighborhood. She bought the old family place from the bank that owned it and had a little money left over to do some repairs. She'd been born a Bailey, but her name had changed with marriage, as had her sister's. When her father died, he was the last in Julia's line to have the name Bailey since he was an only son of Julia's only son. Trudy wanted to be a Bailey and had regretted her name change since the day of her wedding.

"I don't know what they call it now, but we used to say they were shacking up," Josephine said.

Trudy felt as if she was about to nod off, so she took a sip of her tea and pretended to listen. She was thinking of Emily, her daughter who now lived in Chicago. Emily thought her mother had to be out of her mind to buy the dilapidated old place in a small Texas town with half the stores downtown vacant and boarded up. Trudy had to admit it did seem like a crazy thing to do, but she loved the old house, and in Trudy's opinion, her advanced age gave her a license to do what she wanted, even if it seemed crazy to others. Besides, it was a good way to get away from people. She'd grown impatient with most of the human race. Emily accused her of growing cantankerous in her old age after she was left a near-penniless widow.

4

Emily had admonished her that she wasn't to let the adverse circumstances get the best of her. "Remember you're a fighter," Emily had said.

Trudy wanted to tell them that she had never been a fighter, because she'd never had to be. She'd always been taken care of, either by her parents or, she had thought, by her husband. She had no idea how to cope with adverse circumstances.

She was quickly running out of money now. She might even have to start taking in boarders. The thought made her sick to her stomach. It was some small, if strange, comfort to her that she would not be likely to attract boarders in this dying town.

"And now, wouldn't you know it, she's pregnant," Josephine said.

"Mmm," Trudy said. She had no idea who was pregnant.

"Good Lord, it's nearly eleven thirty," Josephine said, glancing at the clock in Trudy's kitchen and standing up quickly. "I left a pot of green beans on the stove. I hope they didn't scorch."

Trudy stood, too, to see Josephine to the door.

"You need to fix that porch roof," Josephine said, looking up at the sagging structure as she left. "It'll fall on somebody one of these days."

"I'll keep that in mind, Josephine," Trudy said.

The house was a big dark place made of wood that had weathered to a silvery color for want of paint. The steps leading up to the wide front porch were in good shape, but Josephine was right: the roof sagged a little, but Trudy ran out of money before she got around to repairing it.

She had heard from Josephine that, before she rescued the old place, it had become Anton's haunted house, infested with teenagers, especially at night, daring each other to wander through the vacant rooms downstairs or climb the stairs to a long hall lined with bed-rooms, some of them still furnished with ancient bed frames and dressers, where the ghost of the dead woman was said to still roam. Recently, she'd learned that the house had added a few ghosts of what people believed to be deceased members of the Bailey family. Trudy never encountered them. Unless that rattling in the basement …

Maybe a neighborhood cat? Not rats. At least she hoped not.

When she bought the house for back taxes, she bought a lot of problems along with it, expensive problems that required plumb-ers and carpenters and electricians and permits as well as an end-less number of supplies. Now, although she was dangerously low on money, it was at least presentable on the inside, but she wished she'd forgone the old-fashioned wallpaper for a light-colored paint and hadn't chosen such dark draperies. Too late to change now. After all, money didn't grow on that tall weeping willows that shrouded the front or the even taller cottonwoods in the back that literally roared in defiance of the wind blowing through their branches.

Trudy had to admit she might not have been able to put up with all the problems with the remodeling contractors if it hadn't been for Adam. He lived in a little house in the back of her property. He'd been there for years. His father and grandfather had also lived there, maybe even a great-grandfather. Trudy couldn't remember.

Trudy and her sister and cousins had often included Adam in their games and adventures when they were growing up, except he was never allowed inside the house unless he was bringing in grocer-ies or had been called in with his father to repair something. Trudy and her cousins and sister called him Adam Again because there had been an Adam who had lived there years ago who had taken care of Grandma when she got too old and blind to take care of herself. Then there'd been another Adam who had lived there when Grandma died and Aunt Maxie had taken over the place. Aunt Maxie claimed her mother never gave that first Adam permission to build his place in the back. He just did it. She couldn't remember when. After Grandma died and Aunt Maxie moved in, she tried to run the second Adam off, but he wouldn't leave. Finally, she just got tired of arguing with him, so she just let it go. Trudy thought her great-aunt secretly was grateful for having the strong, capable man back there, but Aunt Maxie would never admit her gratitude. To her dying day, she said it was a disgrace to have a black man living in her backyard.

To Aunt Maxie's dismay, Adam claimed to be a Bailey, too. Aunt Maxie, like Trudy, was a Bailey by birth. The first Adam said he was descended from slaves who took the name of their owner before the Bailey family moved to Texas from the Carolinas. No one ever took the trouble to find out if it was true. It made no difference to Trudy whether that first Adam had fabricated his ancestry story or not. She could readily admit that she was glad Adam Again lived behind her place.

Trudy went back to the kitchen and noticed that Josephine had left the cake pan on the table. Trudy wouldn't bother to call and remind her. Her request to borrow it was probably just an excuse to come share her gossip anyway. Trudy was about to pour herself a second glass of tea to take to the sitting area by the kitchen. She was going to watch the latest episode of *Better Call Saul* that she had recorded because she always fell asleep if she watched it at night when it was live. She watched something she'd recorded every morning because watching the news made her angry.

As she made her way to the sofa in front of the television, a now-familiar sound filtered up through the new timbers of the floor beneath Trudy's feet. Not a crash this time, just a strange rattling sound.

There was something down there in that basement, or else she was losing her mind. With a resolve that was half anger and half dread, she went back to the kitchen, opened a drawer to retrieve the flashlight, and went to the back door. A cluster of stunted native mesquite brush obscured her view of the slanted wooden door that was the only entrance to the basement. Steps led down to a space under the house. Sometime in the past before Trudy was born, the old entrance to the basement off the kitchen had been closed off and the house's first bathroom built over it. As long as Trudy could remember, there had never been a lock on the opening, which might now be called a cellar door. It was a slanted wooden flap built close to the ground that had to be opened by lifting it up. The only means of security was an oversized rock holding the door down so the wind wouldn't blow it open.

Trudy had just made it down the three steps from the kitchen to the unkempt backyard, which was another project on her to-do list, when she saw Adam waving at her from the back step of his house.

"Hey, Trudy." Adam was a tall, slender man with broad powerful shoulders. When he was a kid, he was just plain skinny. Trudy herself had matured into a rounded shape. She'd given up on dieting, though, and coloring her grey hair was just too much trouble now. She kept it short and grey with soft curls around her face.

"Hey, yourself," she called back to Adam. The July sun was spreading itself like melted butter across the morning.

"You're out awful early," he said, walking toward her across the stretches of patchy grass that were trying to survive in the backyard they shared. The cottonwoods were silent in the stillness, but they already looked thirsty in the morning heat.

"It's nearly noon. I guess you just got up if you think that's early."

He ignored her sarcastic remark and walked toward her. "Where you going with that flashlight? You still hearing noises?"

"I keep telling you; there's something down there."

"Let me have another look," Adam said, holding his hand out to retrieve the flashlight, although he was still a few yards away from her.

She hesitated. "Well … I …" He'd inspected the basement for her before and had found nothing. She was reluctant to ask him to do it again, even if she did hate going down there to do it herself. That outstretched hand was closer now and too tempting to resist.

Adam took the flashlight and turned around to look at her. "You best stay back, Trudy. It'll make you sneeze on account of all that dust. Remember? You sneezed every time you went down there when we were kids."

"I think I'd better have a look at what's making that noise."

"Suit yourself," Adam said and pushed the rock away to open the door. He went down ahead of Trudy but turned himself sideways so he could hold the flashlight on the steps as she descended.

Trudy's eyes scanned the small area as Adam swept the beam of the light from corner to corner. There was nothing to see except a dirt floor and the dust-covered jars on the few shelves against the wall.

"Now, I know I'm not crazy," Trudy said. "I keep hearing a noise coming from down here."

"Could be mice," Adam said.

Trudy answered with a sneeze before she said in a voice that sounded annoyed, "Mice? Never saw a mouse big enough to make that much noise." She was thinking of rats.

"Not likely rats," Adam said, as if he'd read her mind. "Never saw any signs of that. A cat?" Adam offered. That was the same thing Trudy had considered earlier, but now she was convinced it was out of the question.

"A cat couldn't get in with that rock holding the door down."

"Cats have their ways, I reckon," Adam said. "Seen 'em squeeze themselves into little bitty openings like the cracks between the boards."

"Nonsense!" Trudy managed to say before she sneezed again. She headed up the stairs to the opening. With her back to Adam, she couldn't see him, but she could sense that he was grinning and shaking his head at her foolishness for not agreeing with him. She was also keenly aware that he hadn't descended all the way into the basement but had inspected it only with the sweeping of the flashlight's beam.

She turned to him when they were both above ground and told him she'd give him the money to go down to Randall Lumber and Supply to buy a few boards to cover the cracks on the cellar door and a lock to secure it.

"I'd go myself, but I wouldn't be able to get the lumber in my car. You've got that pickup ..."

"Good idea," Adam said, nodding with his face sober, as if the lock and boards were a genius solution.

Trudy replied, "I appreciate it. Couldn't handle long boards by myself." Adam had always been eager to help her when they were growing up. She had been his favorite of all of the cousins. She was glad to see that hadn't changed.

"What? You getting old or something?"

Trudy gave him a withering look and turned away from him. "I'm still not as old as you," she said over her shoulder as she walked toward the steps that led to the kitchen. "Six months younger."

Once inside, she turned on the air conditioner in the kitchen window and went back to the kitchen sitting area. She seldom used the front parlor that had been the lobby when the house was still open to boarders. It always had been and still was the nicest room in the house, even if she now considered striped and flowery wallpaper ugly and the new drapes too dark. She'd put a red velvet Victorian sofa and a dark leather chair in the room, along with some antique tables she'd inherited from her mother. She'd bought old-fashioned standing lamps with fringed shades in a Goodwill Store in Lubbock to place on each side of the fireplace that had been closed up with bricks a long time ago. All of that, she now thought, made the place look like the entrance to a brothel.

She'd found a worn carpet in one of the closets upstairs to place on the floor until she could afford to buy a new one. When her daughter came to visit, she told her not to replace it because worn carpets were fashionable. Trudy thought the entire human race had lost perspective with its fascination for worn carpets and ragged jeans. She didn't say it out loud, though. She didn't want to sound like an old woman.

Trudy had once again just settled on the sofa and turned on the television to watch her recording when her telephone rang. It was a landline with a portable receiver that sat on the kitchen counter. She had a mobile phone, but she was always misplacing it or forgetting to recharge it, so people she knew had learned to use the landline.

The display on the phone printed out a number with an out-of-state area code and the message, "Unknown caller." Trudy turned away. She never answered calls from "Unknown." This time she took the receiver with her and laid it beside her as she once again settled on the couch. The phone stopped ringing.

She had managed to zip through the opening credits of the program she'd recorded and was engrossed in the first scene when something made her glance at the phone again. A message telling her she had voice mail was flashing on the display screen. Probably a charity or a politician wanting money—that was something she ignored.

In that brief moment, the action on the program had advanced to a scene she couldn't connect with the last thing she saw. She'd have to zip back. She went too far back, so she pressed a button to start again. It was the wrong button. The program had disappeared, and a news channel popped up on the screen, showing something about illegal immigrants trying to cross into the US. That was always happening. She didn't want to hear it again.

Everything, it seemed, was conspiring to annoy her this morning. Her solution was to eat a cookie. She was on her way to the cupboard where the cookie jar rested when the phone rang again, and a mechanical voice informed her that it was once again an unknown caller with the same out-of-state phone number. Her level of aggravation rose exponentially. She whirled around and walked back to where she'd left the phone on the sofa with rapid click-clacking steps, ready to tell the caller to remove her name from their calling list.

"What do you want?" she snapped as she pressed the button to activate the phone.

"Aunt Trudy?"

She paused, confused for a moment.

The caller spoke again. "It's Al." There was a moment of silence before he spoke again. "Are you there, Aunt Trudy? It's Albert, your nephew."

It took a moment for Trudy to gather her wits. Al—that was her sister's son, Albert Bailey Daniels from California. For a moment she felt a void in her chest as if her heart had leapt out. Had something happened to Liz, her younger sister, who was well into her seventies?

"Al," she said. She was aware that retort sounded somewhat uncharitable, but she was trying to hold back the temptation to ask if there was something wrong.

"How you doin'?"

"All right," she replied sharply, again.

"I need to ask you for a favor."

A favor? He needed money. Well, she wasn't giving him a penny. He had a good job writing about food and restaurants for some newspaper in LA. Besides, if he really needed money, he could ask his dad. He was an old geezer who spent all of his time on the golf course or on a cruise ship with Liz.

"Aunt Trudy? You still there?"

"Yes." After that one word, she waited, hoping the silence made him uncomfortable.

"Don't worry; I'm not asking for money."

Trudy felt a moment of chagrin mixed with curiosity, but the only word she could come up with was, "Oh?"

"You see, the thing is, you've got that big place, and, well, Mom told me it used to be a hotel or something, and … Anyway, it's got a lot of rooms."

"Where is this going, Al?"

"Well, it's like this. I have a friend who's going to need a place to stay, and—"

She stiffened. "A place to stay?"

"Not for long," Al said. "Don't worry about that. A couple of nights is all."

"Uh huh. Why does he need a place to stay?'

"It's not a he; it's a she."

Trudy paused again before saying, with some suspicion, "I see."

"A woman and her daughter. They're both really nice. I think you'll like them."

"Will I?"

This time the pause came from Al's end of the phone. "Look," he said finally, "I can tell you don't want to do this. I just thought that … Well, never mind. I'll find another way. Sorry I bothered you. Oh, and Mom said tell you hi."

"Wait." Trudy said before he could hang up. "I … well … Why do these people need a place to stay for a couple of nights?"

"Because she's trying to get to Houston, and she's a single mom. Not much money, see. Can't afford motels, so I thought—"

"Why does she want to go to Houston of all places?" Trudy had always hated Houston. It was big and noisy, and the weather was awful.

"She thinks she can get a job there."

"How do you know this woman?" Trudy was suspicious. He'd already ruined at least one marriage with his philandering.

"She's a friend of my wife."

"Alice's friend?"

"Kim. My wife's name is Kim."

"Oh, that's right. Alice was a couple of wives back. Kim's the one that's in real estate or is a house decorator or something like that."

"Kim's a Feng Shui consultant."

Trudy had no idea what a Fung Shui consultant was, so all she said was, "Hmm."

"Well, sorry to bother you, Aunt Trudy. If you're ever in LA …"

"Sorry I couldn't help you, Al."

"Well, thanks anyway, and I'll tell Dad … What's that noise?"

"Nothing to worry about. Just something in the basement."

"You would like Gee Gee and Jazz."

"Gee Gee and Jazz?"

"Gee Gee is Kim's friend. Jazz is her daughter."

"She has a daughter?"

"I told you she's a single mom."

"How old is her daughter?" Trudy was glad she hadn't agreed to have them come. She didn't want a troublesome little kid running around tearing up things.

"Fifteen or sixteen, I think."

A teenager! That was even worse. "Well, tell your mom I said hello."

By the time she hung up the phone, she'd lost interest in the show she'd recorded and had decided to clean the bathroom instead. She was just finishing up when she heard the basement noise again. It was a rickety-rackety sound this time, like dry bones rattling. Trudy grabbed the flashlight from where she'd left it on the kitchen counter and went toward the back door. Just as she stepped out, she heard a low growl of thunder, and she could see that in the time she'd been in the house, the sky had thickened with gray clouds. At the same time, she saw Adam in his pickup driving into the wide space between his house and hers. Several long boards leaned against the tailgate of the pickup.

"Fixin' to rain!" he called to her. "You best get back in the house." He was pulling a blue plastic tarpaulin from somewhere in the back of the pickup. He was trying to throw it across the boards in the back just as heavy raindrops plinked on the hood and cab of the pickup.

Trudy made a futile attempt to cover her head with her flashlight-free left hand. On the horizon in front of her, a branch of lightening flickered, and within a few seconds, thunder roared its approval.

"I was just on my way to check the basement again," she said, shouting against the quickening rain.

"Get inside, Trudy!"

"There's something down there, Adam. There's something in that basement."

Chapter 2

The basement noise continued intermittently during the day while it was raining. It was back the next day, and the next, and even awakened her during the night a few times. Adam was always willing to check the basement for Trudy. There were times when he asked her to wait a few minutes while he finished something he was doing. Sometimes she went down with him, but mostly, she left the basement inspection to him. He never found anything, not when he did the inspection alone, nor when she reluctantly went down with him.

Lately, Trudy had stopped asking for his help, thinking it was probably becoming annoying to Adam. She went down twice without him, although it took her several minutes to unlock the stiff new lock on the door the first time. The next time, the door wasn't locked. That frightened her, so she broke her promise to herself and went for his help.

"I'm sure I locked it when I came out." She was standing in his small living room as she spoke. It was a neat room with no dirty socks or old newspapers lying around. It was a room with no frills,

17

too utilitarian to be called pretty. It smelled of something sweet and spicy.

"New lock," he said, wiping his hands on a kitchen towel. "It's a little stiff, so it doesn't always lock when you think it does."

Trudy had dealt with new locks before. She shook her head. "I don't think so. Someone else must have unlocked it."

"Did you go down to check if there was anybody down there?"

Trudy felt suddenly embarrassed. "Well ... no. I ..."

"Don't worry about it, Trudy. I know you don't like to go down in that dark hole. Never liked it when we were kids either, did you?"

"Adam, it's not that I—"

"Don't worry about it," he said again with a little laugh. "Just leave it to me."

Trudy wanted to say "thank you," but somehow the words just wouldn't form. All she said was, "I'll go with you."

Adam had already started walking toward the cellar, but he stopped, turned toward Trudy, and studied her for a moment. "You sure? It'll make you sneeze."

Trudy opened her mouth to protest, but she gave in to his gaze, which made her think of a cautioning father. "Well, all right. I'll stay up here. I guess I don't like the way it makes me feel."

"Good choice," he said and started out the door again with Trudy following him.

"Check the lock for me, will you?" she said and handed him her key. "You'll need this."

"Guess I will," he said, reaching for it. "Now you go on back inside your house, and I'll let you know what I find."

He found nothing. He told her so as he returned the key to her.

She took the key with a weary sigh. "Do you think I'm losing my mind? I *know* I heard something."

He laughed. "No, you're not losing your mind, Trudy, and I believe you when you say you heard something. Maybe the house settling."

"The house is settling? Adam, you know this house is a hundred years old. It's been settled for a long time." Then, because she still felt a need to thank him, she asked, "Want to come in and have some ice tea?"

He gave her a wave on his way out the door. "No tea, thank you. Gotta get back to work. Bought a bushel of peaches from old Perrin. Now I'm makin' peach preserves. Bring you some when it's done."

Trudy watched him until he disappeared into the back door of his house and went back inside her own house. He was the same Adam Again she'd known when they were kids, still kind, still resourceful and helpful. He had sometimes joined in the games of hide and seek or kickball with Trudy and her siblings and cousins when they were young. Yet, as she had recalled earlier, he wasn't allowed to come into the house unless he came as a helper. It just wasn't done. That must be what they meant by institutional racism. *Cruel times*, she told herself.

She made a silent vow to herself that she wasn't going to think about cruel times or ghosts in the basement anymore. Too troubling. She wanted only peace at this stage of her life.

Her resolve lasted until sometime after midnight. It wasn't the familiar rattling or crashing sound that awakened her this time. Instead, it was wailing—an unearthly bone-chilling sound. Since she'd taken the only downstairs bedroom for herself, the moaning she heard seemed as if it could be coming from under her bed. It went on for perhaps ten seconds after she was awake. She sat up in bed and pulled the covers to her chin, shivering despite the summer heat.

After a minute or two, she slid down in the bed and covered her head, trying to go back to sleep. That made her too hot, and besides, it was hard to breathe with a blanket over her head. She threw the covers back and tried again to sleep, but sleep wouldn't come. When she glanced at her bedside clock, she saw that it was seven minutes after three. With a disgruntled mumble, she got out of bed and went to the kitchen to make coffee. She'd just poured herself a cup when she heard it again—softer this time, but a distinct moaning creeping up from beneath the house.

Her first instinct was to grab the flashlight and hurry across the heavy, dark gloom of the backyard to knock on Adam's door. She got as far as the back step before she stopped, reconsidering. It was a moonless night permitting the stars to sparkle clearly above her. Since the near-deserted town was too far away from city lights and too small to have any of its own, the Milky Way was free to make a gaudy display of itself. When she lived in the city, it was impossible to see the extravagance of the light gushing like spilled milk above her. She took a moment to bask in the experience before she turned toward the cellar door.

The lock was as cantankerous as before. Trudy propped the flashlight against a rock, fixing the beam to shine on the lock. She gripped the shiny new lock with one hand and twisted the key with the other. But it was only after bracing the edge of her foot against the lock and using both hands to turn the key that she unlocked the door. Dropping the key in her robe pocket, Trudy vowed to buy that stuff George used to spray on stubborn mechanical things.

The rain the day before had cooled the air a little. Nevertheless, she was sweating by the time she lifted the heavy and awkward cellar door. It was even heavier than it used to be now that Adam had replaced the old boards with thicker new ones. When she had at last managed to pull the door far enough away from the opening, she let it drop with a heavy thud to the ground. The sound was loud enough to wake the dead, and she turned with some anticipation toward Adam's house, hoping to see a light turned on. Several seconds passed, and the house remained dark.

Trudy picked up the flashlight and headed down the steep, dusty stairs with extreme caution, putting one foot on a step and bringing the other foot beside it on the same step, slowly and deliberately. It was a far cry from the way she used to run down the steps the few times she'd descended into the dark dusty and spidery chasm when she was a child.

She sneezed before she was halfway down, and she stopped on the steps long enough to sweep the light around the small area.

She saw something! A shadowy movement.

Trudy pointed the light toward whatever it was that had stirred. She saw nothing at first, and then … a pair of eyes? She wasn't sure, and she wasn't going to try to make sure. Just as she turned around to head back up the stairs, she sneezed again, this time with such trembling force that she dropped the flashlight. She heard it clatter down the steps and hit the dirt floor. In the same instant, there was blackness. The flashlight must have landed on the switch.

Feeling around the floor with her feet that were shod in bathroom slippers, she felt nothing until something skittered across the top of her right foot. A mouse! She hated mice more than she hated spiders. She wouldn't scream, however. Instead, she turned around toward the stairs.

But where were the stairs? It was too dark to see, and it was so dark inside the cellar that she couldn't make out the opening. There was nothing to do but inch her way toward where she thought the stairs were supposed to be. She crept along, her breath coming in shallow gasps, her back tingling with the certainty that something was behind her, watching.

By the time her foot hit the bottom stair, there was enough light to see the gaping opening above her. She was more certain than ever that there were eyes behind her, trained on her every movement, but she dared not turn around. She began her ascent, but it was dark and her steps were uncertain. Before long, she was crawling up the dusty stairs on her hands and knees. She sneezed four times in quick succession when she finally crawled out onto the sparse grass. As soon as the spasms were over, she ran toward her back door, but she stopped before she reached it. She hadn't closed the cellar door.

Glancing toward Adam's still darkened house, she felt a flare of anger. Why hadn't all the noise she was making awakened him? Damn him! Where was he when she needed him? She wouldn't call out to him or knock on his door. Instead, she went back to the cellar door and lifted it halfway before dropping it with a bang. It didn't make as much noise as she'd hoped, and there were still no lights in Adam's house.

She searched blindly with her hands for the lock, but it wasn't on the latch like it was supposed to be. The forceful crash of the door when she had closed it must have made the lock bounce off. With an angry whoosh of her breath, she kicked at the door and crept back toward the house. What difference would it make that it wasn't locked? There was already something down there anyway.

Trudy didn't sleep for the rest of the night. She got up early, watching the clock so she could call the sheriff as soon as his office opened. While she waited, she would tell Adam what had happened, even if she had to wake him.

Adam waved to her from his back step as she walked out her door. He called out, "Morning, Trudy." She walked toward him and saw that he was holding a cat: big, yellow, and eyeing Trudy with suspicion. "Look at what I found down in the cellar." He was stroking the cat's back and grinning.

"That's not the only thing down there."

"You still think there's a ghost down there?" Adam walked toward her, still holding the cat.

"Ghost or not, there's something down there. I saw it last night."

"You *saw* it? You telling me you saw a ghost?"

"I said I saw something. Don't know what it was," Trudy snapped, sounding defensive.

"What were you doing down there at night, Trudy, by yourself?"

"I heard a noise again, Adam. I'm not sure it was human, but it wasn't a cat."

Adam frowned. "If you heard something, why didn't you wake me up?"

Trudy shrugged. "Thought I could handle it by myself." She still sounded defensive.

"Well, did you? Handle it, I mean? Did you handle it yourself?"

"Dropped my flashlight. Had to come back up the stairs. You didn't find it down there, did you? My flashlight?"

Adam shook his head slowly. "Didn't see any flashlight."

"Then whoever was down there must have … What were *you* doing down there, Adam?"

"Saw the door was unlocked, so I went down to see if there was anybody down there. Finally found the lock and the key on the ground over there." He pointed to a spot near the cellar door.

"Yeah, well, that was me that unlocked the door, then lost the lock. I ought to get a new one anyway. That damned thing you bought was too hard to open."

"Yes, ma'am," Andy said and looked away.

Trudy sighed. She knew Adam didn't like to hear people swear, even mild swear words like "damn." "Sorry, Adam. Shouldn't swear, I know. Sometimes it seems like it's called for, though."

Adam nodded and said, "You were always a little testy, as I remember."

Trudy ignored his remark. "That cat got in after I left the cellar open. I swear there's somebody down there. I aim to tell the sheriff soon as it gets to be eight o'clock."

Adam nodded again. "Good idea," he said. "Tell him you want him to have a look."

This time it was Trudy who frowned and studied Adam's face. "So, you believe me, do you? You believe there really is somebody or some*thing* down there."

"I know you would never lie, Trudy; that's for sure."

Chapter 3

The sheriff knocked on the front door just before noon. Trudy was in the kitchen making a sandwich out of some leftover chicken with a fresh tomato from her garden. She put the sandwich aside and hurried to the front door. She heard the knocking again as she was on her way. There had never been a doorbell installed in the hundred-plus years the house had existed, and Trudy was not inclined to get one now.

When she opened the door, she saw a young man she knew as Hank Richardson. He was tall and slender with a clean-shaven square-jawed face, handsome, probably in his early forties at most. Josephine said he had grown up in Littlefield, just a few miles away. Trudy had met him when she first returned to Anton.

"Hello, Ms. Trudy," he said. "You called about an intruder?"

"In my basement," she answered. "Come on through to the back, and I'll show you." She led him from the front parlor, through the long dining room with its extended table and mismatched chairs where boarders were fed in the past. She led him all the way to the kitchen where she grabbed the flashlight and the key.

"The lock gets cranky sometimes," she said, working hard to make the lock open. "Adam said he'd replace it for me."

"Adam?" the sheriff asked.

"Lives right there." She motioned with her head to Adam's house. "You've probably seen him around town. Adam Bailey?"

"Sure, I've met him. Got the same last name as the original owners of this place. You're kin to them, I hear."

"Bailey is my maiden name, and no, Adam's no kin, if that's what you're really wanting to ask. I know you're curious on account of him being black."

Hank's face turned bright red. "Well, no, I didn't mean to … I mean, I was just …"

"Well, to put your mind at ease, his family has been with the Baileys a long time. Claims his family was owned as slaves by my family back before the Northern Aggression. That satisfy you?"

"Back before the what?"

"Civil War. I forget people don't call it Northern Aggression anymore. It's just that's what people my age were taught to call it back when I was in school, hundred years ago, I guess."

"Here, let me do that for you." Hank held his hand out for the key. Trudy handed it to him, and he opened the lock after only a minor struggle. Lifting the heavy door required even less effort. Trudy proceeded down the steps ahead of him, the flashlight beam lighting the way.

"It was right over there that I thought I saw something." She moved the beam of light to the corner. Hank stepped around her to inspect the area.

"Don't see anything," he said.

"Here, take this." Trudy handed him the flashlight. The sheriff took it and searched the corner again, then walked around the entire perimeter of the cellar room, looking under shelves and behind dusty jars until he had covered virtually every inch of the area.

"I don't see anything, ma'am," he said. "You think maybe it could have been a cat?"

"No." The word came out of Trudy's mouth sharp and definitive.

The sheriff gave her a look she couldn't decipher. Maybe he thought she was just a crazy old lady, but she had no inclination to defend herself.

"Describe the sound to me," he said.

"At first it was just like something or somebody rattling around down here, then they started crying. Or maybe it was moaning."

The sheriff nodded and frowned at the same time, as if he was weighing what she'd just said. "Well, you know, ma'am," he said slowly and deliberately, "sometimes cats make a kinda weird noise that sounds like a baby crying when they—"

"I've heard cats when they're breeding. It wasn't that," she said with the same sharp tone she'd used earlier.

The sheriff looked at her again without speaking at first. Finally, he nodded and said, "You think it was human." It wasn't a question, but it seemed to Trudy to require a response.

"Yes," she said. "It was either that or …"

"Or what?"

"It was human," she said. She wasn't going to tell him it could be a ghost since it would only confirm his suspicion that she was crazy.

Hank took her arm to lead her up the stairs, holding the flashlight so she could see the steps. "Tell you what," he said, "if you hear it again, give me a call, and I'll come over and have a look. Any time. Night or day, okay?"

"Well ..." Trudy took the last step up out of the cellar and turned around to peer into the depths of the chasm.

"I mean it now. We want to get to the bottom of this, don't we?" He handed the flashlight to her, closed the door, and then fished the key out of his pocket and locked it. "Call me. Hear?" He handed the key back to her, tipped his hat, then disappeared around the side of the house, making his way back to his car.

Trudy hesitated before she went back into the house. She was unconsciously twisting the key in her hand while she thought about the noise and the cellar and Hank Richardson's response. At least he was kind enough not to make her feel like a senile old woman, but he must have thought that, just like Adam probably did. Maybe she *was* senile and hearing things that weren't there. Would she be hallucinating next, seeing ghosts or people she used to know who were dead now, people like George, her husband? He wouldn't dare! That would make her angry, and he knew it, and he knew better than to make her angry. Trudy shook her head and was about to start back to the house when she heard Adam's voice.

"What you doing standing out here just staring at nothing, Trudy?"

She turned around to see Adam about to enter his back door. He was carrying a sack from the grocery store. "Just that, Adam. Staring at nothing."

Adam laughed. "Well, all right then," he said as he opened his screen door.

"You just missed the sheriff," she said.

"Did I?" Adam said, holding the screen open with his body. "That Richardson kid's already been here?"

"You know him?" Trudy asked.

"Knew his daddy better. Owned a farm east of town before he went broke during that drought in the seventies and moved to Littlefield. That was after you left," Adam said as he walked toward her, still carrying his grocery sack. "Don't think that kid's been a sheriff more than a year. So you called him, like you said you would."

"Yes, I called him," Trudy said. "I just can't figure out why I keep hearing those noises."

"Find anything?"

"Not a thing." Trudy paused a moment before asking, "Adam, do you think I'm losing my marbles? Like maybe I'm going senile, getting Alzheimer's or something?"

"Why, no. No! 'Course not." He frowned. "Senile? Why, you're no more senile than I am."

Trudy looked at him for a moment, feeling as if she was about to cry. Instead, she laughed. "I guess that's supposed to be a comfort to me."

Adam paused, then laughed with her, grocery sack still in hand. "Got some ice cream in here I got to get in the fridge. You want some? Make you feel better."

For a moment she wanted to hug him for the way he had of always making her feel better, but she settled for a friendly pat on his arm. "Thanks, Adam, but I better not. Gained two pounds overnight from eating cookies."

Adam started back to his house and spoke over his shoulder. "It'll be here when you're ready."

There were no more noises coming from the cellar for the next two days and nights, and Trudy was beginning to feel better, at least most of the time. Occasionally, she worried that the noises she'd heard were all in her imagination and she really was becoming senile. By the third day, she'd decided to quit thinking about it and had gone back to sewing little girls' dresses for the church to take to the homeless shelter in Lubbock. She wouldn't take them herself, but she'd leave them at the church for someone else to deliver.

It was toward the end of the third day, and she had just put away her sewing machine when she heard a knock on the door. She wasn't expecting anyone, especially not this late. It was time to warm up something for supper and watch *Dancing with the Stars*, but she made her way to the front door. Two people were standing there. One of them had striped neon hair, black makeup around her eyes, ragged jeans, and a tattoo on her shoulder of a dog or maybe a wolf. The other one was fairly normal looking: small, with honey-colored hair pulled back in a ponytail, and with eyes the color of hyacinths. She and the younger one were each holding a suitcase.

"Hello, Trudy," the normal one said. "It is so nice of you to do this."

"Do what?" Trudy was still looking at the two of them through the screen door.

"Letting us stay with you until we … Al said he called you … He did call you, didn't he?" The normal one had a puzzled look on her face as she spoke.

"Al called me, all right. I told him …" Trudy sighed and pushed the screen door open. "Come on in." She didn't sound particularly welcoming, even to her own ears, but she couldn't leave two people outside with no place to go this late, could she, even if one of them looked like a circus clown? Damn that nephew! And his mother, her own sister.

As the two stepped inside, Trudy noticed the car parked in front of the house: a faded blue Ford. It looked ancient, and the right front fender had a big dent in it. "I'm Grace," the normal one said, "and this is my daughter, Jasmine. I guess Jasmine is your great-niece." She silently studied Trudy's face for a moment before she spoke again. "Al didn't tell, did he?"

"All he told me was that you are his current wife's friend." Trudy was scrutinizing the two of them equally as intently as they studied her. Grace, she admitted grudgingly to herself, had a rather pretty face. The nose ring and black stuff around Jasmine's eyes made her look like a freak to Trudy.

Grace's soft little laugh was sardonic. "Yes, Kim and I used to be friends before she … Well, the thing is, I was Al's second wife and Jasmine is his daughter." She put her hand on Jasmine's shoulder in a gentle gesture.

Trudy frowned. "No one ever told me he had a daughter. He didn't tell me when he called either!" *So, this little aberration is a part of the Bailey family,* she thought. Jasmine was chewing on a fingernail with a distant look on her face.

"Al didn't mention her? Not surprising."

"Well, he did say something about somebody called Jazz. And Gee Gee. He said your name is Gee Gee."

Grace rolled her eyes. "My name is Grace Elizabeth Ellison. Al called me Gee Gee. And yes, Al insists on calling his daughter Jazz."

Jasmine met Trudy's gaze this time, with her makeup-blackened eyes, analyzing her face. "Yeah," she said. "I hate that name, Jazz. I hate Jasmine too. I'm changing it to Lobo as soon as I'm eighteen."

"Oh." It was the only thing Trudy could think of to say.

"It means wolf," Jasmine said.

Trudy nodded. "Suits you."

Jasmine's surprised look dissolved into a frown. Trudy returned the look with her own frown. "Well," she said, after a while, "there're six bedrooms upstairs. Take your pick. I'll find some sheets for you. Don't suppose you'll need blankets. It's hot up there in the summer. No air-conditioning."

"Thank you," Grace said. She started up the stairs with her suitcase in tow. Jasmine followed her, mumbling something Trudy couldn't decipher.

"Don't suppose you've had supper, have you?" Trudy called out to their backs.

Grace turned around to speak to Trudy and almost bumped into Jasmine. "Yes," Grace said. "We stopped at a McDonald's before we got here."

Trudy felt slightly chastened. It was thoughtful of Grace to do that, but all she did was nod and move away toward the linen closet in the kitchen sitting area to find some sheets for the beds. When she brought the bedding upstairs, she saw that two of the doors were open. One was the first door on the left, and the other was the door to a big room at the end of the hall where there were two beds, one regular size, the other twin size. She'd expected them to choose that room, but she could see from where she stood at the top of the stairs that only Grace was in there, unpacking her suitcase. She could hear Jasmine making noises in the room to her left. She knocked on the door frame.

"Got your sheets," she called.

Jasmine, who had been trying to open the window, turned around toward Trudy. "This window's stuck," she said.

Trudy put the folded sheets on the bed and went to the window. She opened it with one powerful upward shove.

"Awesome," Jasmine said. Trudy didn't know whether that meant "thank you" or not. In the next breath, Jasmine said, "This place is kinda creepy."

"This room is haunted," Trudy said, trying not to show the delight she felt at conveying that to the sullen child. She wasn't disappointed at the response.

"No shit!" Jasmine's blue eyes widened, shining like blue marbles in a black hole.

"No shit," Trudy answered.

"Who?" Jasmine called to Trudy just as she was about to leave the room.

"Who? Oh, you mean who haunts the room?" Trudy shrugged. "Some woman I never met. She died in this room before I was born."

"She was murdered," Jasmine said. "By someone with an ax." It was apparent that she was trying to sound sarcastic.

Trudy laughed. "No, not an ax. They say she was either bitten or stabbed in the neck. Anyway, she bled to death."

"You're shitting me." Jasmine's voice had lost all traces of sarcasm.

Trudy shrugged. "Just telling you what my great-grandmother said."

"Your great-grandmother?"

"Julia Bailey," Trudy said. "She would be your three times great-grandmother, I guess. She and her husband built the house as a boarding house. Don't worry. No one else has died in this room, as far as I know." Trudy started for the door again.

"Who killed her?"

"Oh, it was her dead husband. Haven't seen him around since I bought the place."

"Her *dead* husband?" A nervous little laugh escaped Jasmine's throat. "Are you for real? I don't think so!"

"It was after a séance," Trudy said. "The lady—they said her name was Frances—liked to hold séances in this room. Seems the husband wasn't happy with the woman we were discussing, because she took up with another man right after he died. Then she called her dead husband up one night in this very room and told him to, well, go to hell, so to speak. So I guess he took her with him. She comes back sometimes."

"You really believe that? If you do, you're crazy," Jasmine said.

Trudy shrugged. "Whatever." She picked up one set of sheets and walked toward the door. "Oh, I forgot to mention," she said, turning to face Jasmine again. "There's a ghost down in the basement, too. So far it seems harmless." She saw Jasmine's blackened eyes grow wider and brighter.

"You are fuckin' full of shit!" Jasmine said.

Trudy didn't respond and walked toward the door again. Just as she stepped into the hall, Jasmine called to her, "Am I supposed to put these sheets on the bed myself?"

"Looks that way," Trudy said without turning around. She walked out and opened the door to the room across the hall, then went to the window and opened it as well. Before she left the room, she moved an old rocking chair from the corner to a spot a few feet away from the open window. Before she started up the hall to take the sheets to Grace, she called out to Jasmine, "If you leave your door open, there will be a nice cross breeze in your room." Trudy smiled to herself as she made her way up the hall. The cross breeze would also set the old chair to rocking back and forth with no one in it.

Chapter 4

Trudy was asleep in her bedroom when she heard the noise. There was someone or some*thing* in the kitchen. She got out of bed and opened the door just enough to peer into the kitchen sitting area. Jasmine was spreading her sheets and blanket on the couch.

When Trudy got up the next morning and walked through the sitting area on her way to make coffee, Jasmine was still sleeping soundly. The blanket and top sheet had slipped to the floor. She didn't awaken even when the coffee maker started burbling, and she was still sleeping when Grace entered the kitchen, fully dressed in white shorts and a blue T-shirt with her hair freshly combed, although she wore no makeup.

Grace spied Jasmine on the couch and gave Trudy a surprised, questioning look without speaking. Trudy answered with a silent shrug and a gesture for Grace to have a seat at the kitchen table. Trudy set a cup of coffee in front of her and moved the cream and sugar closer to Grace.

"What's she doing down here?" Grace whispered.

"I think she got scared of the room she chose to sleep in as it's supposed to be haunted."

"Supposed to be?"

"Well, you know, just an old story. A woman was killed in that room a long time ago by a jealous husband." Trudy poured a generous splash of cream in her coffee as she spoke.

"Did Jasmine know about that?"

"I told her, but I don't think she believed me. She said I was fucking full of shit."

Grace's face went white, and she set her coffee cup down carefully. "I'm so sorry. She's out of control."

"Obviously," Trudy said.

For a moment Grace looked as if she was about to cry. Instead, she took a deep breath and got to her feet. "We've got to be going. It's a long way to Houston."

Trudy considered telling her she was getting a late start and would never make it there before dark. But it was none of her business, she decided, so she kept silent.

"What time is it?" Jasmine was sitting up on her makeshift bed. Her straight black and purple hair was sticking out from her head, and she looked as if she was still half asleep.

"Time to get up," Grace said. "Get dressed. We need to get on the road."

Jasmine's response was to fall backward onto her bed. Grace ignored her and picked up her coffee cup to take it to the sink. Trudy felt an unfamiliar stab of something she wasn't accustomed to. Was it pity?

"Let me cook you some breakfast before you go," she said despite herself.

"You've done more than enough for us," Grace said. "Get up and get dressed, Jasmine. Help me get the suitcases in the car."

"Mom!" Jasmine whined. "I'm hungry."

Grace gave her daughter a withering gaze but said nothing.

Jasmine mumbled something under her breath, but she got out of bed and headed toward the stairs. Trudy, seeing her in her short pajamas and T-shirt, noticed how small she was, how thin, how like a young child.

"Fold the bedding!" Grace commanded.

Jasmine pretended not to hear and left the kitchen.

"Kind of an unpleasant little brat, isn't she?" Trudy said.

Grace rolled her eyes. "You have no idea."

Amid Grace's protests, Trudy fried two eggs and four strips of bacon and popped bread in the toaster.

"You're too kind," Grace said as they sat down to eat together.

They ate in silence for a few minutes before Trudy spoke. "What's wrong with her?" She motioned with her head toward the doorway through which Jasmine had left.

"She's unhappy," Grace said.

"I can see that."

After another silence, Grace spoke again. "It's none of your business, but she's mad at me and her father for divorcing."

Trudy got up to bring the coffee pot to the table and filled both cups without saying a word.

"Al … Al can be, well, difficult," Grace said. After another long pause, she said, "I should have known. He cheated on his first wife with me. Then after he married me …" Grace raised her eyes to look at Trudy and seemed about to say more, but Trudy spoke first.

"It's none of my business."

38

"Mrs. Walters, I didn't mean to sound so—"

"Yes, you did. You meant to put me in my place. Don't worry about it. I would have done the same thing. You want some sandwiches to take with you?"

"No, thanks," Grace said. "We—"

"So, you get breakfast, but I don't," Jasmine said, coming into the kitchen. She was dressed in the same black pants and shirt she'd worn the day before. Her hair was still sticking out in spikes, just as it was when she woke up.

"I'm going to put the bags in the car," Grace said.

At the same time, Trudy said, "How do you like your eggs?"

"Got any cereal?"

"Corn flakes."

"Gaw!" Jasmine slumped into a chair and picked up the remnants of a piece of toast on her mother's plate. "Scrambled," she said, chewing.

"Fold the bedding while I cook your eggs."

Jasmine had the bedding folded and her breakfast eaten by the time Grace came back to the kitchen. Her face was red, and she was sweating. Her overall look was alarming to Trudy.

"Are you all right?"

"Car won't start." She glanced around as if she might find the answer to why the car was balking somewhere in the kitchen.

"Don't know much about cars," Trudy said, "but I'll have Adam look at it."

"Adam?"

"Lives behind me. I'll walk over and get him. He'll be out working somewhere and won't hear his phone."

Adam was wielding a hoe, chopping at the weeds in his garden, when Trudy approached his house. He looked up when he saw her. "Morning, Trudy."

"I need a favor, Adam. Good morning," she added as an afterthought.

"Sure."

"You know how to fix a car?"

Adam laughed. "Can't say it's my specialty. Not the modern ones with all the computers. Who needs it?"

"I had some company come in last night. Her car won't start this morning."

Adam leaned his hoe against a wheelbarrow. "I'll have a look," he said.

Grace and Jasmine were both standing next to the car as Adam and Trudy approached them. "It just makes this funny kind of grinding noise when I try to start it," Grace said.

"Name's Adam." He extended his hand.

"I'm Grace Daniels, and this is my daughter, Jasmine."

"Pleased to meet you," Adam said. "Y'all kin to Trudy?"

"I used to be married to her nephew," Grace said. She sounded a little stunned at Adam's enthusiastic attitude.

"Uh huh, I see." He glanced at Jasmine. "Your daddy Trudy's nephew?"

Jasmine shrugged before nodding.

"So, you're a Bailey by blood." Adam studied her odd appearance for a moment. "Just you remember that, little girl. You're a Bailey by blood. Ever' thing's gonna be all right." Before either Grace or Jasmine could respond, he shooed them back to the house. "Just wait inside where it's cool. I'll let you know what I find."

Grace sat on the old-fashioned sofa in the parlor, and Jasmine plopped herself on the floor, her back against the wall.

"Talk about weird," Jasmine said. She turned her head to glance out the window at Adam.

Grace took several seconds to respond. "We need to talk," she said finally.

Jasmine rolled her eyes. "The sound of doom! What is it? Lay it on me." She stretched and yawned. "You're going to say you don't like my attitude again, aren't you? Always the same old ..." She stopped speaking when she saw the tears in her mother's eyes. She stood up abruptly. "Oh, give me a break." She left through the front door, letting it slam behind her.

Trudy had seen the entire scene from the entrance to the enormous dining room. She entered the parlor just as Jasmine left. "Not much of anything Adam can't fix," she said. "You okay?" she added when she saw the tears in Grace's eyes.

"Yes," Grace said as she swiped at her eyes with the back of her hand. She turned her head, refusing to look at Trudy.

"Here," Trudy said, handing Grace a box of tissues she picked up from a table next to the sofa. Grace took one and wiped her eyes again, then blew her nose. Trudy sat down in the chair across from her, waiting.

Grace wadded the tissue into a tight ball and held it in her fist. She stared straight ahead as if she were looking out the front window, but Trudy knew she was staring at something only she could see. In a little while, Grace sighed. "I can't just give up. Much as I want to, I know I can't."

"Right," Trudy said.

"I would if I didn't have Jasmine. I'd just throw in the towel."

Trudy worried about what the metaphor meant, but she didn't say anything. She watched as Grace reached for another tissue, blew her nose again, and came to her feet with the slow movements of an old woman. "I'm going to wash my face, and then ..." She didn't finish her sentence as she started for the stairwell.

"Use the downstairs bathroom. Save yourself some steps. It's clean. Just off my bedroom, there."

Grace walked away toward the bathroom, her shoulders slumped. Trudy watched her until she disappeared, thinking she probably had plenty of stuff that was getting her down. She'd lost her job, lost her husband who was no count anyway, and she had a daughter who was fighting her own descent into chaos. That was nobody's business except theirs, Trudy thought. She'd stay out of it. She had problems enough of her own.

When Grace walked back into the room, her face was shining, probably from a rubbing with a towel, Trudy assumed.

"Is there a basement to this house?" she asked.

"Uh, yes," Trudy said with some reluctance.

"Sounds like somebody's down there."

Trudy felt as if something was crawling on the back of her neck. "Really? Wonder what it could be. The door stays locked."

"Maybe a cat or something?" Grace offered.

"I'll have Adam check it out," Trudy said. Her heart was pounding with a mixture of feelings. First, maybe she wasn't crazy after all. Someone else had heard the noise. Her second realization was that it now felt more important than ever to find out who or what was making those noises.

Grace seemed about to say something when Adam walked in the front door, followed by Jasmine. He was holding an awkward-looking metal object with one long appendage and several smaller ones.

"Your distributor's shot, ma'am," he said, looking at Grace.

Grace stiffened. "Are they expensive?"

"New one set you back, I don't know, maybe four or five hundred."

Her face went pale. "That's … that's a lot."

"Well, you can't buy one here anyway. Haven't had a parts store in Anton since the eighties," Adam said.

"I … I'll have to think about it," Grace said as she slumped down onto the sofa again.

"I guess that means we're stuck here." Jasmine sounded more sad than angry.

Grace didn't respond. She was staring straight ahead at nothing again.

Adam sat down beside her. "Sorry, ma'am. I can take my old pickup and try to find you one in Littlefield. Might have to go all the way to Lubbock. It's a kinda old car. Could be hard to find parts."

"You can take my car, Adam," Trudy said. "It's old, but it runs. Might be low on gas."

"No!" Grace said, coming to her feet. "I don't have five hundred dollars. I'll have to think about it." She glanced at Trudy. "I was so dumb! I signed that prenup with Al. Can't even get child support from him."

"Think about it?" Jasmine said. "You think you can come up with five hundred bucks by just thinking about it?"

43

"I'll get a job." Grace grabbed both of the suitcases and held on to them, looking lost. "There must be something in this town I can do."

"Bank's still open," Adam said. "Maybe they can use a teller."

"Velma Holton's been the teller since the late sixties," Trudy said. "She's not going to leave until she dies."

"The quilt shop that young Frazier woman opened a few months ago?"

Trudy shook her head. "She's barely paying the light bill." She looked at Grace who was still holding on to the luggage and wearing a forlorn expression. Trudy knew all the things she had just said had served no purpose but to pour cold water on any spark of hope the young woman might have had. She pushed out a sigh. "Well, you can stay here until you figure it out." She walked toward the back of the house and to her bedroom where her sewing machine waited on the old table. She still had dresses to finish for the church. All the while, she was asking herself why in God's name she'd offered to let the two of them stay with her.

Adam was the only one who spoke, and all he said was, "It'll be okay, Trudy," as he walked through the house toward the back door. He was still carrying the broken distributor. Trudy thought of calling him back and telling him what Grace had said about the noise in the basement, but she let it go. Maybe it could be a cat after all.

Trudy tried to hang on to the idea of a cat in the basement, but it was to no avail. She heard something again that night, wailing, like a person mourning over something. That noise in the basement was not a cat. It had to be a person—whether dead or alive, she didn't know.

Chapter 5

The next morning, Grace came downstairs wearing a black skirt with a white blouse. It was clear, judging from the way she looked, that she hadn't slept much, if at all, during the night. She sat down in one of the chairs at the kitchen table. Trudy turned on the coffee maker and sat across from her.

"Morning," Trudy said.

Grace, who had been staring at the red flowers on the oil-cloth-covered table, glanced up. "Morning," she said. She stared at the flowers again, tracing one of them with the tip of her finger. She sighed and seemed about to speak but said nothing. A little while later, Trudy got up and poured two cups of coffee.

"Your daughter doesn't drink coffee, does she?" Trudy set a full mug in front of Grace.

Grace gave her a startled look. "Jasmine? No, she won't drink it."

"Milk? Orange juice?" Trudy asked.

Grace seemed not to hear her. "We won't be here long. I promise. I'm going to find a job today."

Trudy nodded. "Okay." As she stirred her coffee, it occurred to her that, if Grace went job hunting, she might be stuck with Jasmine all day. "Is your daughter going to look for a job, too?"

Grace seemed surprised at the question. "She could, couldn't she?"

Trudy nodded. "She could, but she'll probably have to change … you know, change the way she looks."

Grace nodded, looking sad, but before she could say anything, Jasmine shuffled into the kitchen still wearing her pajamas, a pair of men's boxer shorts, and an oversized T-shirt. She'd washed all the purple and black color out of her hair in the shower, revealing a light brown color. Her face was devoid of the black eye makeup and looked shiny, but she still bore a sleepy look. She looked closer to ten years old than fourteen, Trudy thought.

"There's orange juice and milk in the fridge," Trudy said.

Jasmine didn't respond. She laid her head on her folded arms as she sat next to her mother.

"Sit up, Jasmine," Grace said. "It's impolite to lie on the table."

Jasmine sat up. "That noise kept me awake. Kept you awake, too. I heard you get up and then I saw you look out the window." By that remark, Trudy knew Jasmine must have slept on the little bed in the same room where her mother slept. Jasmine turned to Trudy. "What the fuck *was* that noise?" There was an accusatory tone to her question.

"Jasmine! Watch your language!" Grace said.

"My name is Lobo." She turned to Trudy. "Well …?"

"Well, what?" Trudy asked.

"That weird noise, what is it?"

"What do you think it is?"

"How would I know?" Jasmine said.

"How indeed," Trudy said.

Instead of a defiant look, which Trudy expected, Jasmine gave her one of fright. She turned back to her mother, looking as if she might cry, but all she said was, "Why are you so dressed up?"

"I'm going to look for a job today." Grace pushed away from the table and stood.

"At least have a piece of toast." Trudy wondered what made her say that. She hadn't felt particularly maternal toward anyone in years.

"I'll get it," Grace said, going to the cupboard. "You want some, Jasmine?"

"Yeah," Jasmine said.

"The proper response is 'Yes, please,'" Grace said.

"Please!" Jasmine sounded resentful.

"Toast, Trudy?" Grace asked.

"Yes, please," Trudy said, glaring at Jasmine.

"What am I supposed to do while you're gone?" Jasmine asked in a few minutes, just as Grace placed the toast in front of her.

"I don't know. Look for a job, maybe?" Grace said. "We need all the money we can get."

Jasmine tore off a bite of toast with her teeth, like an animal tearing at flesh.

A little while after Grace left, Jasmine came downstairs again dressed in shorts and a T-shirt. She hadn't recolored her hair or applied the black makeup around her eyes, but she still had the ring in her nose.

"I heard that noise again," Jasmine said. "Coming from the basement."

Trudy didn't look up from her work of mixing a marinade for the roast she had thawed in the refrigerator overnight.

"Don't tell me you didn't hear it," Jasmine said.

"Okay."

"Okay, what?"

"Okay, I won't tell you I didn't hear it." Trudy still wasn't looking at her.

Trudy couldn't see the annoyed look on Jasmine's face, but she felt satisfaction in believing she could sense it.

"So, you did hear it?"

"Yes," Trudy said. "Many times."

Jasmine sat down in one of the chairs around the table. "So you think this house is haunted?"

Trudy turned to Jasmine and wearily shook her head. "I don't know what to think. I never believed in ghosts before."

"This house is real old, isn't it?" Jasmine asked. "Sometimes old houses are haunted." Apparently, the ghost had helped her lose some of her belligerence.

Trudy set aside the marinade bowl, opened the refrigerator to retrieve orange juice, and set it, along with a glass, in front of Jasmine. "Not so incredibly old. It was built about a hundred years ago."

"A hundred years! Man! That's like ancient. I don't think I've ever seen a hundred-year-old house before."

"Really?"

"Who built it, anyway?" Jasmine took a sip of the orange juice she'd poured for herself and pulled a paper napkin from the small basket-shaped napkin holder Trudy kept on the table. Trudy was surprised at the dainty way Jasmine touched the napkin to her mouth and then folded her hands in her lap.

"My great-grandparents built it. As I said, that's your three times great-grandparents. They catered mostly to crews that were working on the railroad at first. Later, the clientele became a little more diverse."

"Like the woman in the first bedroom upstairs," Jasmine said, speaking more or less to herself.

"During the Depression, all those homeless men who rode the rails—hobos, they were called—marked this house as a welcoming place." Trudy didn't know why she was talking so much, but she couldn't seem to stop herself.

"Can I have some of that coffee?" Jasmine gestured toward the coffee pot. "And what do you mean by marked?"

"I don't know. They painted on it, I guess, with black paint, the old-fashioned kind that's hard to clean off. If you look real close, you can still see some of the marks on that side closest to the train tracks." She poured two cups of coffee and sat down across from Jasmine. "They had special symbols they used, and they painted them on the sides of houses or barns or telephone poles, things like that. You can barely make it out now, but the one on this house is a circle with an "X" in the middle. That meant it was a good place for a handout. Grandma believed in doing her Christian duty. Oh, there was a kind of crude drawing of a cross that meant the people who lived here liked to talk about religion. Grandma and Grandpa both liked to do that. They were the religious sort."

"Wow!" Jasmine said. "Did you ever talk to any of the hobos?"

Trudy laughed. "That was before my time. I was more of the miniskirts and go-go boots era."

Jasmine almost spewed her coffee out of her mouth. "You? In a miniskirt and go-go boots?"

"Well, yes. Why are you surprised?"

Jasmine looked uncustomarily embarrassed. "I don't know, I just … Well, um … You haven't always lived in this house, have you?" She seemed relieved to have found a way to change the subject.

"Used to visit here a lot when I was a kid, but I never lived here. I lived in Dallas for years with my husband and two kids. I've only been in the house three years. I moved in after my husband died. It had been vacant a long time with nobody around to see after it except Adam, and I wanted to get out of the big city, so I moved in here."

"So the original owners lived here until just a few years ago," Jasmine said. "Maybe they don't like what you've done to the place, so they come back and haunt it."

Trudy forced out a laugh. It had never occurred to her that Grandma might not like what she'd done with the place, and even if she didn't, she wouldn't be the type to haunt it. She'd say that was not Christian.

"Why are you laughing?" Jasmine demanded.

"Well, for one thing, Grandma wouldn't haunt anything, and besides, other people have lived here before I moved in."

"Other people? Like who?"

"Aunt Maxie and Uncle Hollis."

"Who?" Jasmine wrinkled her nose as if the names were displeasing to her.

"Aunt Maxie was Grandma's daughter, my great-aunt. Your three times great-aunt. She and Uncle Hollis were bank robbers."

Jasmine spewed out some of her coffee. "What!"

"Oh, they became respectable citizens later on, and they probably wouldn't have robbed the bank anyway if it hadn't been during the Depression when nobody had any money."

Jasmine's eyes were wide. "You're telling me there were Baileys who were bank robbers?"

Trudy nodded. "Aunt Maxie became a devout Baptist afterward, just like Great-grandma. She chewed me out for marrying a Presbyterian."

"That's a good one," Jasmine said. "A religious bank robber. What else is wrong with this family?"

"More than you can imagine," Trudy said, thinking of her grandfather, Grandma's only son, who went to prison for robbing the railroad.

"Tell me."

"Another time," Trudy said, "but don't get the idea they were all bad. One of the grandfathers several greats back was the preacher who performed the wedding ceremony for Abraham Lincoln's parents."

"Oh my God!"

"Another one died at the Alamo. Bailey County is named for him."

"Died at the Alamo, huh? What's so great about that? They lost that battle."

"Be careful what you say!" Trudy cautioned. "You're in Texas now, and besides, you need to remember that you are a Bailey, too."

"Weird people!" Jasmine said. "Just the type to haunt a basement."

Trudy didn't respond. She sat looking into the dark remains in her coffee cup before she got up and went back to stirring the marinade bowl.

"Somebody ought to have a look down there," Jasmine said.

"Be my guest. The key is hanging next to the door, and the flashlight is in this drawer." Trudy pointed to the drawer with the spoon she held in her hand.

"Flashlight?"

"It's dark down there, and there's no electricity."

Jasmine didn't reply. She waited a while before moving with what seemed like great caution toward the drawer Trudy had pointed to. Without a word, she pulled the flashlight from its resting place and grabbed the key from the hook next to the door on her way out. She was still wearing her makeshift pajamas.

Trudy expected Jasmine to be back in the house quickly, but she had finished mixing the marinade, had the roast soaking in it, and had returned to her sewing, and Jasmine still had not returned. She peered out the glass window on the back door, but she couldn't see anything except the big shrub that hid the cellar door from her view. Her instinct was to step outside and have a look, but she suppressed the urge and went to her bedroom where her sewing machine still sat on the little table, waiting for her. She had sewed two side seams and pinned a sleeve to the arm opening when she heard the back door open and bang against the inside wall with a thud.

"Trudy!" Jasmine's voice was loud, and she sounded frightened. "Trudy!" she called again, then added, "Aunt Trudy!"

Trudy stood up from her sewing machine and walked to the doorway. Jasmine was on her way toward the big dining room.

"What is it?"

Jasmine turned around at the sound of Trudy's voice. Her face was white, and her eyes wide. "Oh my God!" she spoke in a voice barely above a whisper. She staggered to the kitchen table and collapsed into a chair.

Trudy took a step toward her. "What's wrong, Jasmine? Are you hurt?"

Jasmine was trembling. "There's something down there! A fucking ghost. I saw her."

"Her? Do you mean you saw a girl ghost?"

"I thought she was coming after me, but she … We got to call the cops!"

Trudy went to the table and sat next to Jasmine. "All right. We'll call the sheriff. Do you want to talk to him?"

Jasmine shook her head, wordlessly.

"If you want me to talk to him, let me make sure I understand. You heard something in the basement. When? Last night?"

Jasmine nodded.

"You went down to the basement to check, and you saw a woman?"

"A ghost," Jasmine whispered.

"A ghost. I, uh … I don't know if the sheriff will believe that."

Jasmine only stared at Trudy, her eyes wide, her face even whiter than before.

"And you think she tried to follow you when you ran away?" Trudy continued.

"Yes. I mean, I don't know … Yes, yes she did." Tears formed in Jasmine's eyes, and Trudy instinctively reached to cover the girl's hand with her own. She removed it quickly when she realized what she'd done and stood up, expecting Jasmine to react with a string of profanities. The girl said nothing. She just shivered and stared at the door as if she expected to see the ghost walk through it.

Trudy went to the counter and picked up the portable phone. After a pause, she said, "This is Trudy Walters. You need to give me a call, Hank. You know my number." She clicked off the phone and spoke to Jasmine. "He's out. I left a message."

"Shit!"

Trudy took that as a good sign, that she was at least coming out of her stupor. "Why don't you go upstairs and get dressed? Then you can come down here and watch TV. It'll keep your mind off of things while we wait," Trudy said.

Jasmine obeyed silently, almost as if she were a robot. She came back to the kitchen dressed in her black jeans and a T-shirt bearing the name of a rock band Trudy had never heard of. She sat down, picked up the remote, and turned on the television without bothering to change the channel. Trudy had left it on PBS the night before. There was a show on about rose pruning, which Trudy was certain wouldn't hold Jasmine's interest. Nevertheless, she kept her eyes on the screen while she chewed at her fingernails.

Trudy went back to her sewing, but she was as restless as Jasmine appeared to be. She'd stitched the collar on the little girl dress on backward and was in the process of trying to rip out the seam to start over when Grace came in through the back door. Jasmine stood up as soon as she saw her and went to her, throwing her arms around her waist.

Grace was startled. "What …? Jasmine, are you all right?"

"Oh, Mommy!" Jasmine said and buried her face in Grace's shoulder. Grace put her arms around her daughter, and as Trudy entered from the bedroom, Grace gave her a look that was half questioning and half alarmed.

"She went down into the basement," Trudy said.

Jasmine pulled herself away, but she didn't leave her mother's side. "There's a fucking ghost down there. I saw it, Mommy. I saw it with my own two eyes."

Grace looked at her, frowning. "You didn't bring it with you, did you? The weed, I mean. I told you to throw it out."

"No, no!" Jasmine said, her head in her hands. I didn't … I mean I did throw it out, like you said. Well, most of it, but I didn't bring it with me, and I swear … You should have seen it. It was so … Oh, I am so scared." Jasmine sobbed and clung to her mother.

"I believe her. She saw *something*," Trudy said. "I called the sheriff, but I had to leave a message."

Grace pulled away from Jasmine. "I'm going down to have a look."

"You'll need a flashlight," Trudy said. "What did you do with it, Jasmine?"

"I … I don't know," Jasmine said. She wiped her eyes with the backs of her hands.

"Never mind. I have one." Grace rummaged in her purse and pulled out a flashlight hardly bigger than a mascara tube.

"That's not going to be much help," Trudy said, but she followed Grace out the door and was prepared to help her unlock the cellar door. However, when they reached the door, it was still unlocked. "Be careful!" she called out as Grace flung the heavy door back with what seemed to Trudy to take very little effort.

"Do you have a gun?" Grace asked over her shoulder.

"A gun. Oh, yes, I do. It was my husband's. It's in my room, I think, but I've never used it. Don't even know if it works."

"Well then …" Grace didn't finish the sentence. With a resigned sigh and using her little light, she started down the stairs. Trudy lingered at the top. In a little while, Jasmine joined her, still chewing her fingernails. Trudy couldn't see much of anything below. It took her a while to gather enough courage to take a few steps down. Behind her, Jasmine was calling out, "Are you okay, Mom?"

"Damn!" The word from Grace's lips drifted up the steps along with a thud like someone hitting the ground.

"Grace?"

There was no answer. A broad beam of light lit up the underground area, making Trudy think Grace must have stumbled on the flashlight Jasmine had dropped, but at least it seemed she had retrieved it. Trudy took another tentative step down the stairs and stopped again when she heard a scuffling sound and Grace's voice again.

"Who are you? Come out from behind that shelf! Come out!" Grace's voice was loud, but it was impossible to miss the quake of fear as she yelled.

Trudy was tempted to turn around and run up the few stairs she had descended, but it seemed wrong to leave Grace down there alone if she was in danger. She started down again but stopped when she heard more scuffling, the sound of someone crying, Grace swearing again, another voice mumbling in a language she couldn't understand. Trudy felt Jasmine hovering behind her, felt her breathing on her neck before she called out in a frightened voice, "Mom! Mom!"

There was more scuffling, and Grace said, "Go on! Get up the stairs!"

Trudy could see Grace at the bottom of the stairs. She was pushing someone in front of her. The person—it looked like a woman—stumbled and almost fell, but Grace gave her a hard shove, forcing her toward the stairs. Trudy and Jasmine both turned and hurried back up the stairs so Grace and the "ghost" could ascend.

The ghost was indeed a woman—short, with a rounded figure and hair the color of a raven. Her skin was like coffee with cream. Although she was no longer crying, her face was tear-streaked. She spoke rapidly and breathlessly in a language Trudy couldn't understand.

"What were you doing down there in my cellar?" Trudy demanded. "You got no business sneaking around and trespassing on my property!"

The woman shook her head and looked at her with dark frightened eyes. She spoke again, this time in English. "So sorry! Need …" She hesitated and lapsed into the foreign tongue again.

"Good Lord, woman. What in the world are you blabbering about?" Trudy demanded.

"She said she needed a place to stay while she looks for her daughter," Jasmine said. "She's speaking Spanish."

"Spanish? You speak Spanish?" Trudy said. "And why does she think her daughter is in my basement?"

Jasmine spoke haltingly to the woman in Spanish, and there was a brief exchange between the two of them before Jasmine turned back to Trudy. "She says she doesn't know where her daughter is, but she wants to find her. I think she said her daughter was adopted, but I'm not sure that's what she said. I've only had two years of Spanish along with what Gonzo taught me."

"Gonzo? Who's that?" Trudy asked.

"My boyfriend," Jasmine said. "Gonzales Gonzales. Neat name, huh?"

Trudy shook her head. "None of this makes sense. She has an adopted daughter and she lost her in my basement?"

"Ask her again," Grace said. She still hadn't let go of the woman's arm.

57

Jasmine blew air out of puffed cheeks in a frustrated manner to speak to the woman again. Their exchange was longer this time. By the time Jasmine turned to Trudy to translate, the woman was trembling, and Grace had to help her sit down on the cellar door. She still hovered over the woman, watching her with a dragon eye.

"Okay," Jasmine said after the lengthy interchange. "Here's what I think she said: Somebody took her daughter away from her, and now she is adopted by someone. Someone in Texas, she said. Now she's looking for her. She couldn't find any place to sleep except your basement while she tries to find a way to go get her daughter."

Trudy felt herself growing more and more frustrated. "That makes no sense to me. People don't just take kids away from somebody and adopt them out, and even if they did, it wouldn't be to anybody in Anton. That's just crazy."

"She was in jail when they took her daughter," Jasmine said. "I forgot to tell you that."

"Jail?" Trudy was indignant. "Well, that probably means it was for the daughter's own good. She's probably better off with—"

"Wait a minute," Grace said, interrupting Trudy. She moved away from the still-trembling woman. "Is she talking about immigration officials taking her daughter and sending the child to an adoption agency? I read about that. It happens when the parent gets deported."

"You mean she's one of those aliens?" Trudy said.

"If she was, then the jail she was in wasn't a jail in the way you're thinking," Grace said. "I mean, she didn't really commit a crime."

"Of course she committed a crime," Trudy said. "Why do you think they call 'em *illegal* aliens?"

"People aren't illegal." A touch of anger came through in Grace's voice.

"Oh come on, you know what I mean. She came across the border without the proper papers."

Jasmine kept punching at her phone and then speaking Spanish, interrupted the two of them. "She says she came here to the border because her daughter was in danger at home. I couldn't understand exactly what the danger was. I think she said her daughter is stupid."

"What?" Grace said.

"All I can say is, breaking the law is stupid," Trudy said.

Jasmine spoke to the woman again. "Her name is Marta Ramondino," she said, turning to Grace and Trudy. She said something else in Spanish to Marta and then translated. "Her daughter's name is Concepcion, and she was stupid when she was in Mexico."

"That doesn't make sense," Grace said, "that she was stupid when she was in Mexico, I mean."

Jasmine sighed heavily and shook her head. "I wish Gonzo was here. I don't know why she thinks her daughter is stupid."

Marta spoke again, her words spilling out in a wild rocky stream, one word stumbling over the next.

"What did she say?" Grace asked.

Jasmine shook her head. "I don't know. She's talking too fast."

"Well, it's clear she's upset," Grace said. "Who can blame her? If someone had taken you, Jasmine, I—"

"I think we should get her inside," Jasmine said. "Before anyone sees her."

"Inside? In my house? Oh no!" Trudy said. Despite her obvious reluctance, she didn't try to stop Grace and Jasmine when they led Marta toward the back door.

Once Marta was inside, she and Trudy stared at each other for a few seconds, Marta with trepidation and Trudy with curiosity. Finally, Trudy forced air from puffed cheeks, giving a resigned sigh.

"Well, I guess you'd better ask her if she's hungry," Trudy said, turning to Jasmine.

"Yes," Jasmine said after she'd consulted her phone again before she spok to Marta in her schoolgirl Spanish. "And thirsty. She wants to know if she can have *agua*. I mean water."

"Water? Get her a glass out of that cupboard next to the sink. I hope she likes cold chicken. That's all the leftovers I have until I cook the roast. I can warm the chicken in the microwave. And some vegetables if I can find some." Trudy was already rummaging in the refrigerator.

Jasmine spoke to Marta while she got water for her, but Marta didn't answer. She was watching wide-eyed as water came out of the front of the refrigerator. In a little while, Trudy set the microwave-warmed plate of chicken, potatoes, and green beans on the table and motioned for her to sit down. Marta sat, bowed her head over the plate briefly, and crossed herself before she began to eat with a zestful eagerness.

"Good Lord!" Trudy said. "Looks like she hasn't eaten in a month."

The next moment, there was a knock on the back door, startling Marta, her fork clattering against her plate. She stood up abruptly and looked at the window in the door. When she saw Adam's face, she collapsed into her chair again. She spoke in a quiet, relieved voice. "Oh! *Señor* Bailey."

Trudy's eyes widened. "You know him?"

Adam knocked again and pressed his face against the window.

"Come in. You know it's open," Trudy called. "You better tell me what's going on!" she said when he opened the door and stepped inside.

Adam gave Marta a brief nod before he turned to Trudy and said, "I see you found her."

"Adam! Tell me what's going on. How long have you known this woman? You have a lot of explaining to do."

"Yes, ma'am." Adam was trying to look contrite, but he wasn't succeeding. "I reckon I have a little explaining to do. I just wanted to help her, is all, and I didn't want you to get in trouble."

"Get me in trouble? I guess so!" Trudy sounded frustrated. "She's illegal, you know."

"Well …" Adam hesitated as if he was trying to get his thoughts in order. "It's illegal for her to be here if that's what you mean. I was going to get around to telling you about her one of these days, because—"

"One of these days? You should have let me know as soon as you knew."

"Yes, ma'am."

"Don't *yes ma'am* me now, Adam. How long were you going to let me wonder about all those noises? I nearly killed myself going down those stairs at night."

"Yes, ma'am. What I mean is, well, I just kept thinking about how your great-grandma, Ms. Julia, always helped those hobos back during the Depression, and I thought you'd want to carry on the tradition. You know what I mean?"

"Don't try to shame me, Adam. I'm providing food for her now. I don't see how she's survived this long without food."

"I been giving her food when I can. Not always easy for me to go down in that cellar, and she couldn't come out in the open to come to my house."

Trudy shook her head and did her best to look stern. "It seems like she's been in and out a few times, judging by how many times I've seen that cellar door left unlocked. Unless it was you leaving it that way, Adam."

"She had to get in and out, Trudy. She had to go look for her daughter."

Trudy's eyes narrowed as she continued to look at Adam. "How did you know about her looking for her daughter? You don't speak Spanish, do you?"

"Well, not really, but kind of."

"What does that mean?" Trudy demanded.

"I know a few words," Adam said. "Enough to know her daughter was molested when she was in Mexico and that it was likely to happen again, and that's why they left, but then her daughter got taken away from her, so she has to find her."

"It seems you may know more than a few words," Grace said, speaking up for the first time.

Adam shrugged. "I picked up a little bit from people I met."

"Mexicans," Trudy said.

Adam nodded.

"Where do you find Mexicans to talk to?" Trudy asked.

"Just made friends with people coming in down at the Travel Stop on the highway. Drank coffee with 'em. A lot of Mexicans get treated like us Black folk, you know. That makes it natural we'd take up with each other, I guess."

Trudy uttered a noncommittal, "Mmm," before she turned to Jasmine. "You never said a word about her daughter being molested. You just said she was stupid."

Jasmine shrugged. "That's what I thought she said. She said *estuprador*. That means stupid, I think."

Adam stifled a laugh. "It means rapist. She must have been talking about the man who raped either her or her daughter."

Jasmine's eyes widened, but she said nothing.

"Now that you know about her, we have to figure out what to do about her," Adam said. "We can't just turn her in to the immigration men."

"Who says we can't?" Trudy said. "It's our responsibility to obey the law."

Adam stared at Trudy silently for several seconds before he spoke. "Trudy ..."

"What?" She sounded defiant.

Adam didn't answer except to cock his head slightly as if he was waiting for her to say more.

"Don't try to make me feel guilty," she said.

"But what about her daughter?" Grace said. "She was given to someone else to adopt without Marta's consent. That's not right. She needs to find her."

"If she wants to find her, why was she hanging out in my cellar? Why wasn't she out looking for her?"

"That was her plan," Adam said, "but the immigration cops have been patrolling up and down the highway between here and Lubbock for a week now."

"They're on to her!" Jasmine said, sounding alarmed.

"She was planning to hitchhike?" Grace asked.

Adam nodded. "That's what she said. I told her I'd drive her, but even that's not safe. They see a Black man and a Mexican woman together in my old pickup, they going to stop us for sure."

Trudy shook her head and looked away. "It's none of my business. I don't want any part of it."

"How would you feel if somebody took your daughter away from you and gave her to somebody else?" Jasmine said. Her words surprised both Grace and Trudy, but before they could react, someone knocked on the front door. The sound startled all four of them, and they stared at each other speechless for several seconds until Jasmine spoke again. "What if it's the immigration people?" she whispered.

"I'll see who it is," Grace said.

"No!" Trudy was already on her way to the front. "It's my house. I'll take care of it." She could feel all of their eyes on her as she made her way toward the door, and it seemed as if they were each holding their breath. She was also well aware that both Grace and Jasmine were following close behind. She opened the door to Hank Richardson. Her breath caught in her throat for a second before she could speak. "Oh ... hello, Sheriff." He looked even more boyish than usual, with that shock of light brown hair showing on his forehead beneath the brim of his hat.

There was an awkward moment as Hank removed his hat and held it in his hands, staring at Trudy expectantly as if he expected to be invited inside. "Morning, Ms. Trudy. You left a message, said you needed me to check out your basement again."

"Oh!" Trudy's voice was strained with nervousness. "That ..." Trudy felt her face flush and she was once again momentarily at a loss for words. "It, uh … It was nothing. A cat! Yes, it was a cat got in there somehow. Sorry I bothered you."

Hank looked puzzled, but his eyes drifted to Grace and Jasmine, still standing behind Trudy. He gave them a polite nod.

"Oh!" Trudy said again, still sounding nervous. "Forgot my manners. This is my nephew's wife … ex-wife … Grace Daniels and her daughter, Jasmine."

"Pleased to meet you." Hank stepped inside and around Trudy to offer Grace his hand.

"Thank you," Grace took his hand. She blushed at how handsome he was.

Hank smiled and nodded at Jasmine, who had retreated behind Grace. She didn't respond to his acknowledgement of her.

"Thank you for coming, Hank," Trudy said. "I'd invite you in, but I got a mess in the kitchen," she added awkwardly. "Trying to get some canning done, don't you know."

"Sure," Hank said and nodded at Grace. "Glad everything's okay."

"Sorry!" Trudy called to his back as he crossed the big front porch.

Hank acknowledged her with a wave of his hand without turning around. Trudy closed the door, feeling a bit confused about what she had just done.

"That was fu—friggin' awesome," Jasmine said.

Grace put her hand on Trudy's arm in a supportive gesture and whispered, "Thank you."

"Don't get the wrong idea," Trudy said, already on her way back to the kitchen. "I just need some time to think about this."

"You're going to turn her in after all!" Jasmine's tone was both alarmed and accusatory.

Trudy didn't answer, and when they got back to the kitchen, both Adam and Marta were gone.

Chapter 6

Hank got in his pickup and sat for a moment, trying to decide what to do. Trudy wasn't acting normal. That had to mean something was wrong. He wondered for a moment if it could have anything to do with that woman and her daughter who were visiting her. Could they be threatening her somehow?

He dismissed the thought and started his pickup to drive back to the office. That woman and girl didn't look threatening, not that a person could always go by looks, but his gut told him that wasn't the problem. That woman—didn't Ms. Trudy say her name was Grace? She was pretty. Didn't look old enough to have a daughter as old as that one lurking behind her with her hair sticking out in all directions. How much longer would she be in Anton? Not that it mattered, he told himself. He had other things to think about.

The next possibility was someone else, someone who had something to do with that noise Trudy had at first insisted was coming from her basement. It was entirely possible someone was hiding out down there and putting Trudy's life in danger. He couldn't immediately come up with a reason for why anyone would do that. Trudy

Bailey wasn't a wealthy woman, so it wouldn't be likely she was being extorted for money.

Maybe someone in trouble, a prison escapee who was threatening her not to reveal they were hiding out in her basement. There had been no alerts about escaped criminals in the area, though. Just the usual illegal aliens coming up from Mexico, but the last alert was at least two weeks old. That one had probably made his way to Dallas by now, where he could blend in and hide out better.

Nevertheless, Hank knew it was a possibility there could be someone hiding out down there. Just because there was no one there the first time he looked didn't mean the person hadn't come back. Hank parked in his usual spot in front of his office and went inside. He'd check out any new alerts that might have come in, and regardless of whether he found anything or not, he'd have another look at that basement.

"Ms. Trudy okay?" Hank's secretary, Clara Stearn, asked as he entered his office. Hank had known Clara all of his life. She and his mother had been friends since high school. His mother had talked Hank into giving Clara a job after her husband died. Hank had been reluctant, but there were no regrets now. Clara kept him organized.

"I hope so," Hank said. "Said it turns out it was a cat causing all that commotion in her basement."

"Bless her heart," Clara said. "I know it's scary living all alone in that big old place."

"She's got somebody there now. Said it was her nephew's ex-wife and her daughter. At least that's what I think she said."

"Nephew's ex-wife? That must be Liz's son. Were they from California?"

"Don't know," Hank said, trying to get away to his desk.

"I'll bet it is. That boy has been married half a dozen times. That happens a lot in California, you know. Liz should have stayed in Texas and raised her kids here."

"Anything important happen while I was out?" Hank asked, ignoring Clara's pontificating.

"Just another illegal supposed to be in the area. I tried to call you on your radio, but I got no answer. I guess you were in Trudy's house when I called. Left a note on your desk."

Hank murmured his thanks and hurried into his office. So there *was* an illegal in the area. Perhaps his hunch about Trudy's basement was right. He picked up the note and scanned it quickly. The notice had come from an ICE facility in Sierra Blanca, Texas, just outside of El Paso. Some woman had escaped and was believed to be on her way to Lubbock.

Hank picked up his telephone to punch in the number for the ICE facility. He'd need more information.

• • •

Trudy's first instinct was to look out the window of her back door in search of Adam and Marta, although common sense told her they wouldn't be back there. Adam wasn't that much of a fool. He was, however, sitting in his rocking chair on his back porch reading a newspaper. He seemed to sense that Trudy was looking at him. He folded his newspaper and stuck it under his arm as he stood up from his chair.

"How you doin', Trudy?" he asked as Trudy came out onto her back step.

Trudy waited until Adam got closer before she spoke in a quiet voice. "He's gone. Where's Marta?"

Adam answered with a jerk of his head toward his house. "Got her hidin' out in the bathroom 'til I see if it's clear," he said. "You say he's gone?"

Trudy nodded. "Don't know if he'll be back."

"You think it's okay if I let her outta the bathroom? She doesn't like being in my house. Best I can figure out, she thinks it's not proper to stay in a house with a man that's not her husband."

Trudy hesitated before she let out a puff of air and said, "I guess so. Can't keep her closed up in a bathroom forever."

"No, ma'am," Adam said and turned around and headed back to his house.

"You knew she was under there all this time," she said to Adam's back.

Adam turned around slowly. "Yes, ma'am."

Trudy's hands came up to rest on her hips in a demanding gesture. "Why'd you keep it from me?"

"I didn't know how you would take it," he said.

Trudy planted her hands even more firmly on her hips. "Didn't know how I'd take it? I believe I have a right to know when somebody is camping out in my cellar. You should have told me."

"I reckon you're right." Adam didn't sound at all contrite, which irritated Trudy a little. She shook her head and relaxed her angry hands-on-hips position. "I would never have thought you'd do a thing like that, Adam."

Adam held her eyes with his own in what could have been a defiant expression. "Didn't turn her in to the law, did you?"

"Well … no, but …"

"Wanted to help her just like I did, I reckon."

"I didn't say anything about wanting to help her," Trudy snapped. She didn't miss the slight hint of a smile playing at Adam's lips before she turned around and walked toward her back door. "Bring her back in. I got to figure this out," she said over her shoulder.

Grace and Jasmine were sitting at the kitchen table waiting for her when she stepped inside.

"Did you find her?" Jasmine asked.

"She'll be here in a minute," Trudy said. She was busy pulling five tall glasses from her cupboard.

Jasmine pressed her. "She with Adam?"

Trudy didn't answer. She pulled a jug of tea from her refrigerator.

"Can I help?" Grace asked.

Trudy filled the glasses with ice from her refrigerator then poured the tea. She took all five on the table one at a time.

"What's this?" Jasmine asked.

"Tea," Trudy said. "It helps you think."

Jasmine took a sip and wrinkled her nose. "Tastes funny."

"It's sweet tea, Jasmine," Grace said. "We're in Texas now. Get used to it."

Jasmine took another cautious sip as Adam and Marta entered through the back door. Marta wore a frightened look and held back, staying close to the door.

"Coast is clear?" Adam asked.

"Come on in," Trudy said. "Drink your tea."

Adam turned toward Marta, took her arm, and led her to the table. He pulled out a chair and motioned for her to sit.

"*Asseyez-vous*," Jasmine said and then added, "Oh wait, that's French. I meant *sentar*."

Marta gave her a puzzled look just as Adam said, "*Sentarse*."

71

When Marta was seated, Trudy turned to Adam. "How in the world was she going to get to Lubbock? How did she get this far in the first place? And why was she hanging out so long in my basement?"

Adam nodded. "Well, Trudy, I reckon you got a right to know all of that. First, she got this far by walking and sometimes jumping on the top of freight trains and by paying a smuggler. Second, she was hiding out in your basement on account of she hurt her leg bad jumping off a train. She's been waiting for it to heal. Third, we don't know how she's going get to Lubbock. I've been trying to come up with something. Like I say, the cops see a Black man hauling a Mexican woman around, I'll be sure to get stopped. Thought I might put her in the back of my pickup and cover her with a tarp or something. Problem is, I don't know if that old wreck of mine will make it all the way to Lubbock."

"Mom can drive her in our car soon as we get that generator."

"Distributor," Adam said.

"Whatever," Jasmine said at the same time Grace replied, "Yes. I'll be happy to do that."

"Got to hide her out 'til then," Adam said.

"She's not hiding out in my basement anymore; I'll tell you that for sure," Trudy said. The room grew silent as all four sets of eyes turned toward her.

"I reckon I could take her in," Adam said, "but I only got one bed."

"It's cruel," Jasmine said, her eyes boring into Trudy's.

"Now that you know she's here, I reckon I could stay in the basement and give her my bed," Adam said. "That way, won't look like something improper going on."

"How long before that distributor gets here?" Grace asked.

"Best guess is two more weeks," Adam said.

"You can't stay in that dirty old basement that long," Jasmine said.

"Sure, I can. I'll just—"

"Will you all just hush?" Trudy said, setting her tea glass on the table in a manner that made the room grow quiet again. "I have some say in this. It's my basement." She looked around the table, trying not to look as uncomfortable as she felt. "I've got four empty rooms upstairs. Well, three, because you can't count the one that's full of junk. They all have perfectly good beds in them. She can stay there until we get this figured out."

"Figure what out?" Jasmine said. "We take her to Lubbock to find her daughter, that's all."

"Do we know where in Lubbock to look?" Trudy asked. "Do we know what to do if we find her? What if her adoptive parents won't give her up? "

"You're not thinking of turning her in to immigration, are you?" Jasmine sounded angry.

Trudy didn't answer.

Chapter 7

Trudy put sheets on the bed in the room next to Grace and Jasmine's room. Ever since Jasmine's experience with a "ghost," she had moved in permanently with her mother and was sleeping on the twin bed in the corner. She showed Marta the room and did her best, with Jasmine's help, to explain that she could take a shower in the bathroom at the end of the hall. There was no question that Marta needed a shower after such a long sojourn in the basement and who knew what before that. When Marta finally realized that she was to have the opportunity to bathe, she smiled for the first time since she'd shown herself. Trudy had provided the nightgown and dress from her own collection since she and Marta were at least close to the same size. Trudy was a little taller and had a bit more girth.

Jasmine's stumbling and inept attempt to explain about the bath, and later about the clean nightgown and a dress for the next day, had taken quite a long time using her translation app on her phone. The explanation might have gone much quicker with Adam's help , but he would not accompany the group upstairs to the bedroom and bath, saying it was not proper for a gentleman to do such a thing. Instead, he went back to his house where he disappeared inside and did not show himself again.

Later, when the summer sky was just beginning to deepen to royal purple, Grace and Trudy were in the kitchen cleaning up after supper while Jasmine and Marta were upstairs in their separate rooms. Trudy heard a knock on the front door. Grace had heard it, as well. They exchanged surprised and wary expressions before Trudy threw her dishtowel across the back of a chair and walked toward the front door. She didn't like the idea of every knock on the front door making her nervous. Things had never been that way before. Now, Marta's presence had changed everything. That made Trudy angry. If her daughter was around, she would say Trudy was becoming a crabby old woman who couldn't handle change. That thought made her even more angry.

Her anger and frustration, no doubt, showed on her face when she opened the front door to Hank.

His first words were, "Are you all right, Ms. Trudy?"

"Of course! Why do you ask?" She knew she sounded defensive.

A little frown crept across Hank's brow. "Just thought you looked upset," he said.

"Well, I guess I'm not used to having somebody come to my door this late," Trudy said, scowling.

She expected Hank to reply with an apology, but all he did was smile and look past her. "Evenin', ma'am," he said.

Trudy turned around to see Grace standing behind her.

"Hello, Sheriff," Grace said. "Is there trouble? Something you came to tell us about?"

"No trouble," Hank said. "At least not yet. I just stopped by to give you some information."

"In that case, come in, please," Grace said. "Have a seat." She pointed to one of the antique chairs in the parlor. Trudy was taken aback at Grace's impudence. What business did she have inviting someone to come in and take a seat? It wasn't her house or her parlor.

Nevertheless, Hank stepped inside, removed his hat, and sat down. Grace sat in the chair next to him and turned slightly sideways so she could see him. "What sort of information, Sheriff?"

"Please call me Hank," he said. "Everybody else does, ma'am."

"Grace," she said.

Trudy sat down heavily on the sofa and rolled her eyes at the sweet sound of Grace's voice and the smitten look on Hank's face. "What is it, Hank? Get on with it. It's getting late."

"I just came to ask you to watch out for an illegal that's supposed to be coming through here."

"An illegal," Trudy said. It was a statement, not a question.

"A woman," Hank said. Just as he spoke, Trudy saw Jasmine making her way down the stairs.

"An illegal woman, from Mexico, I suppose." Trudy's voice was a little louder than it needed to be, and she was pleased to see Jasmine turn around and head up the stairs again. Trudy hoped it was to make sure Marta stayed in her room.

"Yes, from Mexico," Hank said. "Although they think she's originally from Guatemala. Got the information from immigration in Sierra Blanca."

"ICE, you mean," Grace said.

"Yes, ma'am," Hank replied.

"Is she dangerous?" Trudy asked.

"Not that I know of," Hank said. "Just illegal."

"People aren't illegal," Grace said. "I think you mean immigrant."

Hank blushed and looked uncomfortable. "Well, I wanted you to know about it in case …"

"In case what?" Grace asked. Trudy wished she'd keep quiet. The sooner they got off the subject, the better it would be for all, she felt.

Hank looked at Trudy when he answered. "In case that noise you heard in your basement turns out to be the illegal, I mean the immigrant."

Trudy frowned. "You mean the cat. We caught it red-handed down there. He was chasing mice. Need to get an exterminator out here. Guess they'll have to come all the way from Lubbock. Or I could just encourage that cat to stay."

"Yes, ma'am," Hank said. "Do you mind if I take another look?" he asked as he stood up from his chair.

"Be my guest," Trudy said, forcing herself to stay seated. She was keenly aware that Hank had turned his face toward the stairwell.

Hank frowned. "Do I hear voices coming from up there? You taking in boarders, Ms. Trudy?"

"Oh, that's just Jasmine," Grace answered before Trudy could get her wits about her. "She's talking on her phone to her boyfriend, in California."

"His name's Gonzo," Trudy added. She thought it must have sounded stupid.

"Gonzo," Hank said, sounding as if the word made an odd taste in his mouth.

"He's from California," Trudy offered as an excuse. In the next breath, she added, "Want me to go down to the basement with you?"

"No need," Hank said on his way to the door. "I'll just have a look and let you know if I find anything."

"You do that," Trudy said.

"Good night, Hank." The sound of Grace's voice made Hank turn toward her again and give her another smile and a nod just before he put his hat back on.

Trudy and Grace watched from the front window as Hank went to his police car and pulled out a flashlight. He turned it on as he walked around the house toward the back. The two women looked at each other silently for a moment, each trying to shed her alarm.

The next voice they heard was Jasmine's, as she hung over the banister, looking down at them. "Is he gone?"

"Went to have a look in the basement," Trudy said.

"Shit."

Grace gave Jasmine a warning look. "I don't like that word. Please stop using it."

Jasmine came all the way down the stairs. "Do you think he knows she's here?" she asked.

"Not yet," Grace said, "but he came to tell us an immigrant woman is coming through here on her way to Lubbock."

"I heard that part," Jasmine said. "Why is he in the basement? He must know something."

"He's just being careful," Grace said. "He thought maybe the noise Trudy kept hearing might be the woman, but Trudy assured him it was a cat." She turned to Trudy, smiling, "I think you diverted him."

Once again Trudy didn't answer. She was asking herself what in the world had made her decide to hide a woman in her house instead of turning her in to the authorities as she should have done.

"Cool," Jasmine said, giving Trudy an appreciative smile. "Now, all we have to do is get her daughter back to her."

"That's not going to be as easy as you may think," Grace said. "It will probably take a lawyer to get it done."

"Lawyer?" Trudy said. "That's expensive. I don't have that kind of money, and neither do you."

"At least she can stay here until we figure something out," Jasmine said.

Trudy gave her a withering look and once again sat down heavily on the couch. First her basement, then her house, and now her entire life was being taken over by forces she couldn't seem to control.

Chapter 8

The next morning, Jasmine came down to breakfast late, still dressed in the men's boxer shorts and T-shirt that passed for pajamas. None of that was unusual. However, she looked even worse than she customarily did. Her hair, which she'd made no attempt to comb, was sticking out even more than usual. Her eyes were red and bleary, and she shuffled into the kitchen like a woman five times her age. She sat down in the chair at what had become her usual place at the table and breathed a heavy sigh.

"Are you all right, Jasmine?" Grace had a concerned look on her face.

"My name is Lobo." Jasmine's words came out sounding weary rather than surly.

Grace was growing impatient. "What's wrong with you?"

"Just tired. Didn't sleep much."

"You're sick!" Grace said.

"No, just making a plan for how we can help Marta."

Marta, who had come to the kitchen early to help Trudy, looked up at the sound of her name.

"It's a pretty good plan, and I think we can pull it off. We're going to have to use your car, Trudy."

"To drive her to Lubbock, where we don't know where to go or what to do after we get there," Trudy said. She walked toward the coffee pot and picked it up, ready to refill everyone's cups.

"You need to listen to my plan," Jasmine said. "You're right that we need a lawyer to help us, and you're right that we probably can't afford one, so here's what we are going to do first: we're going to rob that bank down there on Main Street."

Trudy splashed coffee over the rim of the cup she was refilling, making a bronze-colored stain on her white tablecloth.

"Don't be ridiculous, Jasmine," Grace said, dabbing at the stain with a paper napkin.

"Lobo," Jasmine said. "You'd better get used to it. And it's not ridiculous. It's a family tradition."

Trudy stirred the sugar in her coffee slowly, but she didn't react beyond that even though she knew what was coming next, and a part of her wasn't ready to discount the idea.

Grace frowned. "What do you mean, a family tradition?"

"Trudy told me about her aunt who—"

"Great-aunt," Trudy said.

"Her great-aunt," Jasmine continued. "Anyway, she and her boyfriend robbed a bank."

"It was only because it was the Depression and they needed the money bad," Trudy said.

"So do we. We need money bad."

"She got caught and went to jail," Trudy said. Marta turned her head from one of the three women to another as she tried to discern what their conversation meant.

"Well, we've got to be smarter than she was," Jasmine said. "For one thing, that's why you have to get used to calling me Lobo. We've all got to take new names, except Marta. She'll probably be okay since we won't tell her anything about it, but you, Mom, and you, Trudy, you've got to have an alias. Adam too if he decides to help."

Trudy laughed. "Oh, Jasmine, you're something else."

"You don't think I'm serious?"

"Sure you are." Trudy sounded sarcastic.

"Jasmine ..." Grace began.

"We'll wait until we get the car fixed, 'cause nobody here will recognize our car," Jasmine said. "It will just be the three of us. Adam, if he's willing, will be waiting in Trudy's car somewhere on a back road. We'll ditch our car, and Adam will drive us to Lubbock, like he's our chauffer. We'll get the hotel reservations ahead of time using Mom's credit card. They reservations will be under my name, Lobo Wolf. We'll lay low for a while, then contact the lawyer. Or maybe we'll do that ahead of time. We can look up one on the Internet. If he asks for payment ahead of time, we'll use the credit card for that too. Don't worry, Mom. We'll pay off the credit card with money we get from the heist."

Trudy nodded, her expression solemn. "Good plan, except for the fact that your mother's credit card can be traced back to her."

Jasmine was silent for a beat before she spoke. "Shit."

"If you use that word again, I'm going to ground you," Grace said.

"You can't ground me if we're on the lam," Jasmine replied.

"Where did you learn an expression like that, like 'on the lam'?" Grace asked.

Jasmine didn't answer. "I've got to give this some more thought," she said. "In the meantime, you two need to be thinking about what your names will be." She got out of her chair and went to the refrigerator, pulling out a jug of orange juice. "Got any Captain Crunch yet?"

Grace pushed her chair back and stood. "I've got a job interview at the insurance agency." She turned toward the door. "Don't rob any banks while I'm gone."

Jasmine, with her head in the refrigerator, said, "We can't do it without you, Mom."

For the first time since they'd all sat down, Marta spoke. "No bank rob," she said, shaking her head fiercely.

Jasmine bumped her head on the inside wall of the refrigerator as she straightened and turned toward Marta. "What?"

Grace turned around and took a step back toward the table. "You understand English!" she said.

Marta shook her head. "No. *No entiendo mucho inglés, pero entiendo rob, y entiendo banco. Estás hablando de robar un banco!*" She pointed a finger at Jasmine and shook it to emphasize each word. *"No robaré un banco!"*

"Oh no!" Jasmine shook her head vigorously from side to side. "Not you. Us! *No usted! Nosotros!*"

Marta glared at Jasmine with an expression that seemed to indicate she didn't understand before she turned abruptly and marched out of the room.

"What was that all about?" Grace asked.

"She thinks we want her to rob the bank for us," Jasmine said.

"Well, for heaven's sake!" Grace said. She looked at her watch. "I have to hurry. I don't want to be late." She pulled a mirror out of her purse to apply lipstick.

Trudy went to the cupboard, barely able to keep from laughing out loud while she took an inordinately long time to pull a box of cereal from a shelf. When she finally composed herself enough to turn around, she placed the box on the table in front of Jasmine. "Still no Captain Crunch. Still just cornflakes," she said.

Trudy expected another grumbling complaint from Jasmine, but she said nothing and appeared distracted as she poured the corn flakes into a bowl. She was obviously perfecting her plans for the robbery. Trudy sat down at the table and leaned toward Jasmine. "Remember Aunt Maxie and her boyfriend—both went to prison for that robbery attempt."

Jasmine waved her spoon in a dismissive gesture. "I told you; we have to be smarter. Just leave it to me."

Before Trudy could reply, Marta walked into the kitchen, headed for the back door. She was wearing the dirty slacks and tattered shirt she'd had on when she came out of the basement. She carried the rest of her belongings in the paper sack she'd had before.

"Where are you going?" Grace asked, intercepting her as they both headed toward the back door.

Marta didn't answer, and before Grace could stop her, Marta was out the door. Grace was right behind her.

"Please, Marta. No one is going to rob a bank," Grace said. "Jasmine is just a kid. She's always saying dumb things."

Marta replied in rapid, angry Spanish. Trudy stuck her head out the back door and told them both to be quiet. "You're going to bring out the entire neighborhood," she said. Jasmine stood behind her, towering over her.

All of the racket brought Adam to his back door and out on his porch. "What's going on out here? Trudy, you all right?" he asked when he saw her standing at the back door. His gaze turned to Marta. "What—?"

"You've got to tell Marta she's not going to have to help us rob the bank," Grace said when she saw Adam.

Adam held on to the rail to steady himself as he walked down the steps of his porch. "Rob a bank? Who's going to rob a bank? What bank?"

Marta spoke to him in Spanish, sounding near tears. Grace interrupted her. "Jasmine was talking crazy stuff about robbing a bank so we'd have the money to help Marta hire a lawyer. Tell her nobody's going to rob a bank. Tell her Jasmine is just a crazy kid."

"I'm not crazy!" Jasmine yelled, still hovering behind Trudy. She turned away in a snit, to retreat to her room.

Adam grinned and shook his head before he spoke to Marta. Trudy came out of her house and walked toward the three of them. She could tell that Adam was speaking haltingly with long pauses and lots of "uh, uh" between sentences. Obviously, his Spanish was limited. As if she needed further confirmation of that, Marta wore a puzzled frown and leaned closer to Adam as if she was trying to understand, all the while constantly interrupting Adam with her spiel of Spanish. Finally, she seemed to relax. The only word Trudy's high school Spanish had allowed her to understand was "niñita." Didn't that mean "little girl?"

Adam was telling Marta that Jasmine was just a stupid little girl. She couldn't remember the word for stupid. *Loco? Estupido?* She hadn't caught either word in Adam's discourse. It didn't matter. Marta had calmed down. Trudy shook her head and rolled her eyes in a gesture that could have meant disgust or relief, or both.

Adam laughed softly. "It's okay, Trudy. Everything's straightened out. Y'all better get Ms. Marta back inside before somebody sees her."

The warning was too late. Trudy saw Hank's police car on the street in front of Adam's house. He slowed down long enough to get a good look at everyone standing outside. There was no doubt in Trudy's mind that he had seen Marta. He sped up a little and rounded the corner to Trudy's street. She knew he had stopped in front of her house. Next, he would be knocking on her front door. Before that happened, however, she would have to think fast and decide whether or not to try to hide Marta again.

"That was Hank. The sheriff, I mean," Grace said. "I think he's coming here." She glanced at Marta. "We've got to get her out of sight."

"Too late," Adam said. Just as he spoke, Hank appeared from around the corner of the house.

"Got company?" he asked, directing his gaze at Marta.

No one spoke.

The back screen creaked as it opened, and Jasmine stepped out on the step. "Oh shit!" This time Grace didn't correct her.

Hank moved closer to Marta and spoke to her in a soft voice, speaking Spanish. Marta nodded and tears ran down her face.

"What did you say to her?" Jasmine demanded in an angry voice.

"Let's go inside," Hank said. He took Marta's arm and led her toward Trudy's back door, still speaking to her in quiet Spanish.

"What's he saying to her?" Grace whispered to Jasmine.

"I don't know. He's speaking too fast," Jasmine said. "The fucker better not be telling her—"

"Jasmine!" Grace wasn't able to say more as she kept her worried eyes on Marta, but Jasmine got the message.

Trudy led the way into her house through the back door and, without speaking, sat down at the kitchen table. The others followed.

Jasmine hoisted herself up to sit on the kitchen counter, and Hank leaned against it, looking grim. Trudy did not follow her custom of offering ice tea or coffee.

Hank breathed a sigh before he spoke. "How long has she been here?"

There was another long silence before Trudy finally answered. "Don't know for sure."

"How long have you known about her being here?"

"Not long." Trudy was well aware of how vague her answer was.

Adam, looking uncomfortable, shifted his position.

"You should have told me about this, Trudy." Marta was sniffling audibly. Grace pulled a paper napkin from the spiraled brass holder in the middle of the table and handed it to her.

Trudy took her time replying. "Yeah, I know I should have ..."

"No you shouldn't have!" Jasmine blurted. "They just want to lock her up, then send her back to Mexico or Guatemala ore wherever she's from without her daughter. You did the right thing, Trudy. Don't let some bastard tell you that you didn't."

Without correcting her daughter, Grace sat in agonized silence along with everyone else. Hank still leaned against the counter, looking at the floor.

"I don't know if you know her story, but ICE told me everything. She got sent back to Mexico. I don't know ... Maybe she didn't know how to apply for amnesty; maybe she just didn't want to. But they sent her back and left her daughter here. Daughter's just a young girl, name's Conception, eleven years old, more or less. Somehow she got set up for adoption, and some family from Lubbock took her."

Jasmine lashed out at him. "We know the story, you moth—" A warning look from Grace kept her from saying more.

87

Hank pushed himself away from the counter. "I have to report this to ICE," he said.

"Oh no! Do you really have to?" Grace asked. "She's not hurting anything just being here."

Hank's shoulders slumped and his face looked haggard. "Well, I—"

"You can't blame her for wanting to find her daughter," Grace added, interrupting him. "Wouldn't you want to find your daughter if you had one?"

"I ..." Hank didn't seem to continue for a few seconds. "Look, I need to think about this. I'm going back to the office. Y'all just keep her here and don't say anything about it to anybody until I figure it out."

"You're going to go back to your office and call ICE," Jasmine said.

"No." Hank's voice sounded strained and tired. "I won't call ICE without telling you. Now, y'all just sit tight until I get back." He went to the back door and opened it. Grace followed him as he stepped outside.

Marta was still sniffling, and Adam put his hand on her shoulder, looking miserable himself.

Jasmine looked as if she might cry as well. "If he's lying and calls ICE, I'm going to ..." Her voice cracked, and she was unable to voice her threat.

Trudy sat at her kitchen table, looking at the old-fashioned picture of her great-grandmother hanging on the wall of the sitting area. She was wondering how the quiet and peaceful life she'd found here in the old family house had turned into such turmoil. Staring at the picture, she was struck by the hardness of Julia Bailey's mouth. Life certainly hadn't been quiet and peaceful for her. She'd built this place after she sold the farm her husband couldn't seem to make profitable. The boarding house was to be their salvation. She made it work with the tenacity of a bulldog and a miser's frugality. Her Baptist faith was as ferocious as she was, and she used it alternately like an attacking lion and a purring kitten, improvising as needed. How else could she have survived the death of children, a bank-robbing daughter who went to prison, and an economic depression that threatened her at every turn?

Trudy could admire her, but she hadn't planned on having to emulate her. She wanted to take the easy way out and send all these people around packing. They could solve their own problems. All she wanted was to be left alone.

Misery and self-pity boiled inside her until she was suddenly and unexpectedly startled by a knock at the front door. Everyone else, it seemed, had been similarly affected. They stared at each other silently and wide-eyed for a few seconds before Jasmine sprang from her chair.

"I'll see who it is," she said, on her way to the front door.

Trudy stood before Jasmine had taken more than two steps. "No! I'll get it," she said. She could feel the eyes of all of them on her back as she walked away. By the time she got to the door, she had managed to control her breathing, but her heart seemed to be doing flip-flops.

She opened the door to a uniformed man holding a badge for her to inspect.

"Immigration and Customs Enforcement," he said. "I need to talk to you, Mrs. Walters."

Chapter 9

For the first few seconds, all Trudy could do was look at the man in the dark blue shirt. He also wore a cap with the letters "ICE" embroidered on the front.

"What did you say?" Trudy asked when she could finally speak. "Immigration or something?"

"ICE," he said, thrusting his badge forward. "Immigration and Customs Enforcement."

Trudy did her best to appear confused. "Are you sure you have the right house? I'm not an immigrant."

"I understand, ma'am, but I have to ask you some questions," the man said.

"About what?"

"Official business."

"About me being an immigrant?"

"No, ma'am, not you. Other people."

Trudy hesitated again before she spoke. "Well … all right, I guess." She didn't move from her spot in the middle of the doorway where she was blocking his entrance.

The man tried to see around her. "May I come in and sit down? This may take a while."

Trudy hesitated again before she spoke. "I guess we can sit on the front porch." She nodded her head toward the two rocking chairs that rested there. The man frowned, and a look that might have been suspicion or even anger moved across his face. "You see, I promised my husband before he died that I wouldn't let strangers in the house. I'm sure you understand."

The man mumbled something indistinct.

"I'm not even supposed to admit that I'm a widow, but I'm afraid I just did when I told you my husband had died." She slumped her shoulders and tried to look elderly and confused as she made her way to one of the rocking chairs.

The blue-clad ICE man sighed audibly and stepped to the other chair. Before he sat down, he slipped his hand in his pocket. Trudy supposed it was to turn on a recorder, but she pretended not to notice.

"All right, ma'am," the man said, giving Trudy a smile that she could only describe as fake. "My name is Nathan Duckworth. My friends call me Nate."

"How do you do, Mr. Duckworth."

"Yes, well, as I said, I'm with Immigration and Customs Enforcement. You may have heard it referred to as ICE." He was obviously following a memorized script. When Trudy didn't reply, he continued. "And you are Mrs. Walters, aren't you?"

"Bailey," she said. "That's what I go by now. Ms. Trudy Bailey." She emphasized the "Ms." It had not occurred to her until that moment that she could do that—use the "Ms" title and go back to calling herself Trudy Bailey.

Duckworth took on an uncomfortable expression. "You're not Mrs. George Walters?"

"Not anymore. Walters was my late husband's name. He's dead now. I told you that. So, I'm Trudy Bailey again."

Duckworth frowned again. "Is that your legal name? It is my understanding that—"

"What difference does it make if it's legal?" Trudy said, interrupting him. "It's the name I go by."

Duckworth nodded in a way that made him rock back and forth. "Very well, Mrs... uh, Bailey—"

"Ms. It's Ms. Bailey."

"Ms. Yes, of course. Whatever. What I need to ask you about is a woman by the name of Marta Ramondino."

"Who?"

"Ramondino. Marta Ramondino."

Trudy frowned. "Well, now, that's an odd name."

"Yes, well, the thing is, she is believed to be here in this area. I'd like to know if you know anything about her."

"Why would I know anything about her? What'd you say the name is? Rumy Deeny?"

"Never mind. Have you seen anyone in this area who appears to be of Hispanic descent?"

"Hispanic descent. You mean, like from Mexico? Or do you mean Spain?"

"Mexico. Or more precisely, Guatemala." Duckworth was frowning again; it was more of an annoyed frown this time.

"Well, let's see, several families live over there on the other side of the old Baptist Church. The old one, not the new building. One of them goes by the name of Sanchez. Always makes me think of

Sancho. You know, like in Don Quixote? I think maybe one family is Garcia. You see I don't know any of 'em all that well on account of they go to the Catholic church, and I'm Baptist, but I never heard any of 'em called … What was it? Rumma something?"

"Ramondino. She would be a woman probably in her thirties traveling alone."

"Traveling alone? My, my. When my husband was alive, he would never allow me to do that. Said it was dangerous."

"Yes, well, have you seen a Hispanic woman in her middle to late thirties you didn't recognize here in Anton? Dark hair, dark eyes, about five-three or four, 120 pounds?"

"Good Lord, why would a woman want to come to Anton?"

"She may be on her way to Lubbock."

"Oh," Trudy said and waited.

"She's a fugitive, wanted by the federal government."

"Oh dear, that sounds serious."

"It is serious, ma'am," Duckworth said, straightening his shoulders and, Trudy could swear, puffing out his chest. "She's in the country illegally."

"Illegally? My goodness!"

"Just keep an eye out," Duckworth said as he stood.

"Oh, I will."

"Notify Sheriff Richardson if you see her."

"Sheriff Richardson," Trudy repeated, trying to sound confused.

"Thank you for your trouble." Duckworth made his way down the steps.

"No trouble," Trudy said. She was silently going over everything each of them had said, making sure that nothing she had said was a lie. She was not so much worried about the damage the lies would do to her soul as Julia might have been, but lying to the federal government was an altogether different matter.

She watched as Nathan Duckworth got into his car and drove away, heading west. She hoped he was on his way to El Paso. When he was completely out of sight, she got up from the rocking chair and went into the house. She found Adam, Grace, and Jasmine still in the kitchen, all of them silent and looking frightened. Each of them kept their gaze on Trudy.

"I thought you had a job interview," Trudy said, looking at Grace.

"I called to tell him I'd be late. Now I have to wait until five o'clock. He sounded angry."

Trudy's eyes shifted to an empty chair. "Where's Marta?" she asked.

No one spoke.

"Don't worry; he's gone," Trudy said. "Where is she?"

"Bathroom," Adam said. "Hiding."

"Hiding in the bathroom?" Trudy said. "You think he wouldn't look there if I hadn't got rid of him?"

"We couldn't think of anyplace else," Jasmine said. "We were afraid he'd look in the basement and in Adam's house. But if the bathroom was locked … I mean even a fed dick wouldn't force his way into a locked bathroom, would he?"

Trudy collapsed into one of the chairs around the table. "See if you can get her to come out. Talk to her in Spanish, Adam. Tell her everything's okay for now." She watched Adam make his way toward the bathroom before she added, "We've got to figure something out. We've got to get her out of here."

"She's going to need a lawyer," Jasmine said. "We should have robbed the bank."

"Maybe the ACLU could help?" Grace said. "Or do you have to be a citizen for them to help you?"

"It wouldn't be hard at all," Jasmine said, ignoring her mother. "I've got it all planned out. I'll be the one to go in first, see, because they won't suspect a kid. Then I show them the gun while the rest of you ... Do you own a gun, Trudy?"

Trudy wasn't listening. Instead, she was watching Adam and Marta as they walked toward the table. Marta was unmistakably frightened, leaning heavily on Adam.

"El se fue. Esta' bien por ahora," Adam said.

Whatever it was he said didn't seem to calm Marta, Trudy noticed. Marta looked around the room nervously as if she expected the ICE man to approach her from any corner. Everyone watched Marta in silence as Adam helped her ease into a chair. All Trudy could think was that none of this was in her plan when she decided to move back to Anton and live a quiet and peaceful life.

All eyes were still on Marta, and no one was speaking when another knock at the front door startled them all. Now all eyes turned to Trudy. She could feel her heart pounding again, and her first thought was to run out the back door, maybe hide in the basement, maybe just keep running. Instead, she stood up slowly and made her way to the front door. At the same time, Adam and Marta stood up quickly and in unison before they both headed toward the bathroom.

Once Trudy was in the parlor, she hesitated at the front door, staring at the wooden panels and trying to summon the courage to open the door. Maybe she could tell Mr. Duckworth that she wasn't feeling well, and he would have to come back later. Maybe she would tell him to get the hell off of her property.

It wasn't Nathan Duckworth standing before her when she finally managed to open the door, but Hank Richardson. He had an odd expression on his face that made Trudy think he was either angry or deeply troubled, or both.

Trudy could manage only one word. "What?"

"Ms. Trudy, I, uh, I believe you had a visitor a little while ago."

"What makes you think that?"

Hank took off his hat as if he was preparing to enter the house. "Well, he came by the office and told me he'd spoken with you."

"So?"

"Sorry 'bout that," Hank said, looking more uncomfortable by the minute. "I told you I'd let you know if … Well, I thought he'd come by the office first. But he didn't. He started going around town asking questions."

"Going around town?" Trudy said. "He was trying to talk to everybody?"

"Seems that way."

Trudy relaxed a little. At least he hadn't singled her out. She hoped that meant he didn't know as much as she had feared.

Trudy's silence seemed to make Hank uncomfortable. "I was wondering if he, well … you know, if he …"

"If he what?" Trudy asked.

"If he, uh, well, if he found what he was looking for."

"Didn't act like he did," Trudy said.

Hank's expression changed completely. He smiled and even seemed to relax a little. "That's good. No, not good; that's not what I meant. He's a law officer, and so am I. It's important that we …"

Trudy pushed the screen door open. "Why don't you come inside, Hank, before you have a seizure or something?"

Hank stepped inside and looked around the room as well as down the hallway that led to the kitchen. Hank and Trudy each saw Jasmine at the same time when she made a surreptitious attempt to stick her head around the corner.

"Go on upstairs and get dressed, Lobo," Trudy said. "Gettin' close to noon. High time you changed out of your pajamas."

Jasmine hesitated a moment, looking over her shoulder toward her mother before she stepped into the hallway and scurried up to the parlor and the stairway without saying a word and looking as if she was embarrassed. Her embarrassment surprised Trudy.

Hank kept his eyes trained toward the kitchen, apparently hardly noticing as Jasmine rushed past him.

"You lookin' for Grace?" Trudy asked.

Now it was Hank who appeared embarrassed. "No, I …"

"Grace!" Trudy called. "Come here to the parlor. We got company." She knew Hank wanted to see her pretty ex-niece, but her summons was as much for her own benefit as it was for Hank's. After what she'd already been through, she needed a backup. Adam, she hoped, would stay in the kitchen, keeping an eye on the bathroom door.

"Oh, hello, Hank," Grace said as she entered the parlor, pretending to be surprised.

"Ma'am," Hank said, giving her a nod.

Trudy sat down in one of the old chairs, knocking the antimacassar on the back askew in the process. "Ya'll have a seat," she said, motioning toward the sofa. They each took a seat, one on each end, leaving a long swath of space between them.

97

"Hank was just telling me that ICE man—Duckworth was his name—stopped by his office," Trudy said. She saw Grace's eyes widen in nervous surprise.

Hank cleared his throat. "I'm sure y'all know he was looking for illegal aliens. He probably told you that when he stopped by there."

Grace said nothing but glanced at Trudy for reassurance.

"That's what he said," Trudy said.

"Far as I know, he didn't find any," Hank said, looking first at Trudy and then at Grace.

Trudy said nothing, and all Grace said was, "Oh."

"He did mention a name," Hank said, appearing only slightly less uncomfortable than he had when he first arrived. "Said her name was Marta Ramondino. Seems I remember somebody by that name."

Grace shot a nervous look toward Trudy.

"Go on," Trudy said, speaking to Hank.

"Seems this woman was separated at the border from her daughter."

"Sorry to hear that," Trudy said.

Hank nodded. "Too much of that going on."

Grace looked exceptionally nervous. She looked down at her hands when Trudy shot her a warning look.

"I want y'all to know that I did get information about the woman being here in town and that the feds would be here to look for her," Hank said. "I told him I hadn't seen her. He came on over here anyway. Nothing I could do about that."

"Guess not," Trudy said.

Hank cleared his throat and shifted his weight as he sat on the sofa. "It's no concern to you, I'm sure, but the feds think the woman—Marta Ramondino? They think she's trying to get to Lubbock because for some reason she thinks her daughter got adopted by somebody there."

Trudy nodded in a noncommittal way, while Grace stared straight ahead, her hands clinched and her shoulders stiff.

"Point is," Hank continued, "it wouldn't be wise if anybody in town did happen to see her and try to help her get to Lubbock."

Grace shot another quick glance toward Trudy. Trudy cupped her chin with her hand and pretended to look interested.

"Now, I understand wanting to help," Hank said, "but I wouldn't want anybody in Anton to get in any kind of trouble just for trying to do the Christian thing."

"Sure," Trudy said.

Hank rubbed a hand across his face as if he were trying to wipe away any trouble that might surface. "Thing is, I'd like to help people like that woman myself. Help her find her daughter, I mean. But I would want to do it in a legal way. You understand?"

Trudy nodded. "That's your job, keeping things legal."

"I would have to give it some thought," Hank said. "I mean if anything like that ever came up, taking her off to Lubbock, I mean, which it hasn't as far as I know. But if it did, I would have to take the time to give it some thought and hope that nobody took it on themselves to jump the gun 'til I came up with something, if you know what I mean."

"Sure," Trudy said again.

"I believe I would start with Christian Rescue Services in Lubbock. That's an adoption agency that handles foreign children." Hank looked at Trudy and then at Grace. "Don't know why I'm telling you this. It's just the kind of red tape law officers have to go through. Just boring information to you, I'm sure."

"Always red tape," Trudy said.

Hank stood and reached for his hat. "I got to get back to the office."

Trudy stood to see him out. "Thanks for coming by," she said. She closed the door and turned to look at Grace who looked as if she was about to be sick.

"I heard everything!" Jasmine said as she came bounding down the stairs, dressed in shorts and a T-shirt, her hair still damp from the shower. "He was trying to warn us. I hope the bastard doesn't change his mind and turn us in to the feds."

"I think he was trying to help us," Grace said. "What do you think, Trudy? Trudy?" she said again as she watched her make her way to the hall entrance.

Trudy turned around and looked at Jasmine. "How far along are you on that bank robbery plan?"

Chapter 10

For two nights in a row, Trudy didn't sleep much at all. Or was it three? Maybe she'd never sleep again. All she could think about was the woman called Marta Ramondino who was in one of the rooms upstairs. She probably wasn't sleeping either. After all, she had more to worry about than anyone.

Grace looked as if she hadn't slept in a month, but she had landed the job at the insurance agency, and she went to work every day. The past two days she'd said almost nothing at supper time, and she'd gone to bed early. Marta was just as quiet. Jasmine was anything but quiet. She stayed busy all day going over her plan to rob the bank, and for the last two nights, all she'd done was talk about the revisions she was making to the plan. The current plan called for Trudy to enter the bank and ask to withdraw a large sum of money; Jasmine hadn't decided on the amount yet. While she was dealing with tellers, Adam would make his way to the basement and set off some kind of device that would make a lot of smoke. While everyone would be trying to flee the bank, Jasmine would scoop up all the money in the vault that had to be opened to accommodate Trudy's unusual request. Grace would drive the get-away car with Marta crouched on the floor in the back.

Interesting plan, Trudy thought. Crazy as hell. It would never work.

As Trudy stirred the pot of green beans she had gathered from Adam's garden, she glanced out the kitchen window and saw him sitting on his back porch with Jasmine who was doing all the talking. She was probably filling him in on the latest plan for the heist. From Trudy's vantage point, she could see neither approval nor disapproval on Adam's face. He did look as if he was enjoying the entertainment, however.

Trudy replaced the lid on the beans and was about to start making the cornbread when she heard a noise at the front door. She was halfway up the hallway to see what was happening when she heard a familiar voice, followed by another equally familiar voice: Grace and Hank. Grace would be just now arriving home from work. Hank's presence made Trudy curious enough to take a few steps closer to the parlor so she could eavesdrop.

Grace's voice came through first. "Oh no! Oh my God! Who ...?"

"Some drug runner," Hank said. "Some guy from Mexico. He was found this morning in his car by the side of the road. Bullet wound in his head."

Trudy took another step forward, eager to learn who was dead, but she stopped when Hank continued speaking.

"Feds are already on the case," he said. "They think it was another illegal that killed him."

"Do the feds think it was Marta?" Grace's voice sounded choked.

"They haven't ruled out anyone at this point," Hank said.

"We've got to protect her ..."

"Don't say anything!" Hank warned.

"Oh! No, I won't." Grace's voice shook as she spoke.

"Thing is, if anybody was harboring an alien, especially one that's a suspect in something like that, and if I knew anything about it, I'd be obliged to let ICE know about it. Trudy could be arrested."

"Oh no!" Grace said. "You wouldn't ... I mean you couldn't ..."

"Yes, I would have to."

"I ... I don't know what to do." Grace sounded as if she might cry.

"Whatever you decide, don't tell me," Hank said. "I'm leaving now." Trudy heard the creak of the front door as Hank pulled it open. "It's not necessary that anybody knows I was here."

"Thank you," Grace said in a voice so low Trudy could hardly hear her. "I ... I don't know how I'll ever repay you for your kindness."

"Well, when this is over, maybe you could buy me a cup of coffee."

"Oh yes," Grace said. "Of course, I can do that. I'd love that, actually."

"You would?"

Whatever Grace's answer to that was, Trudy couldn't hear it. Grace was already out on the front porch with Hank. Trudy walked closer to the opening into the parlor and tried to see the two of them out the front window. They were on the front porch all right, and they were standing awfully close together, it seemed. Trudy turned around and made her way down the hall to the kitchen and out the back door. She had to talk to Adam.

She was relieved to see that Adam sat alone on his back porch with Jasmine nowhere in sight.

"'Evening, Trudy," he said when he saw here.

"Where's Jasmine?" Trudy asked.

"Took off down the alley toward town. I reckon she's gone to check out the bank again. Her plan is coming along. Kind of alarming, I'd say."

"At least it keeps her busy," Trudy said.

"It does that," Adam agreed. "What you looking so upset about? Beans didn't cook up right?"

"They're just fine, Adam." Trudy turned her head to look over each shoulder. "I got to talk to you about something else."

"Let's hear it."

"It's about Marta Ramondino."

"Uh oh!"

"We have to get her out of here. She might be wanted for murder, and I might be, too."

Adam sat up straighter in his chair. "My God, Trudy, what are you talking about?"

Trudy told him everything she had overheard from Grace and Hank. "I never meant to get involved in any of this, Adam. I just wanted to come live a quiet, peaceful life in Anton, with no boarders, I might add. I sure didn't plan on having the unholy mix I've got living with me now."

"Lord-a-mercy!" Adam said. Trudy knew his response wasn't to her whining about having too much company. He was thinking of Marta. His next remark proved her correct. "You're right. We got to get her out of here."

"You know she won't go anywhere without her daughter," Trudy said. "And now that she knows she's in Lubbock, she won't consent to go anyplace else."

"Well, we got to get her to Lubbock to find her daughter. Then we'll figure out what to do next."

"You have to go with me, Adam."

"Me? Go with you? Why?"

"Because … because I don't want to do this by myself."

"You can do anything you set your mind to, Trudy."

Trudy felt deflated. All she could say was, "Well …"

"But if you want me to go with you, I will. We'll take your car, and Mrs. Ramondino can hunker down in the back seat so nobody will see her. You can drive, and I'll sit in the back seat on account of it would look odd to have me in the front with you."

"Adam, this is the twenty-first century. You can sit in the front seat with me."

"You got more faith in the twenty-first century than I do."

"Never mind that, Adam. We have to act fast. Leave tonight. Get some stuff together. I'll turn off the burner under the beans and get Marta. Grace and Jasmine will have to fend for themselves tonight."

Adam shook his head. "That just doesn't sound like you, Trudy. You've always been such a stickler for being a law-abiding citizen. What's got into you?"

"I'm still law abiding," Trudy said. "I just don't believe in the Gestapo coming around and picking up people just because they're looking for their own kid. Any mother understands the need to do what it takes to protect a child."

"Marta's breaking the law just by being here," Adam said.

Trudy gave him a caustic look. "Whose side are you on? You've always been a kind man up until now."

"Yeah, well …"

"Marta will probably go back to Guatemala once she finds her daughter, so everything will come out lawful in the end."

"She won't go back to Guatemala, Trudy. Why do you think she came here in the first place? She's running away from something. She's caught between a rock and a hard place."

Trudy shook her head. "I've never known you to be so unwilling to help before. I just don't know what's got into you."

"I never said I wouldn't help." There was a sharper than usual tone to Adam's response. "You just haven't thought this through."

"If I had time, I'd think it through, but right now I got the feds breathing down my back. Hank said I could be arrested."

"Good Lord, Trudy, you've got yourself in a mess."

Trudy looked at Adam without speaking, but impatience stewed inside her threatening to encase him in the escaping hot steam. He stood up from his chair and opened the screen door.

"I'll get my stuff together," he said. "Meet you at the car in twenty minutes. That long enough for you to get ready?"

"More than long enough," Trudy said. She was already on her way to her back door.

Grace and Jasmine were both in the kitchen when Trudy got back inside. Grace was pulling something out of the refrigerator, while Jasmine sat at the table with her chin in her hands. Marta was nowhere in sight.

"Want me to slice some of this leftover roast to go with the beans?" Grace asked. "Jasmine, you can make a salad."

"Whatever you want," Trudy said. "I'm leaving."

"What do you mean you're leaving?" Grace asked, turning around quickly and letting the refrigerator door slam behind her.

"Taking Marta to Lubbock before the feds find her. Adam's going with me. You two can stay here."

Jasmine stood up suddenly, knocking her chair over in the process. "Stay here? No way!"

"Yes, you must," Trudy said. "I don't know how long this will take."

"I'm going with you," Jasmine insisted. She turned toward the hallway. "I'll get my backpack and some clean underwear."

Grace dropped the knife she'd pulled out of a drawer into the sink. "I'm going, too," she said.

"You can't," Trudy said. "You have to go to work."

"No, I don't."

Trudy gave her a warning look. "Show some responsibility for your daughter. You can't just arbitrarily decide not to go to work."

"Yes, I can. I quit today."

"You what?"

"The bastard wanted me to sleep with him."

Trudy's eyes widened. "Sid Anderson wanted you to sleep with him? I've known him all my life. He took over that agency when his daddy retired."

"Not Sid, Mason. He runs things now."

"Oh, that's right," Trudy said. "Sid retired ten years ago. That kid of his was never worth the bullet it would take to shoot him."

Jasmine turned around in the hall doorway to stare at Trudy. "Geez, Trudy, that's kind of a violent way to put it. Why don't you just say he was never worth a shit?"

"You're wasting my time," Trudy said. She turned away toward her bedroom to gather clean underwear and at least one change of clothing. She threw everything into a small bag and was on her way to the stairs to fetch Marta when she saw her. She was holding tight to Grace's hand, while Jasmine tried to balance a backpack and another small bag.

Trudy didn't want to take the time to argue, so all she did was ask Jasmine, "Did you explain to Marta what's going on?"

"I tried," Jasmine said. "I wish Gonzo was here."

"Oh sure, that's all we need," Trudy said under her breath. No one seemed to notice as they hurried out. As Trudy was locking the back door, she could see that Adam was already waiting in the back seat of the car.

"We picked up a couple of passengers," Trudy said, hefting an arthritic knee to get behind the wheel.

"You ride in the front, Adam," Jasmine said. "Mom and I will ride back here with Marta. That will be less conspicuous. Three women in the back with two elderly people in front."

Elderly? Trudy almost said it aloud, but she didn't want to take any more time than it was taking already for Adam to move to the front and the other three to settle into the back. It was going to take her a while to come to terms with the idea of being elderly.

As they drove away, Trudy could see in her rearview mirror that Marta was clearly upset. Why wouldn't she be, since she probably didn't understand what was happening. Jasmine and Adam each had tried talking to her. Jasmine kept checking her mobile phone and typing in phrases, obviously to translate what she needed to say to Marta. Adam tried to help with his own more proficient Spanish. However, none of what either of them said appeared to comfort Marta.

Chapter 11

Sitting next to the unkempt American teenager in the back seat of the car, Marta couldn't help thinking of her own daughter. Concepcion was younger and not as brash as this child known as Jasmine. Or at least she hadn't been that way the last time Marta saw her, almost a year ago. Marta could see how Jasmine and Grace took their relationship for granted. Perhaps she'd been that way herself once before the cartel came into her life.

Los Enojados, they called themselves. They demanded money from Carlos, her husband, to keep the little store that was his livelihood safe, they said. The store made barely enough to feed his family, and some days, nothing at all. When he couldn't pay, they killed him, along with Nando, their son, who was only fourteen and who had helped out in the store. They were the same ones who had brutally raped her.

Marta tried to erase the sight of Nando's and Carlos's bloodied bodies from her mind, tried not to remember when they came back and raped her and then demanded that they also have Concepcion, who was only eleven at the time.

She'd seen them approaching the little hut that she and Concepcion shared with her aging mother. She turned to Concepcion, who was helping her grandmother mix flour and water for tortillas to be cooked on the fire outdoor.

"Run! *Mi hita!*" Marta said. Her voice was quiet but anxious.

Concepcion looked at her mother with wide, frightened eyes just before she started toward the door. Her grandmother caught her skirt and pulled her back, motioning toward the only window in the tiny hut. Concepcion's grandmother helped her out of the window, and Marta watched her run. She barely disappeared into the thick green of the jungle before three men from *Los Enojados* walked in the open doorway.

Marta backed away as soon as she saw the men, trying to position herself between the men and her mother.

"Hey, don't be afraid," one of them said. "We didn't come here to hurt you. We just came for a nice visit with your daughter."

Marta said nothing in reply and fought against the instinct to look out the window to make sure Concepcion was still out of sight.

"Where is she?" another of the young men demanded.

"Don't know. She left this morning. Hasn't come back."

All of them laughed, sounding to Marta like a three-headed maniacal beast. Within seconds, one of them took a step toward her. "Too bad, but I'll take what's available. I'm horny as hell." The young man grabbed her blouse and forced it down, exposing her breasts. He laughed again and pulled at her breasts, causing Marta to cry out. At the same time, she heard her mother's cry.

"Go on, old woman. We don't need you around," one of them said.

Marta never saw her mother leave, and in the next minute she was on the floor with someone holding her arms above her head while another forced himself inside her. Marta was vaguely aware of her mother's cry and then a thud as if she had fallen to the floor, but she was unable to see what had happened as the three took turns with her.

When it was finally over and the three had left, Marta felt for a moment as if she could not move. Yet, she forced herself to her hands and knees and crawled to where her mother lay on the floor. Blood was trickling from her mother's temple and down her cheek.

"Mamá!" She cradled her mother's head in her lap and saw her eyelids flicker.

"I saw!" the old woman said. "I saw what they did to you. I tried to …" Her voice dissolved into sobbing.

Marta helped her into bed and bathed her face. "I'm all right now, Mamá. Don't cry. Rest, while I look for Concepcion."

It took the rest of the day, pushing herself through the tangles of the jungle, before Marta found Concepcion cowering near an *estanque* under some vines.

Mamá was no longer crying when they finally returned. She encircled both of them in her arms. "You have to leave," she said. "It's not safe for you. They'll be back wanting more and more until there's nothing to give, then they will kill you just as they did Carlos and Nando."

"Leave?" Marta said. "How can we leave? Where will we go?"

"U.S.," Mamá said. "Like Carlos did."

Carlos had made the journey to the U.S. twice. Each time he was gone a year before he had come back with enough money to keep them from starving.

Marta shook her head. "He said it was hard. He said he would never take his wife and children with him."

"And you think it is not hard here? We are almost starving without the store. And you think *Los Enojados* won't be back? You think you can keep them from Concepcion?"

Marta glanced at Concepcion and read the stricken and dull look in her eyes. It was then that Marta knew her daughter had witnessed what had happened. Still, she resisted, thinking it was better to try to protect her daughter at home than to risk her life on a dangerous journey. It was not until several weeks later that Marta came to terms with her circumstances.

As they started their long walk toward the border, they were both stricken with awful diarrhea. Then Conception started her flow with no way to buy pads. They encountered *Los Enojados* more than once but somehow managed not to attract their interest.

The Mexican desert just before they reached the border was the worst part of the journey. Neither of them had known such thirst before, and they would not have survived had they not been with a group of others seeking refuge.

How happy they were when they reached the border! Concepcion smiled for the first time in days, and Marta felt almost giddy. Some in the group had done this before and knew how to cross the river in the shallow part and how to turn themselves in and ask for asylum. It seemed so easy when they described it. How was Marta to know that the worst was yet to come?

No one had told them that the laws in the US had changed, that Marta and Concepcion would be separated, that Marta would be branded a criminal and locked in a cell just for coming into the country and no chance to tell them she wanted asylum. She could still hear Concepcion's screams as she was led away, still feel the anger and frustration when no one could tell her where her daughter had been taken.

Marta had tried to explain all of this to the one called Adam, but she was not certain that he understood any of it. His Spanish was only a little better than her English, although her knowledge of the foreign language was growing. She could understand better than she could speak. Coming up with the correct words still proved to be a challenge.

She had understood a little of what Trudy and her group were talking about as Trudy drove to Lubbock. Jasmine's voice was loud and insistent.

"I have to, Mom. I have to find hair coloring when we get to Lubbock. I just hope it really is a big enough town and not like Anton. I mean, you can't find *anything* there. It's like Podunk."

Marta had no idea what Podunk meant, but she continued to listen to Jasmine's rant.

"My hair has been its natural color since the second day were got here. I can't stand it."

"You look better with your hair natural," Grace said. "All those garish greens and purples distract from your pretty face."

Garish—another word Marta didn't know, but she could guess at what it meant. How lucky they were to have nothing more than hair coloring to worry about. She liked Grace. She was kind and quiet, so unlike her daughter, a *nina mimado*. The child was smart, though, so there was at least hope that she would outgrow it.

"It is taking longer to get there than I thought," Jasmine said, obviously growing restless. "How do we even know Lubbock is where we're supposed to look for Marta's daughter?"

Adam turned partway around to address Jasmine in the back seat. "She said she found out from someone that that's where she went."

"Someone? Who? How do we know whoever it was told her the truth? Besides that, she could have gotten it wrong since she doesn't even speak English."

"I guess she got a translator," Adam said.

"You guess?" Jasmine said. "That's not very reassuring."

Adam gave her a smile. "Have faith, little girl," he said before he turned around to face the front again.

Marta could hear Jasmine mumbling low enough that Adam couldn't hear. "I'm not a little girl."

The truth was that it hadn't been easy finding out where Concepcion was sent. She'd asked over and over again where she could find her daughter. Most of the time she was ignored; sometimes she was told she'd be notified later.

She was consumed with worry. She was losing weight. She felt sick most of the time. But she wouldn't give up. An angel visited her one day while she was in the jail somewhere in the U.S. Marta liked to think of the woman as an angel, at least. She was one of the guards where Marta had been held. She'd seen the woman in her dark uniform frequently, walking along the row of cells, checking locks, peering into cells, but rarely speaking.

Marta had spoken to her more than once, always asking the same question in her poor English, "Please, where *mi niña? Se llama Concepción.*"

Most of the time the guard ignored her until one day she whispered to Marta in Spanish, *"Ella ha sido adoptada. Ella está en Lubbock, Texas."*

Adopted? Another family had taken her? What right did anyone have to do that? Marta was more distressed than ever until the next morning when the same guard returned. She pretended to bend over to tie her shoe while she surreptitiously slipped a small piece of paper under her shoe and pushed it into Marta's cell. Five words were hand-printed on the paper: *"Christian Rescue Agency, Lubbock, Texas."*

The words looked foreign and indecipherable to Marta at first until she remembered how the English language always had the words out of the logical order. It meant *Agencia de Rescate Cristiana.* However, if she were ever to find Concepcion, she would have to use the words in English. She slipped the little sliver of paper into her bra, but the guard was frowning, shaking her head, mimicking putting something in her mouth. She was telling Marta to swallow the paper! Marta took the paper out of her bra, took one more look to imprint the foreign words on her brain, and stuffed it into her mouth, waiting for her saliva to soften it enough to swallow without the words gagging her.

She never had a chance to thank the guard because she was deported early the next morning. She had been told she would be held in Mexico until she could be sent back to Guatemala. She was there for another week, still unable to sleep, but she was no longer losing weight. She would eat to keep up her strength so she could get to Lubbock, Texas, to find her daughter. She had no idea where Lubbock was, but she knew about Texas. She had crossed the border there and turned herself in at a lonely place in the desert called Antelope Wells, just outside of El Paso, Texas. Somehow, she had to find her way back and then locate a place called Lubbock.

Escaping the cell in Mexico wasn't as hard as she had feared. She had simply slipped out of the line of other prisoners as they were lined up to march outside. She was able to walk out of the gate in the front when she bribed the guard posted there with a watch she had stolen from another prisoner. It wasn't the last time she would resort to theft before she made it back to the border. She stole fifty-two dollars from a woman's purse she managed to grab from a shopping cart and used the money to bribe a Spanish-speaking man at a gas station to draw a map for her so she could find her way to Lubbock.

Nothing was easy after that. She had to walk, afraid of asking for a ride. She had to sleep in dirty sheds or on the ground and had to steal food or money to buy it. She'd been accosted twice and raped once.

When she ended up in Anton, she realized the map she'd paid for was not accurate, but she was determined to find her way to Lubbock, nevertheless. Trudy Bailey's basement was supposed to be no more than a place to sleep for a night while she figured out how to correct her mistake. Trudy, it seemed, had proven to be another angel—one with a sour disposition, *una grunida.*

Now, it seemed, *La Grunida* had lost her angel power. The *adolescente impudente* confirmed that after pecking at her telephone and then telling Marta in bad Spanish that a man had been murdered and that she and *La Grunida* might be suspects.

Marta knew that a lawman had been to the house to ask questions. Did *La Grunida* kill someone? That didn't seem possible. She might have a sour disposition, but she surely wasn't a killer. The girl was only being dramatic, trying to get attention.

Chapter 12

The Christian Rescue Agency was located near downtown in a sprawling one-story building a few blocks behind the courthouse. Grace found it by searching on her phone.

"What do we do now?" Jasmine asked as they waited in the car, parked along the side of the building. "Do we just go in and ask where she is?"

"Don't think so," Adam said. "Won't get an answer that way. They'll want to protect their clients."

Grace was staring at the unimposing building. "If only we could get inside and search their records ..."

"That's not likely, either," Adam told her.

"I wouldn't say that." Trudy was staring at the building.

Adam frowned and shook his head. "I'm afraid to ask what you mean by that. Wait!" he said when he saw Trudy opening the door on the driver's side. "Where do you think you're going?"

"Inside," Trudy said. "I'm just going to look things over. Ask a few questions. People don't think old women like me look suspicious. Elderly women," she said, pinning her gaze on Jasmine.

"Can I go with you?" Jasmine was already scrambling out the door on her side of the back seat.

"No, you can't," Trudy snapped.

"Why not?"

"Because you might look suspicious to them. The way you dress …"

"That's not fair!"

"Well, honey, isn't that the whole reason for you doing it, to not look like everybody else? In other words, to attract attention?"

Jasmine replied to Trudy in a defiant tone as Trudy walked away, but Trudy pretended not to hear her. She was glad now that she hadn't had time to change out of the polyester pants and shirt she'd put on that morning. If she'd had time, she'd have dressed in the new black and cream pant suit she'd bought from Chico's the last time she was in Lubbock. The saleslady had said it made her look ten years younger and ten pounds lighter. Wasn't true, of course, but she liked the way it looked—chic. That was the last thing she needed now.

A young woman—a girl, actually—sat at a desk facing the door. She looked up when Trudy entered. Her face and arms looked plump, but her shiny shoulder-length black hair, green eyes, and glossy-lipped smile made her appealing.

"Can I help you, ma'am?" she said.

"Well, I hope you can. You see, I …" Trudy pretended to be out of breath. "Mind if I sit down?" She motioned toward the straight-back chair close to the desk.

"Of course, I don't mind!" The girl said. "Can I get you some water?"

"That would be nice, dear."

The girl stood up quickly and walked toward a water cooler, while Trudy eyed the files behind the desk: alphabetical, with the letters in bold print and slipped into slots on the front of each drawer, a key dangling from the keyhole in front of the file cabinet.

"Here you are, hon." The girl handed Trudy a paper cup full of water before she sat at her desk again. "Now, how can I help you?"

Trudy took a sip of the water. It was so cold it made her teeth ache. "Oh, thank you. This is so good. It's hot out there, and I just can't take the heat like I used to."

"Know what you mean. That's Texas for you." When Trudy responded only by taking another tiny sip of water, the girl added, "This is Christian Rescue. We're an adoption agency. Were you by any chance trying to find the Social Security office? It's one block over on the next street."

Trudy feigned a moment of confusion. "Social …? Oh no, I'm here at the adoption agency on purpose." She forced a little laugh. "Oh, don't worry, dear, I'm not here to adopt. I'm too old for that." She gave another little laugh.

"We do have an age limit," the girl said, still smiling congenially.

"Of course," Trudy said. "I'm just trying to locate my granddaughter. Her name is Concepcion. My daughter married a man from Guatemala, and then there was a big mix-up when—"

"I'm sorry," the girl said, her smile fading. "I can't give you any information on adoptions. We have to protect our clients, you see—company policy."

"But if a mistake was made and my granddaughter wasn't supposed to be adopted—"

"You'll have to take that up with the courts, and if a decision is made in your favor, you can get back to us through your lawyer." The smile was completely gone.

"I see," Trudy said, doing a good job of looking crestfallen. She sat for a few seconds longer, contemplating what her next move would be, before she asked, "Could I use your restroom? I'm afraid I drank too much water."

The girl took her own few seconds of hesitation. "Well ... I guess that won't hurt anything." She pointed to the hallway behind her. "Down that hall. First door on the right."

Trudy hurried toward the restroom. She hadn't been lying when she said she'd had too much water. Her cranky aging bladder could only take a little at a time. She let out a sigh of relief as she plopped down on the toilet, grateful that she had made it on time. She could hear voices through the thin walls of the restroom, and she assumed that meant whoever was on the other side could hear her restroom noises, too. Didn't matter—she was too old to be embarrassed by such things.

She stood up and was about to flush the toilet when she realized that noise would signal that she was almost ready to come out of the room. She wasn't ready for anyone to know that yet. There were still things she needed to know. Pressing her left ear against the wall—her hearing was still good on that side—she listened closely. The sound was muffled, but she could make out a few words.

"Another one?"

"Yeah. Why do they ..." She couldn't make out the rest of the sentence.

"You do, really?"

"Well, she said the kid's name was … So odd like that … The only one is… be finalized by …"

The conversation was mostly unintelligible, but Trudy kept listening until the discussion changed to something about a potluck dinner at someone's pool. She flushed the toilet, washed her hands, and walked out to find the girl back at her desk. Trudy gave her a smile and mumbled, "Thank you," as she walked out.

Jasmine was the first to greet her when she got back to the car, parked on the side street. "God! What took you so long? I'm dying in this heat!"

"You should have gotten out of the car and stood in the shade," Trudy said, pointing to a scrawny elm tree growing next to the sidewalk across the street.

"Like that would help," Jasmine grumbled.

"Did you learn anything?" Grace asked.

"Maybe," Trudy said. "I'll have to come back, uh, sometime." She almost said she would have to come back tonight, but she thought better of it. No point in complicating things by revealing the half-baked plan she had in mind or in having anyone insisting on accompanying her.

'Well, I'm not waiting out in the heat again next time," Jasmine said.

"No, of course I won't make you do that again," Trudy said.

Jasmine frowned. "You're not planning on coming back without us, are you?"

"Why would I do that?" Trudy could feel Adam's gaze burning her face, but she wouldn't turn to look at him.

Trudy took everyone to an early dinner at J&M, her favorite barbecue place. Jasmine complained that she'd rather have pizza, but she ate the spicy ribs she was served with gusto. Trudy resigned herself to answering questions about her visit to the adoption agency:

"Yes, that is most likely the right agency," "No, they wouldn't give me information without a lawyer," "Yes, it probably will take a while to get what we need," "Yes, it will probably be expensive," "My next plan is to hire a lawyer, of course," "No, I was only kidding about robbing a bank, Jasmine."

During dinner and the barrage of questions, Trudy kept an eye on Marta, thinking that maybe they shouldn't have brought her to a public place. But what was their other choice? They certainly couldn't leave her alone in the hotel where they had rented rooms for the night. Jasmine and Adam had done their best to explain to her that they'd found the agency but would not be allowed to see her daughter yet, that it would require time and money. As a result, Marta hardly raised her head during dinner but stared at her hands, folded in her lap, and ate almost nothing, not even the ice cream and peach cobbler.

"Are you going to hire a lawyer tomorrow?" Jasmine asked during the ride back to the hotel.

"No. I think it's best to wait and get a good recommendation," Trudy said.

Grace, who had said very little during the trip, spoke up from the back seat. "Maybe Hank could help."

"Hank?" Trudy asked, sounding doubtful. "Well, I guess he may know some criminal lawyers. Maybe one of them could recommend an immigration lawyer."

"He's on his way here," Grace said. "Said he'd meet us at our hotel."

"When did he say that?" Trudy was uneasy, and it showed in her voice. She didn't need Hank around to make carrying out her plan even more difficult than it would be anyway.

"He called me while we were at the restaurant. The Feds think they know who killed the drug dealer, so you and Marta are off the hook."

"Thank God," Trudy said.

Trudy had heard Grace's telephone ring and noted that she had walked outside to take the call, but she thought it was most likely Mason Anderson calling to ask her to come back to work. Grace had been silent after she took the call.

"Why is he coming here?" Trudy asked after a while.

"He thinks we may need help," Grace answered.

"Oh … that's nice of him," Trudy said, pretending to be happy for the offer. "But I don't think there's anything he can do. You can call him back and tell him—"

Grace interrupted. "He's already on his way."

Should have never introduced the two of them, Trudy thought. *Should have known there'd be some kind of attraction. This would surely mean nothing but trouble.*

She was so annoyed and lost in her thoughts that she wasn't aware that Adam had spoken to her several times.

"Trudy! Did you hear me?"

"What? Yes. Yes, of course I hear you."

"You got this figured out?"

"No," she said a little too quickly as she pulled into a parking space in front of the hotel. Adam stared straight ahead without answering. "I'm tired," she said as they waited for the elevator. "I'm going straight to bed since I'd like to get up early in the morning and go home."

Grace frowned. "But Hank will be here soon. He may have—"

"You can let me know what he has to say in the morning," Trudy said, interrupting her.

"Well, okay," Grace said. "Just keep in mind it may not be feasible to leave early in the morning, in case Hank has some important news, maybe even a plan."

"I'll keep that in mind," Trudy said as she and Marta exited the elevator. The others stayed inside the elevator as it took them up another level. Trudy unlocked the door to the room she shared with Marta and allowed her to enter ahead of her. "If you're as tired as I am, you'll want to go to bed, too," she said to Marta and gestured toward one of the queen-size beds in the room.

Marta nodded as if she understood, then disappeared into the bathroom. Trudy took the opportunity to get into bed quickly, pulling the covers up to her chin so Marta couldn't see that she was still fully clothed. She was pretending to be asleep when Marta came out of the bathroom. She kept pretending for what seemed like an eternity before she heard Marta's even breathing that signaled she was asleep. Trudy slipped out of bed as quietly as she could, reached for her shoes and handbag, and tip-toed out of the room.

The first thing she saw when the elevator door opened on the main level was Adam sitting in one of the comfortable chairs facing the elevators.

"Shit!" she said under her breath.

"Now, Trudy, that's no way for a lady to talk." Adam stood and walked toward her.

"What are you doing down here?"

"I might ask you the same thing, but I'm scared I know the answer. You're fixing to do something crazy."

"Crazy? Why would you say that? I just came down her to … uh …"

"Whatever it is, I reckon I better be with you."

Trudy stared at him without speaking.

"You going back to that adoption place?" he asked.

"Well …"

"Weren't thinking of breaking in, were you?"

Trudy looked away. "Of course not. That would be crazy."

"How you going to get in?"

She didn't respond. She was busy putting on her shoes.

"Break a window? Kick down the door?"

"Certainly not! I have a key."

Adam's eyes widened. "You stole a key?"

"I didn't really steal it. It was just there on the desk, and I—"

"Oh my God!"

"It's not really breaking in if you unlock the door, is it?"

Adam turned away from her and let out a puff of air.

"It was just a thought. I wasn't going to steal anything, you know. I just wanted to see if I could find the records about where that girl is. Just a thought. Crazy, like you said. Now, go on up to your room and go back to bed."

"Trudy," he said, turning back to her. "Trudy …"

"What?"

"I'm not letting you out of my sight."

Trudy stared at him again, feeling trapped. Finally, she turned away toward the door leading to the parking lot. "Suit yourself," she said over her shoulder.

He got to the car before she did and held the driver-side door open for her. "You don't have any idea how to do this," he said when he was seated next to her.

"Do you?"

"Now's not the time to be asking that."

When they reached the building that housed the Christian Rescue Agency, Trudy drove into the wide front parking lot.

"You can't park here," Adam bellowed, loud enough to startle Trudy. "Park the car somewhere that's dark," he said. "Over there. See? Behind that building next to the agency."

Trudy obeyed without protesting. When she was parked, she grabbed her handbag and was about to get out of the car.

"Leave that here," Adam said, nodding toward her purse.

"In the car? What if somebody steals it?"

"What makes you think there'd be any thieves around here?" Adam asked in a sarcastic tone. He picked up the handbag. "Take your keys out and pop the trunk."

Trudy obeyed and waited while he tossed her purse in the trunk, then had to hurry to catch up with him as he walked away toward the adoption building.

"Is the key for the front or the back?" he asked.

"I don't know. Front, I guess."

"We'll try the back first," he said, taking the key from her. There was no light in the back of the building, and he had to fumble to get the key into the lock. Even when he was successful inserting it, the lock wouldn't turn. "I'll try the front. You stay here," he said.

"No way. I'm coming with you." She followed him to the front where it was flooded with light. While he fumbled with the lock again, she watched the street, hoping it would stay free of passing cars.

"Not working here either," Adam said. "Guess we have to go back to the hotel."

"Not yet," Trudy said. "Maybe there's something else we can try to get inside, like a window maybe."

"No, Trudy. I'm not going to break a window, not even for you." He took her arm and pulled her gently away from the front door.

"We could at least try," Trudy said. "Maybe they left one open."

"No, we will not try. Come on, Trudy. We're going back."

Trudy pulled away from Adam as they passed one of the low windows. It was a sash window that opened from the bottom. She gave it a push upward, using both of her hands and all her strength, but it didn't budge.

Adam took her arm again. "You satisfied now? Come on. Get in the car."

"That's not the only window in the building. I distinctly remember seeing one near the back door."

"Aw, for crying out loud, Trudy!" They rounded the corner of the building to the back. Trudy hurried toward the window she'd seen earlier. Adam stood away from her, hands in his pockets and shaking his head.

Once again Trudy used all her strength to push the window open. It slid up with ease, and Trudy's mighty effort caused her to stumble backward and fall, hitting her bottom with a hard thud on the hard-packed dirt next to the building.

Adam cried out and ran toward her. "Good God, Trudy!" He put his arms under her armpits to pull her up. "Are you hurt? Did you break anything?"

"Well, if I did, you shouldn't be pulling on me like that." When she was on her feet, she dusted herself off with her hands and winced as she touched her bottom. She wasn't about to admit how much her tail bone ached and give Adam the opening to call her a pain in the butt. She moved toward the window, grimacing with each step and biting her lip to keep from crying out.

"Where the hell are you going?" Adam called to her.

"Did I just hear you use a swear word, Adam?" Trudy asked without turning around. "I thought that was against your religion."

"You're enough to make a man lose his religion. And I don't mean in the form of temptation."

"Flattery will get you nowhere," she said and tried to heft herself up over the window ledge. After several tries and worsening pain in her buttocks, she called to Adam without turning around to look at him. "Come give me a boost," she said.

"Won't do any such thing," Adam said. Trudy turned around to see him standing feet apart and arms folded in front of him.

She shrugged and turned back to the window. Throwing both of her arms across the window sill as far as she could reach, she gave herself a push with both of her feet and tumbled, headfirst, into the building, landing on her stomach. At least the landing wasn't as hard as the one that landed her on her butt, although she wouldn't consider it an easy landing. She was temporarily out of breath from the blow to her midsection. She managed to pull herself up to her knees, but that was as far as she got. With nothing to hold on to, it was impossible to boost herself to a standing position. Besides that, her knees hurt. When had she lost the power in her legs to get herself up from the floor? Maybe it was the extra weight in her belly that made it so hard. Whatever, she was stranded.

There wasn't enough light to see much of anything, and she had dropped her little flashlight as she splayed herself on the floor when she entered, but she thought she saw a dark form hulking a few feet in front of her. She rolled herself forward, arms in front of her, and tried to crawl toward the form, but the pain in her knees slowed her down. She paused, still on her hands and knees, pondering whether or not she could bear the knee pain long enough to go farther when she heard a whispering voice coming from the open window behind her.

"Trudy, is that you? What in God's name are you doing?"

"Is that you, Adam?"

"Yes, it's me. What's wrong with you? Are you hurt?"

"I can't get up."

"Well, my Lord!"

"Don't my-Lord me. Get in here and help me up, that is if you're not too old and crippled yourself."

Adam already had one of his long legs swung over the window-sill. "I'm coming in, and I'm getting you out of here. I don't want to hear any argument from you."

"Just hurry. My knees are killing me, and I can't turn around and sit. That hurts, too."

Adam mumbled something Trudy couldn't decipher, but in the next few seconds he was standing behind her with his arms looped under her armpits, boosting her to her feet.

"Oh, thank goodness," Trudy said. "I hope nobody saw you crawling in." She bent over to massage her knees, then brought her hands to her backside to try to rub out the pain still lodged there. She took a deep breath and turned toward the window as Adam pulled her toward it. That's when she saw the little flashlight barely visible in the dim light coming through the window. She pulled away from

Adam's light grip and bent over to pick it up, groaning from the pain the effort caused in her backside.

"Where do you think you're going, woman?" Adam asked as Trudy turned on the pinpoint light and limped toward a door that appeared to be leading toward the building interior.

"I'll just be a minute. You go on and wait for me outside in case I need you to help me out."

"No! I will not let you … Trudy! Trudy, you come back here!" Adam kept his voice low, but that didn't hide his frustration.

Trudy opened the door and recognized the hallway she'd seen before when she had used the restroom. The front office with the file cabinets would be at the end of the hall. Adam was directly behind her.

"You going to get us both arrested, Trudy."

"Not if we're careful."

"How did I ever get myself mixed up with the likes of you?"

"You can crawl back out of that window any time you want to," Trudy said, approaching the desk.

"Hush, woman. You're crazy, plumb crazy."

Trudy opened the desk drawer and, with the help of the flashlight, quickly found the key to the filing cabinet. "Here, hold this so I can see what I'm doing," she said, handing the light to Adam. He took the light and held it for her, while she quickly opened the top drawer. "Bring that light a little closer so I can read the names on these files," she said.

Adam complied, but she could sense him seething as she ruffled through the tabs on the files, alphabetically arranged. The last one was "H." The "Rs" for Ramondino would be in another drawer. The third one down, she estimated.

"You're taking too long," Adam said.

"Don't make me nervous," Trudy answered.

"Don't make *you* nervous? How the hell do you think you're making me feel?"

"You're swearing again."

Adam mumbled, once again something indecipherable.

"Ah!" Trudy said. "Here it is. Ramondino!"

Adam leaned closer to have a look for himself as Trudy opened the file. A picture of a frightened-looking dark-haired young girl was attached with a paper clip to a few pages of paper. "That's her!" Adam said. "See, she looks just like Marta."

"Anybody in here?"

Trudy and Adam froze, both wide-eyed and staring at each other. Trudy switched her flashlight off. In the same moment, there was a knock on the front door, only a few yards from where they stood, and the same voice again. "Police! Anybody in here?"

Adam grabbed Trudy's arm to pull her away, but Trudy resisted long enough to replace the file and close the filing cabinet drawer as quietly as she could. Holding her breath, she moved with Adam toward the back.

"There's somebody in there. I can hear you!" the voice at the front called out. That was followed by a loud thud as someone was apparently trying to smash in the door.

Trudy and Adam had barely made it to the back when they heard another thud followed by the sound of splintering wood. Trudy glanced around the room and saw that a little splash of light was coming through the open window where they had entered.

There was another louder sound of splintering wood, and Trudy and Adam moved as one toward the window. Behind them, they heard the sound of footsteps, obviously inside the building. The footsteps stopped, and Trudy paused to catch her breath. Before she could exhale, Adam jerked her into motion again.

"Police! If you're in here, drop any weapons and come out with your hands in the air!"

That was followed by another voice. "Everything looks okay here, Sarge. Doesn't look like anything was taken."

That was followed by what seemed to Trudy to be an interminable silence. She hoped that meant that the policemen were still busy inspecting the front area.

Trudy and Andy had barely made it to the window when they heard footsteps again, moving toward the back. Adam picked Trudy up by her waist and shoved her headfirst out of the open window, then stepped over the windowsill to help her to her feet.

"Run, Trudy!" Adam said in a hoarse whisper as he sprinted toward the car. He turned around to see Trudy attempting an awkward limping run. He turned back toward her and once again caught her around her waist, this time with one arm, as he headed for her car. He used her key fob to open the doors as well as the trunk then shoved her into the front seat and slid his own body into the back. He issued another command. "Drive!"

Trudy started the car and drove toward the parking lot exit. "Sorry about that," she said. "Can't run very fast. My butt hurts."

Adam mumbled something under his breath in response, and Trudy didn't dare ask him to repeat it.

When she had pulled out onto the street, she said, "I got the address for where Conception is living. I hope I remember it long enough to write it down when we get back."

"Tell me the address," Adam said. "Two heads are better than one."

"It's on 76th Street."

"You sure?"

"I remember that much because that's my age."

"Old woman."

"Hush, that's disrespectful."

"What's the house number?"

"It was either 5802 or 2205."

"That narrows it down."

Trudy glanced at him through her rearview mirror. "It actually *does* narrow it down. There are only two possibilities."

"Right."

"You sound smart-alecky, Adam," Trudy said, looking at his reflection again just in time to see the flashing lights of a police car behind them. In almost the same instant, they both heard a siren.

Adam turned his head to look behind their car, and Trudy pulled to the right side of the road and stopped the car. Neither of them spoke as the policeman approached the driver's side and shone the beam of his flashlight into the interior of Trudy's car.

"You all right, ma'am?" the policeman asked, his eyes on Adam.

"Yes, I'm fine. I just had to go pick up my gardener. His car stalled, and he needs a ride home."

"Uh huh," he said, still aiming his flashlight at Adam. "Driver's license?" Trudy pulled her license from her purse and handed it to the policeman. "You live in Anton."

"Yes, sir."

"Long ways to drive to rescue a gardener."

Trudy shrugged. "Well, I reckon I was the only one he could think of to call."

Handing Trudy her license, the policeman asked, "Did you by any chance drive by that adoption office back there on?

"Adoption agency?" Trudy asked.

"It's called Christian Rescue."

"Oh. Uh, I'm not sure," Trudy said. "Did we drive by that place, Adam?" she asked over her shoulder.

"Kinda hard to see from the back seat," Adam said.

"We think somebody might have tried to break in. Just wanted to see if you noticed anything," the policeman said.

Trudy shook her head. "I didn't see anything like that. Did you, Adam?"

"No, ma'am."

The policeman moved the beam of his flashlight all over the interior of the car again. "All right," he said. "You're free to go. Be careful on the road at night."

"Oh, I will," Trudy said. She started the car and watched, again through her mirror, as the policeman turned his car around and headed back in the direction of the adoption agency. She breathed an audible sigh of relief as she drove away toward the hotel.

Trudy had driven several blocks before Adam spoke up from the back. "Your *gardener*?"

"It's all I could think of."

"I believe that's what they call systemic racism."

"I believe it's called keeping your ass out of trouble."

Adam snorted, but Trudy knew it was to cover a laugh.

The next morning, Trudy brought Marta a breakfast tray from the buffet so she wouldn't have to be seen in public again, then called everyone else to a meeting in the room she and Marta shared to give them the information she had gathered at the adoption agency.

"You have an address?" Grace asked. "How did you manage that?"

"Detective work," Trudy said.

"Internet?" Jasmine asked.

"Something like that," Trudy answered, doing her best not to look at Adam. At the same time, she was wondering if there was some way she could have found the information on the Internet without risking what she and Adam went through the night before. It was hard to keep up with the times.

"Cool!" Jasmine said.

"So what do we do now?" Grace asked. "Do we just drive by and look for her?"

"Not a good idea," Adam said.

"*Mi hija! O, mi hija! Ahora, tengo que orinar.*" Marta stood suddenly and hurried toward the bathroom.

"What did she say?" Trudy asked.

"She said she has to pee," Jasmine said.

"Maybe Hank will know what to do," Grace said. "He was supposed to be here last night, but he got delayed because he had to help some woman with her plumbing."

"Josephine," Adam and Trudy said at the same time.

"She's always got plumbing problems," Adam said. "Floods her kitchen every once in a while. She can afford a plumber, but she calls Hank."

"You ought to go help her," Trudy said. "You know about plumbing."

"She won't let me in her house," Adam said.

"Why? Cause you're black?" Jasmine asked. "That's shitty."

THE LAST OF THE BAILEYS

Before Grace could correct her daughter's language, there was a knock at the door along with a voice. "Law enforcement. Open up!"

"Stop trying to be funny, Hank," Grace said just as she opened the door. It wasn't Hank. The man standing in front of her wore the uniform of Immigration and Customs Enforcement.

"Ms. Trudy Bailey?" the official asked amid the stares of everyone in the room.

"Yes?" Trudy said.

"You're under arrest, Ms. Bailey. Put your hands behind your back."

Chapter 13

Trudy had never been inside a jail cell before. It looked cleaner than she expected. Nevertheless, she was certain that it was not clean at all. How many times had that cot been slept on? Did they wash the bedding? Was that thing over in the corner supposed to be a toilet? Was she supposed to sit down on it? The sink looked okay, but where was she supposed to shower?

Above all that, how was she going to get out of here? She had been read the charges: harboring an illegal alien. She'd heard the statement that anything she said could and would be held against her.

She didn't have a lawyer, but Grace had shouted to her as she was being led away, "Don't say anything, Trudy! Don't say a word! I'm trying to get you a lawyer."

How was she going to do that? She had even less money than Trudy. Now, it seemed to Trudy that the waning years of her life would be spent rotting in a prison. That was definitely not the way she had planned it.

Trudy was sitting on her bunk in an orange jumpsuit that she wished was a little roomier through the hips. She was staring at the wall opposite her when a guard showed up on the other side of the steel bars. She was a short woman with a stocky build and hair dyed red and cropped short. Her face was young in Trudy's eyes, maybe mid-forties. It was an angular face, unaccustomed to smiling.

"You got visitors," the guard said. "Stand up and walk toward me."

Trudy obeyed. The guard frisked her through the bars, then asked her to turn around and frisked her again. She unlocked the cell, and in a movement so quick it seemed hardly perceivable, she pulled Trudy's arms behind her back and snapped on a pair of handcuffs then repeated the entire frisking routine.

She led Trudy toward a booth with glass in the front, shielding Grace and Jasmine, and a telephone on a shelf, just like in the movies. Who'd have thought? She said nothing out loud and waited while the guard removed the handcuffs and locked Trudy inside.

"I'll be standing outside," the guard said as she unlocked the handcuffs.

"Call out when you're done. You got forty-five minutes. Total."

Jasmine stood several feet away behind Grace who stepped forward and picked up the phone. Trudy sat in the chair provided for her.

"Oh my God, Trudy. This is awful. Try not to worry. I'm trying to find a lawyer."

"Won't I get a public defender?"

"I'll call the ACLU."

Trudy shook her head. "I don't know …"

"Look, Hank is going to help, too. He'll speak up for you. That should count for something, him being a policeman. He'll be here soon to talk to you."

"I don't see how he can help. Is he going to tell them Marta wasn't at my house?"

"Don't say that, Trudy!" Grace said, looking alarmed. "Don't say she was at your house. You didn't invite her! Don't say anything about it at all, except to the lawyer."

Trudy knew Grace was right. She shouldn't say anything except to a lawyer, but things had gotten out of hand, much worse than she ever thought they would. She was scared out of her wits. "They tell me it could be up to five years in prison and a ten-thousand-dollar fine. I can find the money somewhere. Borrow it from the bank maybe, but—"

"It won't be that much," Grace said, interrupting her. "It never is. That's just the maximum."

"But five years in prison!" Trudy continued. "I might not even live that long."

"Stop it, Trudy! We'll get you out of this. You believe that, don't you?"

Trudy hesitated before she answered with a lie. "Yes."

"Good. Now, here's the thing: Hank is going to talk to the lawyer when we get one, and he'll explain everything. Don't worry; he knows what he's doing, and as I said, he'll be here soon to talk to you."

"Adam …?" Trudy asked.

"Oh yes, he'll come see you," Grace assured her. "You and I both know he will. I haven't talked to him about it, but—"

"You haven't talked to him? Why not?"

"Well, I can't find him."

Trudy felt a jolt of worry. "Can't find him? Is something wrong?"

Grace shook her head and frowned. "Oh no. I don't think so. He just … you know … had some business to take care of."

"Business? What kind of business?"

Grace frowned again and mouthed, "You know."

"Oh. Sure," Trudy said. He was hiding Marta, of course. She tried to listen to the rest of what Grace had to say to her: more reassuring bromides, how she should keep her courage up, how she was sure Hank had all the solutions. Eventually, Grace turned around and looked over her shoulder at Jasmine.

"My time's almost up," Grace said. "I promised Jasmine I'd save some time for her."

As Grace put down the phone and stood to make way for her daughter, Jasmine moved toward the booth like a purposeful stalker.

"Listen to me. This is all bullshit," she said, "and I don't give a flying fuck about what they say is legal. It's bullshit. And a public defender? Don't even think about it. We got to get a *real* lawyer, no matter what it costs. Don't worry about that." She looked both ways over each shoulder before she continued in a whisper. "You know that plan I have? The one to," she wiggled her eyebrows, "earn a little money?"

"You mean about the bank?"

Jasmine looked alarmed. "Bank? I don't know what you're talking about." She put a finger to her lips in a shushing gesture. "Anyway, as soon as I can get back to Anton, which I can assure you won't be long if I put my mind to it, I'm putting my plan into action. I think I can get Adam to help out in the way, you know, in the way you were going to help."

"I never agreed to help."

"No, but I know you would if … Listen, just play along with them and the whole public defender thing until me and Adam can get things in order."

"You don't even know where Adam is," Trudy said.

"And that's a good thing," Jasmine said. "If we can't find him, that means the cops can't. But don't worry. He'll show up. He's got to."

Before Jasmine could say more, the guard knocked on Trudy's door and bellowed, "Time's up!"

Just before Trudy put her phone receiver down, she saw tears shining in Jasmine's eyes. The would-be-tough kid was trying to hold them back. She brought the receiver back to her face and said, "Don't worry, Lobo. Everything will be okay." Jasmine hadn't heard her because the phone had already been turned off.

When the red-haired guard took Trudy back to her cell, she told her she would be allowed an hour in the community room to watch television at six-thirty. Trudy didn't want to watch television, so she asked the guard to bring her the day's paper to read.

"What? You scared of the population? Or you just think you're too good to mingle with the hoi polloi?" the guard asked.

"I just want to read the paper," Trudy said.

It was an hour before the guard showed up with the paper, which she thrust through the bars, letting it fall on the floor.

Trudy had skimmed through a front-page story about local politics and was reading a Dear Abby column about a woman whose husband's best friend had moved in with them. She felt some sympathy, since she'd had a few surprised additions of people living with her recently. The more she read, however, the more trivial the problem seemed compared to those of her own, not to mention those of Marta and Concepcion. She flipped through the pages to find the comic section. Even that couldn't hold her attention, so she settled on the daily horoscope. Apparently, she needed more excitement in her life in order to make her existence more meaningful.

She was still looking for something to take her mind off jail and off Marta, Concepcion, and the possible whereabouts of Adam when the guard showed up outside her cell again.

"You got another visitor," she said in a voice that sounded like a machine gun firing. "There's a limit of three a day, not counting your lawyer." She waited a few seconds before she shot a command at Trudy. "Stand up. Get over here. I ain't coming in to get you."

Trudy stood and went to stand in front of the bars to go through the same ritual she had earlier.

"All right, come on," the guard said, leading the handcuffed Trudy toward the visitor booths. As they walked up the hall, she said, "You might like to know, this one's a cop."

Was that a gesture of friendship? Trudy wondered. A kind of warning? Probably not. There was too much glee in the guard's voice. She felt her heart pounding with fear. Wasn't she supposed to have a lawyer when she talked to any kind of cop? As soon as the guard opened the door, Trudy saw Hank, wearing his sheriff's uniform, and relief left her feeling weak. She all but fell into the chair across from him once the handcuffs were off.

Hank held the phone to his face, but he seemed unable to speak. All he could do was look at her with a stricken expression. Trudy thought for a moment that he might be about to cry. Finally, he spoke.

"Ms. Trudy ..."

"Yes?" Trudy said after what seemed like an inordinately long pause.

"I ... I just want you to know, I didn't say anything to that guy from ICE about ..."

"Never thought you would," Trudy said.

"It's just that … Well, they did an investigation. You know, asking around, asking neighbors, I mean. Seems somebody must have seen some things."

"Yeah." Trudy could well imagine Josephine seeing some things.

"We'll get you through this, Ms. Trudy. Grace is trying to get you a lawyer." Hank's face brightened a little when he said that.

"So I hear."

"ACLU."

Trudy nodded.

"Never thought much of that outfit before," Hank said. "Always heard they were kind of like Commies, but I guess they have their place."

"Yes, they do."

"I sure hope we can get you out of this."

Trudy nodded again. She wasn't feeling any better. She didn't see how she was going to get out of this. After all, she had, in fact, harbored an illegal alien. She was guilty. She was going to prison.

"Listen," Hank said, leaning toward her. "Don't you admit anything you don't have to, not even to the lawyer." When Trudy didn't reply, Hank took on a worried expression. "Of course, you have to tell the truth, but you don't have to say *everything*. I tell you I've seen some lawyers that are so smart they can get a murderer off. It's all in the twists and turns of the law."

"A murderer?"

"I didn't mean it like that," Hank said quickly. "You're not a murderer. I just mean you didn't really do anybody any harm, now, did you?"

"Did you find who murdered that guy?"

"Well. Yes and no." Hank paused and added, "You don't have to worry about it, though."

"What do you mean, yes and no."

"The Feds know who did it, they just haven't found them yet. Just don't worry. We're all working to get you through this."

Trudy wanted to cry, but she had to hold up. Everyone was trying to help her, including Jasmine. Her eyes widened at the thought of Jasmine. "Don't let Jasmine go back to Anton unless somebody's with her all the time."

"Well ... sure." Hank sounded puzzled. 'She's not likely to go by herself, you know."

"I mean it. Don't let her go back to Anton."

"Uh, okay."

"She's planning to rob the bank."

"What? What bank?"

"The Anton Bank."

Hank laughed.

"Don't laugh. She's serious," Trudy said.

"She's a kid. She can't be serious."

"She's a teenager. She's serious."

Hank frowned again. "Why would she want to do a thing like that? Don't we have enough trouble already?"

"More than enough." Trudy rubbed her wrists where the handcuffs had irritated them.

"She wants to get the money to pay a lawyer."

"Grace will get you a lawyer."

"Apparently, Jasmine thinks a lawyer has to be expensive to be good. Just watch her, okay?"

Hank's expression grew even more troubled before he said, "Okay. I'll keep an eye on her." He was silent for a second before he added, "She should know there's no way she can pull it off."

"Maybe not, but she can cause a lot of trouble trying to pull it off." While Hank was shaking his head in disbelief, she added in a whisper, "Now tell me, where are Adam and Marta?"

"Damned if I know," Hank whispered in reply. "I figure Adam has taken her somewhere to hide her. I know! I know!" he said, holding up his free hand as if to defend himself from what he knew Trudy would say. "I'll find 'em! I was on my way to check on 'em, but I wanted to stop by and see how you're doing first. Now, I guess I'd better go check on Jasmine."

Trudy ducked her head and breathed a sigh. "Thanks, Hank. I know you've got your hands full."

"You might say that."

"I should have turned that woman in the first time I saw her coming out of my basement."

"Yeah. You should have notified me," Hank said.

"What would you have done about it?" Trudy asked.

Hank looked at her for a long time before he answered. "I guess I'm no better at this than you are."

Chapter 14

Adam had followed Marta into the bathroom as soon as he had heard the knock on the door to Trudy's room in the hotel. When Marta saw him close the door, she gave him a look that was part surprise and part fear. Adam responded by holding a finger to pursed lips as a signal for her to be quiet.

A quick glance around the bathroom revealed no window. There was only a combination exhaust fan and heater in the ceiling, mounted flush against the plaster with no screws or hinges visible. He knew how to loosen it, but even with his six-foot-plus stature, it was too high to reach. He could hear the ICE officers in the bedroom and knew he had to think of something quickly before they opened the door.

If he stood on the toilet, he could reach the ceiling and the cover to the fan, but since the fan wasn't directly above the toilet, he would have to lean forward in a precarious position that would put him in danger of falling on his face. He saw it as his only option, however, so he closed the lid to the toilet and stood on it. He took a pocketknife out of his pocket, a multi-tooled Swiss Army knife he'd bought years ago. Tilting his body forward, he could barely reach the fan cover, so he moved forward until his feet were on the edge of the toilet and bent forward again.

Marta, who had remained silent until that moment, drew in her breath in a frightened manner and stepped in front of Adam to steady his legs. Adam wasn't certain that her gesture was at all helpful and, in fact, might even cause him to tumble forward, taking both of them down. He didn't speak, however. He kept prying at the cover until it loosened and was hanging by wires from the interior of the ceiling. He caught it before it could tumble to the floor and make a noise that would attract the ICE men. Once it was in hand, he tried to push the wires aside to afford better access to the opening. In the process, he lost his balance and regained it only by planting his hands on Marta's shoulders.

One look at the opening told him that it would be a challenge to get his broad shoulders through the opening and only a little less difficult for Marta to squeeze through.

Adam went first, inadvertently loosening one of the boards in the frame of the opening, but once his shoulders were through the opening, he used his arms to pull the rest of his body upward. Marta watched with frightened eyes from below until Adam signaled for her to stand on the toilet and reach toward him. She followed his instructions, but she wasn't tall enough to grasp the sides of the opening and boost herself up. Adam had to lean over the edge to grab her wrists and pull all 120 pounds of her up and all the way out of the opening until she was lying, belly down, on the rafters of the building.

Just before the bathroom door opened and the ICE men entered, Adam had stuffed the wires in a tangled mass into the crawl space and replaced the covering in what he knew was a less-than-perfect way. It proved good enough, however. When the officers came in to inspect the bathroom, they didn't notice that the covering was slightly askew.

The crawl space in the ceiling was sweltering as Adam and Marta lay sprawled on their stomachs across the rafters, waiting for some sign that the officers were gone and not daring to make a sound as long as they could hear voices. All the while, Adam was searching for a possible way out of their confinement. When he saw light coming through a vent several yards away on the side of the building, facing away from the front, he felt a flicker of hope. It wouldn't be easy to reach, however, since it would require walking in a stooped position across a long stretch of rafters. He also knew that the grate that covered the opening would likely be attached with screws on the outside of the building. His handy pocket tool would be of no use. If they were to escape through the vent, he would have to kick it out from the inside. Even if it was possible to do, he knew it would make noise that would attract maintenance people and curious onlookers. The only thing to do was to wait until the ICE police left and crawl back into the bathroom the same way they had exited.

It was a long sweltering wait. Adam's shoulders ached from the effort needed to keep from rolling off the rafter he was balanced on. He was face down, with the rafter pressing uncomfortably into his stomach. Sweat dampened his clothes and stung his eyes. Marta, he knew, was suffering the same agony as he was, but he didn't dare twist himself around to check because of the risk of making noise that would attract the police.

After what seemed an eternity, Adam heard the door to the bathroom open and heard the voices of the policeman.

"Nobody in here," one of them said.

"You sure?" another asked. His question was followed by the sound of a shower door opening.

"No window. No way for them to escape."

"The exhaust vent?"

"Naw, too narrow. Both of 'em are too big to squeeze through there."

The door opened and closed again. Adam didn't move. He could still hear voices coming from the bedroom. Eventually, the door to the hallway opened and closed again, and the room was silent. Still, Adam didn't move, and neither did Marta. They waited several minutes before Adam inched forward toward the vent and pushed it open. It fell to the floor with a resounding clatter. Adam involuntarily sucked in his breath and held it. There was no response to the noise, however, so he inched forward and stuck his legs through the opening, letting himself down as far as he could go, then drawing his shoulders together to make himself as small as possible so he could force himself all the way out of the opening, breaking some of the plaster loose around the opening in the process.

Once he was through the gap, he stood on the toilet and reached a hand up to help Marta. This time she came down headfirst. Adam surmised that it was to keep her skirt as close to her body as possible. He grabbed her arms and pulled. The loosened plaster and boards made her descent through the opening a little easier, but her head-first exit had been a mistake. She tumbled out of the crevice, falling on top of Adam. He grunted at the impact, but Marta didn't make a sound. She pushed herself off Adam quickly, then stood and offered a hand to help him up.

Adam nodded his thanks, then set about trying to get the vent cover in place again. The new damage to the opening made it more difficult, but he managed to get it in place in a precarious manner. Marta had already cleaned up the plaster from the floor by the time he finished.

Carefully, Adam opened the door a crack and looked outside. Since no one had come to look during all the noise the two of them had made, he was fairly confident no one was in the bedroom, but, he told himself, it never hurt to be cautious. The room was empty, and he signaled for Marta to follow him. The fact that the keys to Trudy's car were still on the lamp table where she had placed them when they returned earlier surprised him. How did she leave without her car? It wouldn't be likely that they all left in Hank's patrol car, would it? He didn't have time to ponder that now, however. He picked up the keys and signaled for Marta to follow him.

He unlocked the car and opened the back door and, using elaborate sign language and his limited Spanish, persuaded Marta to lie down on the back seat. He knew it had been a mistake to take her out in public when they went to that restaurant, and he wasn't going to make the same mistake twice. Once Marta was prone on the back seat and out of sight of anyone looking at the car from the outside, he drove away, trying not to look like someone who was stealing a car. He didn't know where he was going, but he knew he had to get Marta away from the hotel in case law enforcement showed up again.

Marta was talking to him from the back seat, but he had no idea what she was saying.

"*No comprendo,*" he said.

"*Usa el telephono!*"

She was telling him to use the telephone? Of course! The way Jasmine had used it, to translate Spanish and English. Adam pulled his phone from his hip pocket and stared at it, holding it with one hand while he drove the car. Translation would require an app—one that he didn't have. But there was something called an app store. Is that where he would find it? He and Trudy had joked about how the world of technology had left them behind, but it was no laughing matter now. He had to figure this out. He couldn't do it while he was driving, though, and if a cop saw him staring at his phone, he was sure to be pulled over and charged with something like texting while driving while being black.

He put the phone down and drove a few more blocks until he saw a big building just ahead: a Costco Warehouse with its over-sized parking lot. Maybe there was a God after all. He pulled into the parking lot and drove around until he found a space far enough away from the entrance that he wouldn't be likely be watched.

Finding an app store on his phone and then figuring out how to use it took him some time, and since he'd never purchased an app before, he had to put the phone down to pull his wallet out of another pocket and find his credit card. Once that was done, there was the matter of using the app. It wasn't as difficult as he'd thought it would be. In a little while, he had typed in English, "I don't know where to take you, but I have to hide you somewhere."

The translation came back: *"No se' a dónde lievarte, pero yo agave para esconderte en alguna parte."*

Adam tried to relay the sentence to her, but it was met with a troubled frown from Marta. He knew then that his pronunciation was less than perfect. It apparently got even worse when he tried again. Finally, Marta took the phone from him and read the words in one glance. She said something in Spanish. Adam thought she was saying, "I want to go to my daughter."

"You can't do that! Someone is sure to see us," Adam said aloud before realizing he'd have to write it. He typed his protest.

Tears pooled in Marta's eyes when she read the translation, and she began speaking in Spanish, the words tumbling out too rapidly for Adam to understand. It took him several minutes to realize that the translator could be switched to Spanish to English. He managed to explain to Marta how to use it, but she had no expertise with typing, so several more minutes passed before she handed him the phone with the explanation that she would get out of the car now and walk to the house where she'd learned her daughter was living if Adam refused to drive her. The sight of those tears clutched at Adam's heart. He didn't know whether they were tears of anger or of desperation, but he knew it didn't matter. Marta would find her daughter one way or the other.

With a sigh of reluctant resignation, Adam started the car and drove out of the parking lot headed for 76th street. Finding the street wasn't a problem, since he knew where the numbered streets began. Houses were numbered beginning with 814. He stopped long enough to write Marta a translated text, telling her to watch for 2205. She nodded her compliance, but he soon realized the house numbers were descending to the 700s. Turning the car around, he drove the opposite direction for fifteen blocks to the 2200s. Long before he reached that block, however, he noticed houses had given way to strip malls and gas stations. Trudy had said the number could be 2205. There was no such number.

The other number Trudy thought she remembered was 5802, so he kept driving until he reached a dead end somewhere in the 3800s. In front of him was a metal barrier and beyond that an open field of weeds and grass. When he turned around to look at Marta and saw the expression on her face, he knew she understood their situation.

He turned the car around and drove to a cross street, hoping to find a way to get back on a route to the 5800 block, if it even existed. He'd driven for almost an hour before he found 76th Street again. The numbers began with 5001, however, and the street was only five blocks long. There seemed to be no such number as 5802. Adam turned the car around once again and headed down the street.

"Trudy got it wrong," Adam said. "Maybe she's got some kind of—what do they call it—dyslexia or something? Or maybe she was in such a hurry to get out of that place before she got caught that she just didn't get a good look. Or she forgot. She's no spring chicken, you know. We start to forget things after a while. Whatever. She sent us on a wild goose chase." He was speaking in English and knew he was blabbering on without Marta understanding. Still, he had to do it, had to get it off his chest. He might have gone on if Marta hadn't come out with a loud screech and started talking in rapid Spanish that, once again, he was unable to understand.

Marta was pounding on his shoulder and gesturing at something behind them. That was enough to let him know he had to back up. He kept driving backward until Marta said in an excited voice, *"Aqui! Aqui!"*

Adam stopped the car long enough to see why Marta was so excited. A young girl, slender and pretty with dark hair and olive skin, stood in the yard. She was dressed like any teenager in jeans and a T-shirt. He also noticed that the house number was 6208—another sign of Trudy's dyslexia?

"Concepcion!" Marta said and reached for the door handle. At that same moment a woman came out of the house and called out something to the girl, and the girl ran toward the house. The sight of the woman was enough to make Marta pause before she opened the door. Adam took advantage of that pause to step on the gas pedal and drive away.

"*No! Para el coche!*" Marta cried. That was followed by an outburst of Spanish that Adam thought was probably good that he didn't understand.

Adam kept driving until he was forced to stop at a red light. Picking up his phone that he'd placed on the seat beside him, he was attempting to write a message to Marta to tell her that it was best not to attempt to approach Concepcion until they had spoken with the lawyer Grace had promised to contact for Trudy. Before he could finish typing, Marta opened the door in the back where she was sitting and, weaving her way through the stopped cars, made it to the sidewalk and was running back toward the house where she'd seen her daughter.

Since Adam was in the middle lane at the stop light, it took him several minutes to get to the outside lane so he could turn off of the street, merge back on, and head in the direction Marta was going. He caught up to her a little more than a block from the house Marta was trying to reach. He stopped the car beside her and lowered the window to shout, "Get in. If you're that determined, I'll take you to her."

Marta didn't stop. She picked up her pace and kept running toward the house, letting Adam know that she hadn't understood him. He shook his head in frustration and drove to the house, stopping in front of it. He got out of the car until she made it to the edge of the property. Marta stopped, her face crumpled with anger when she saw Adam coming toward her, but she lunged forward, trying to sidestep Adam.

When he caught her in his arms and restrained her, she struggled to get away. "I'm going with you," Adam said before he loosened his grip. Marta looked at him with a puzzled expression, but when he gestured with his arms like an usher showing her the way, she walked toward the house, glancing nervously at Adam as he walked beside her.

Adam rang the doorbell for her, and they waited only a few seconds before Concepcion came to the door. Marta and Concepcion stared at each other without speaking.

"Who is it, Connie?" a voice from somewhere in the house called.

Chapter 15

Jasmine had washed the green and pink and most of the purple from her hair. She used the blow dryer in the hotel bathroom to fashion it into a sleek, straight style. She'd removed her strategically frayed jeans and T-shirt and replaced them with a pair of regular jeans and a plain white top she'd taken from her mother's suitcase. The jeans were baggy on her skinny frame, but she thought that it would help make her look like a starving waif. She worried that the sneakers she wore looked too expensive, but that couldn't be helped unless she wore her mother's preppy-looking loafers. She wasn't going *that* far. Besides, they were too small for her.

Once she felt she was sufficiently disguised, she walked the short distance from the hotel to the loop road and the exit that would take her to Highway 84 and eventually to Anton. She stood with her hand out and her thumb extended for almost an hour before someone in a pickup finally stopped a few feet ahead and started backing toward her.

"Where you headed, kid?" The driver was an old man. Jasmine thought he looked like he was at least forty. He was wearing a cowboy hat like every other man she'd seen in West Texas. He was clean shaven, but his face was a ruddy red, just like his hands.

"I'm headed for Anton," Jasmine said.

"Well, get in. I'm going as far as Shallowater. You can just about walk the rest of the way." The man reached across the seat to open the door for her. "You kinda young to be out hitchhickin', ain't ye?" he asked.

"I'm nearly eighteen," Jasmine said. "I'm just small for my age."

"Uh huh." The man dropped a cigarette butt on the pavement from the open window on the driver's side. Jasmine thought it looked like a reefer. "Name's Bobby. Bobby Lightner." When Jasmine didn't reply, he asked, "What's your name?"

He caught her off guard. "Uh, my name's uh Toni. Toni Bailey."

"You kin to them Baileys that used to live in Anton?"

"No, I don't think so," Jasmine said. Why hadn't she come up with another name? She wasn't thinking fast enough. She had to get her act together or nothing would work out. "My family lives in California," she said.

"Then why you goin' to Anton?"

"I'm supposed to meet my father there. His name's Ramon Gonzales."

"Meskin name."

"Yeah. I'm half Mexican. Bailey is the name of my adopted father."

Bobby Lightner said nothing in reply, and they drove in silence for several miles. Jasmine was grateful for the silence, but she couldn't relax completely since she was trying to concentrate on keeping her story straight. Bobby hardly slowed down when they came to

Shallowater, and within a few minutes, they were all the way through town, still on the highway.

"Hey!" Jasmine turned around to look behind them. "Wasn't that Shallowater?"

"Yep," Bobby said.

"Isn't that where you said you were going?"

"Changed my mind."

Jasmine felt a tinge of nervousness. "So where are we going?"

"Anton. Ain't that where you said you wanted to go?"

"Yeah, but how come you—"

"Listen, kid—Toni—I'm takin' you all the way into Anton. It ain't but just a few miles, but I'm keeping you off the highway. You got no business out on the road hitchhiking like that. You never know who will pick you up. You could get raped or killed."

Jasmine stared at him, her eyes wide. That thought hadn't occurred to her.

"You ain't never hitchhiked before. I can tell," Bobby said.

Jasmine didn't reply. She was still thinking about what Bobby had just said. Maybe he was right. Maybe she shouldn't think about hitchhiking back to Lubbock once she got the money. But if she had money … Yeah, she told herself, with money, she could afford to take a taxi back. Did Anton even have taxis? She'd certainly never seen one, and it was a really small town. She'd think about that later, though. For now, she still had to deal with Bobby Lightner. He was asking her more questions.

"So, where you supposed to meet your dad?"

"Uh … in front of the bank. No! I mean drug store. In front."

Bobby looked at her with a squint and a frown. "So, which is it? The bank or the drug store."

"Drug store," Jasmine said. "It's the drug store."

"You sure?"

"I'm sure."

They had driven only a short distance further before Bobby glanced in his rearview mirror and said something under his breath that sounded like, "Oh, shit!" In the next second came the screech of a police siren.

Jasmine felt every nerve in her body shudder. She held her breath as the policeman approached Bobby's side of the pickup.

"License," the policeman said.

Bobby pulled his wallet from a hip pocket and extracted his driver's license.

"You got a taillight that's broke. Hanging by a wire," the policeman said.

"Oh yeah, I gotta get that fixed," Bobby said.

The policeman gestured with a nod of his head toward Jasmine. "That your kid?"

"My niece," Bobby said.

The policeman frowned, and suspicion darkened his eyes. "Get out of the car, please." He stepped back, his hand on the butt of his gun. "You too, Miss," he added with a nod toward Jasmine. She complied and went to stand beside Bobby when the policeman told her to. He searched the interior, patting the seat with his hands, bending over to look under the seat, and finally opening the glove compartment. He rummaged around the inside and pulled out a small plastic bag. Jasmine recognized the contents: pot. Looked like a fraction of an ounce, she thought. Maybe not even enough for one joint.

The policeman opened the bag and sniffed before he looked at Bobby. "This yours?"

Bobby took a deep breath. "Yeah, I guess it is."

"No, Uncle Bobby! You don't have to lie for me," Jasmine said, turning to the policeman. "It's mine. A kid I know gave it to me, and I hid it in there so Uncle Bobby wouldn't see it."

"Who gave it to you?"

"A kid in Lubbock."

"You know his name?"

"Gonzalez," Jasmine said, speaking before thinking. "Name's Gonzalez Gonzalez. Weird name, I know. I call him Gonzo."

"You know where he lives?"

"Lubbock." Jasmine's mouth was dry, as if she had just smoked a joint herself.

"Where in Lubbock?"

"I don't know. I'm not from there. I'm from California. I'm just visiting my uncle Bobby."

The policeman looked at Bobby. "You know the kid she's talking about?"

Bobby shook his head. "Never heard of him."

The policeman studied the bag in silence for a few seconds and looked at Jasmine again. "Don't be taking this stuff from anybody, you hear? It can get you in trouble." He stuffed the plastic bag into his shirt pocket and turned to Bobby. "Keep an eye on her. You don't want her to get into trouble while she's here."

"I'll do that," Bobby said, looking stricken.

They watched the policeman get in his car before they both got back into the pickup. Bobby turned to Jasmine and spoke first. "Thanks, kid. I owe you one."

Jasmine shrugged.

"Listen, I want you to know I don't use that stuff all the time. Just now and then. No harm in once every week or so, you know."

"Sure."

Bobby puffed out his cheeks and blew the air out slowly as he started the pickup and drove once again toward Anton, neither of them speaking. Jasmine knew Bobby was embarrassed by what had just transpired. When they reached the town, Bobby drove the short distance to the drug store and parked in front of it before she opened the door and jumped out. "Thanks!" she said. Before she could close the door, Bobby spoke again.

"Get back in. We'll wait here until your daddy shows up."

"Oh no! You don't need to do that." Jasmine was alarmed. This thing was much more complicated than she had expected.

"Get back in," Bobby growled. "You're just a kid. I ain't leavin' you by yourself."

"I'm not a kid. I'm eighteen, and I've already been married once. Got a divorce. I can take care of myself."

"Yeah, sure you can."

Jasmine waited, still standing on the sidewalk for several seconds. Bobby's scowl grew darker as he started the car. "Suit yourself, kid."

Jasmine watched until he turned onto the highway leading back to Shallowater and Lubbock. When he was out of sight, she hurried across the street on her way to the Bailey Boarding House, no more than four blocks away if she cut through alleys and backyards. Trudy had given both Jasmine and her mother keys to the house so that, if they should be out late at night, they could come in without bothering her. Trudy had made it quite clear that she didn't like to be bothered.

Neither of them had used their keys, however. There was no place to go in Anton, no reason to stay out late, no reason to cause any bother to Trudy. Jasmine had reason to use it now, though. She had to get Trudy's gun. The idea of having a gun in her possession frightened her a little, but it gave her a jolt of excitement too. She pushed away both emotions and made her way through weed-filled alleys that sliced through the space in the backs of houses and across backyards when the alleys ran out, all the while holding onto the waist of her jeans so they wouldn't fall off her hips. The alleys were full of weeds that had a green, pungent smell despite being slightly wilted from thirst and the relentless yellow ball of sun that took possession of the sky every day. The backyards were either dusty and void of grass or damp from moveable sprinklers spewing big droplets of water on lawns that ranged from lush to struggling.

Within a few minutes, she was in the wide space behind the boarding house and Adam Bailey's house. She picked up her pace and ran through the stretch of spotty Bermuda grass that both Trudy and Adam called their backyard. She opened the screen door at the back of the boarding house and tried to insert the key in the lock. The key was too big. If it didn't fit the back, it had to fit the front. She held the key in her fist and grasped the waist of her jeans to run around the wooden-frame building. Just as she rounded the final corner, she stopped and looked both ways to make sure no one was on the street who might see her. There was nothing in sight and only the sound of a motor that was at least a block away, so she hurried up the steps of the porch and pushed the key into the lock. She felt a surge of relief when the key turned, and she heard the lock click.

The house smelled old as she stepped inside, the same scent she had noticed when she first entered weeks ago. It wasn't stinky old, just old, like a hundred years of beeswax furniture polish and laundry soap and pots of beans and pot roast. She'd grown used to the smell over the short time she and her mother had lived there, but the house felt creepy now. It was too full of quiet, too heavy with antique furniture and silent old memories. She stood in the parlor for a moment, not moving, as if she were waiting for something or someone.

She knew she had to shake herself out of her paralysis, though, and get on with her task. The gun, she surmised, would be in Trudy's bedroom somewhere. She moved toward the downstairs bedroom, dreading the thought of opening drawers and going through Trudy's belongings to find the gun—old lady panties, oversized bras, panty-hose, and God only knew what else old women stashed away.

As she opened the door and stepped inside Trudy's bedroom, she noticed first that the bed had been made up carelessly with the bedspread slightly askew, the pillows on top of the spread instead of folded under it the way old-fashioned people made a bed. A faded robe that she'd seen Trudy wearing in the mornings was draped care-lessly over the handlebars of an exercise bike with dust on the seat that spoke of underuse.

There were two chests and a dresser in the room as well as two nightstands, one on each side of the bed. All of them held papers and books and an assortment of knickknacks on the top. Where to start? The nightstands maybe. Wouldn't she want the gun within easy reach in case of an intruder?

Jasmine could hardly believe her luck when she opened the drawer of the nightstand closest to the door and saw the gun lying there on top of more papers and a couple of wadded tissues. She held her breath as she picked it up. She'd never held a gun before.

Grace was firmly against guns for just about any reason, and her dad, though he owned a handgun and some hunting rifles, had never offered to teach her to shoot.

The weapon felt strange in her hand, and she hesitated a moment before she dropped her hand to her hip, then pretended to draw the pistol from a holster and pointed it at the window.

"Don't move or I'll blow your head off!" She dropped the pistol to her thigh, raised it again, and said, "Hand over the money or I'll blow you to hell." She giggled and tried a quote she'd read in a book about Annie Oakley. "I ain't afraid to love a man, and I ain't afraid to shoot him, either."

With that, she pointed the gun at the window and used her free hand to pretend to cock the gun repeatedly as she called out "Pow, pow, pow." She turned around, blowing at the barrel of the pistol. The final exhale made the waist of her loose jeans slip down over her hips and knees to her ankles.

"Oh fuck!" she said and bent over to retrieve her pants. In the process she dropped the gun. The weapon fired as it hit the floor, startling Jasmine and causing her to stumble backward, entangling her feet in the drooping jeans. She fell on her butt. Her heart thrashed as if it were trying to escape her chest. All she could do was sit on the floor, breathing heavily, trying to make sense of what had just happened. Were there more bullets in the pistol? No, not bullets; you were supposed to call them ammunition or rounds or something like that. If not, how did she load them in? Did she even need to? Would the sight of the pistol be enough to accomplish the heist? Maybe the whole thing was a bad idea. Maybe she should just forget about it.

She sat a little longer, trying to calm herself, and as she sat, she remembered Trudy in that jail. She was a grouchy old lady, crazy too, for thinking her house might be haunted. But she'd opened her house to her and her mother, maybe a little grudgingly at first, but it kept them from being homeless. She fed them, too. That meant something, didn't it? The reason she was in that jail now was because she was trying to help Marta. Some people would think she was crazy for doing that. Even if she was crazy and an old grouch, she didn't belong in that jail, and she deserved the best lawyer money could buy. Jasmine was going to see to it that she got that.

Resolute, she hiked up her jeans, and held onto them, scurrying from the bedroom toward the stairs. She hurried up the stairs, aware that the bank would soon close. She paused as she passed the "haunted" room, recalling the frightening noises she'd heard. Without hesitating a second longer, she ran down the hall to the room she shared with her mother. She slammed the door shut once inside and leaned against it, waiting to catch her breath.

When she was certain there were no more sounds penetrating the walls, she quickly locked the door and hurried to the closet to find a pair of jeans that would fit. There was nothing there that she deemed suitable. She wanted something that would help her come and go unnoticed, but she owned nothing to fit that requirement. It would be useless to choose another pair of her mother's jeans, even if there had been any available. It appeared she had taken the two pairs she owned with her. There were a few pairs of her shorts she wore on occasion folded and resting on a shelf in the closet. She discounted the idea of wearing those now, however, thinking they would make her look too young because of her skinny legs. She owned two dresses of her own. One was a black-and-white-printed halter dress with tombstones—too recognizable even if she didn't wear the leather choker with sharp metal spikes that went with it. The other dress was purple with a cut-out front that was supposed to show the curves of a bosom that Jasmine didn't have. Besides the unflattering front, it was thigh-length and made her legs look as skinny as her shorts did. She'd bought it because she thought it would look good with her black combat boots, if she could just grow some tits.

She'd have to resort to a belt to keep her mother's jeans from falling to her ankles. The first problem was that she didn't own a belt. The second problem was that, apparently, Grace didn't own one either. She learned that when she went through all the drawers. She was about to give up and look for a couple of large safety pins when she spied the frayed pink belt to her mother's bathrobe on the floor of the closet. Within a few seconds, it was secured through the loops of the baggy jeans she wore and tied in the front in a ragged bow. She pulled her T-shirt over the bow, then grabbed a silk scarf she'd seen earlier in her mother's dresser drawer and looped it around her neck. When the time was right, she would cover her face with it.

For now, though, all she had to do was retrieve the gun and be on her way. The pistol was still on the floor in Trudy's bedroom where she had left it. When she entered the bedroom, she noticed for the first time the splintered baseboard where the bullet had struck—no, the round—that had discharged when she dropped the weapon. Next to the splintered board was an old-fashioned standing jewelry chest. All she had to do to conceal the damage was move the chest a little to the left. When that was accomplished, she picked up the gun, carefully this time, and held it barrel down and away from her body as if it might discharge on its own again at any time.

She was still holding the gun with two fingers and a thumb at arm's length as if it were a piece of rotten meat when she reached the front door. Knowing she couldn't be seen carrying the gun that way as she made her way to the bank, she swallowed hard and thrust the weapon into a front pocket. The thought that it might go off again and blow off one of her toes made her hesitate until she remembered the most important mission she'd ever undertaken. Trudy needed her. She couldn't quit now.

Once the front door was open, she looked both ways to make certain no one was watching before she stepped out and used the key to lock the door. If there was enough money left over after they paid the lawyer, Jasmine vowed she would have Trudy install locks that could be secured from the inside with a key for the outside. She'd also have her install air-conditioning. But why should she care? As soon as the car repairs were done, she and her mother would be out of here! She could use the money for a new car, or maybe a new house, back in California where they belonged. It all depended on the size of the heist.

Money filled her thoughts as she made her way back to the alley leading to Main Street and the Anton State Bank. A cold feeling on the back of her neck replaced the daydreams with the sense that someone was following her. Stealing a glance over her shoulder, she saw no one. There was only the sound of a car perhaps a few blocks away. The sound didn't seem to be coming any closer, so Jasmine continued toward the alley. She picked up her pace as she ran across Trudy's and Adam's back lawn. When she reached the alley, she looked behind her again. Seeing no one, she slowed to a walk because she was afraid her movement might cause the pistol to go off again, and anyway, she didn't want to be out of breath when she reached the bank. It was important to appear calm. Nervous, out-of-breath robbers always got caught. She'd learned that from watching television.

Main Street was empty. Heat swirled along with a twisting dust devil on the street. Sweat formed under Jasmine's arms and across her forehead.

Two cars were parked in front of the insurance agency where her mother had worked for a while. Next to it, Cathy's Corner Crafts wouldn't open until one or two o'clock, depending on when Cathy got around to it. The door to Angie's Beauty Parlor was wide open to help the fan in the opening circulate air through the tiny shop. A woman—Jasmine assumed it was Angie—stood in the doorway and waved to her when she saw her. Jasmine didn't wave back. No point in doing anything anyone would remember.

Jasmine was eager to get to the bank where there would be air-conditioning, but by the time she reached the doors, she hesitated with her hand on the brass handle. Did Aunt Maxie Bailey hesitate when she robbed the bank in Lubbock? Probably not. A Bailey wouldn't be afraid. Maybe she wasn't afraid, but she couldn't have been smart either. After all, she got caught and went to prison. A lump of sour-tasting fear formed in Jasmine's throat. She forced it away when once again she remembered Trudy sitting alone in a jail cell with nothing but a public defender to come to her aid. She opened the door and stepped inside, pulling the silk scarf over her face as she entered. The bank lobby appeared to be empty except for the single teller who didn't even look up from her work behind the stall. The icy feeling on the back of Jasmine's neck had returned. She turned around quickly at the sound of a voice.

"You okay?"

"Why are you following me?" Anger mixed with fear clutched at Jasmine's throat as she looked at Bobby Lightner's face. She pulled the scarf down and left it clinging to her neck.

"Following you? I just happened to come into the bank at the same time you did."

"You're lying. I know it."

Bobby tilted his head as he studied Jasmine's face. "You in some kind of trouble?"

"Of course not. Why would you even say a thing like that?" Jasmine couldn't keep her voice from shaking.

"Nobody shootin' at you?"

"Shooting at me? You *are* crazy!"

Bobby didn't answer, but his gaze as he continued to study her face became more intense.

"You've been spying on me," Jasmine said. "Otherwise, how would you know about …" She stopped speaking and drew her lips tight between her teeth before she gave away more than she should. This bank robbery was proving to be a lot more complicated than she'd counted on.

"Go ahead," Bobby said, gesturing toward the teller, who by now had raised her eyes from her work and was watching the two of them intently. "Take care of your banking business. I'll wait, since you came in ahead of me."

Jasmine turned to glance at the teller. "No, I … Uh, I'm in no hurry. You first."

Bobby made no move toward the teller. He kept his eyes on Jasmine. "If you're in some kind of trouble, you ought to tell some-body. I'd tell you to go to the sheriff's office, but he ain't there. That's the way it is in these one-horse towns."

"Mind your own business. You're acting creepy."

"I heard that gun shot after you went into that big old house. That where you live? Or did you just break in? Why is somebody shooting at you?"

"Nobody is shooting at me!" Jasmine shouted.

"Excuse me," the teller said. "I'm going to have to ask you two to leave if you …" The front door opened, and she stopped speaking when she saw who had just walked in. "Hank! Thank God. You got here just in time." She nodded toward Bobby and Jasmine. "These two are causing a disturbance."

"What's going on, Jasmine?" Hank asked.

"Jasmine! Please tell me you're not robbing the bank." Jasmine was chagrined to see that it was her mother speaking. She had come into the building with Hank.

The teller sucked in her breath. "Oh my Lord!" She backed away from her station with her hands raised. "Do something, Hank!"

"Relax, Stella," Hank said. "Nobody's robbing anybody." He took a step toward Jasmine. "You should have told us you wanted to come back to Anton. Your mother has been out of her mind with worry."

"Well, I'll be damned," Bobby said with a little laugh. "You was planning on robbing the bank?"

"No, she wasn't!" Grace said. She turned her gaze back to Jasmine. "Why are you wearing my jeans and my Hermes scarf?"

Jasmine touched the scarf she had tied loosely around her neck to make it easy to slip over her face. "It's not a real Hermes. You know it's a knock-off."

"You were going to … do that thing wearing my clothes?" Grace sounded near tears, but instead of scolding Jasmine more, she went to her daughter and pulled her close. Jasmine didn't resist. She put her head on Grace's shoulder and, despite her effort not to, sobbed into the cotton fabric of her mother's shirt.

"Come on, you two," Hank said, making a show of ushering them out. "It's okay, Stella. This was just a little misunderstanding. You know how teenagers are."

"Misunderstanding?" Stella said. "I don't think … I mean none of my teenagers ever … I don't want that kid back in this bank again."

"Don't worry about that, Stella," Hank said, giving Jasmine an extra shove toward the door. "She won't be giving you any more trouble."

"She better not. I tell you, I'm a nervous wreck. I don't know if I can stay here by myself after this."

"Take the rest of the day off," Hank said over his shoulder. "Martin's gone fishing out in Ruidoso. He'll never know."

"But he's the president of the bank," Stella protested, "I can't just—"

"If he was here, he'd tell you to take the rest of the day off. You know he would. Now, go on home."

"Well, if you think …"

"Go on," Hank said, still trying to get Grace and Jasmine out of the building. Bobby followed them on to the street.

"Rob a bank!" Bobby said and laughed again. "I never would have figured that out. Is that why she's carrying a gun?"

"A gun?" Hank asked.

At the same time, Grace said, "Oh my God," and gave Jasmine a look that was part disbelief and part anger.

"So your name's not Toni? It's Jasmine?" Bobby said.

Jasmine ignored him and looked at her mother. "I wasn't really going to use it. It was just for show."

"Let me have it!" Hank's voice was harshly commanding.

Jasmine lowered her chin and, feeling sheepish, pulled the pistol from her pocket and handed it to Hank.

"We're going to have a talk," he said as he took the gun from her and examined it briefly. "That's Trudy's gun! Did you steal it?"

"No." Jasmine's voice was almost a whisper. "I was going to put it back when I was done."

"When you was done robbing the bank," Bobby said. He appeared to be trying hard not to laugh.

"How did you know about the gun? And who are you?" Hank asked.

"Bobby Lightner," he said, offering his hand. "Live in Shallowater, and I picked up this little girl when she was hitchhiking outta Lubbock."

"Hitchhiking?" Grace was alarmed. "Jasmine, are you out of your mind? You could have been—"

"Raped, killed, both," Bobby said. "I warned her about it."

"The gun?" Hank said. "Did she show it to you?"

"Nah, she didn't have a gun when I picked her up, but something just didn't seem right. Know what I mean? She was acting kinda weird. Thought she might be in some kind of trouble, so after I dropped her off, I kept my eye on her, and ..."

"You *were* following me," Jasmine said. "That's just creepy."

"So, I see that she kinda checks things out over there by the bank, then she takes off through the backway, so it was kinda hard for me to follow, but then I seen her trying to get in that big old house. She finally gets inside, and I think maybe everything's okay. Maybe she lives there, you know, but then I heard a gunshot. I knew it came from that house. I was parked a little ways away, so I drive over there, and I seen her through that front window. She looked okay, so I waited, then she left, so I go over to your office, you know, the sheriff's office, but you wasn't there, so I come back looking for her, and that's when I seen her going into the bank. That bad feeling I had was gettin' worse, so I followed her into the bank. She was still acting real funny, but I never figured she was fixin' to rob the place until y'all showed up."

By the time Bobby finished his account, Jasmine was sobbing again, but she was standing apart from her mother and Hank.

"Hank is not the only one who is going to give you a good tongue lashing," Grace said.

"We'll go to Trudy's place and sit down for this talk," Hank said.

Grace turned to Bobby. "You're welcome to come with us at least for a cup of coffee," she said. "It's the least I can do to thank you for looking after my daughter."

Bobby thanked Grace for the offer but excused himself with the apology that he had to get back to Shallowater. Jasmine would have liked to have him stay as a foil for what she knew would be a humiliation for her. Nevertheless, she steeled herself for what she knew was to come. She knew she would be told it was a foolish and immature act. She would be cautioned never even to think of doing it again. She would mostly likely be threatened with having privileges taken away, as if there were any privileges left for her now that she was in Texas. She couldn't have predicted the added humiliation of the fraying bathrobe belt finally breaking just as they stepped into the lobby of the old boarding house. Before she could catch them, her mother's jeans slipped down to her ankles again, leaving her standing there in her underwear.

Chapter 16

S he said her name was LaTonya Jones, and she asked Trudy if she wasn't kinda old to be in for a felony. Trudy's first instinct was to move to another table in the common area and sit by herself without answering. She hadn't asked LaTonya to sit at the table with her anyway. She didn't move, though. Instead, she told LaTonya a person should never be too old to learn new things.

Trudy had said that without looking at the big woman. She'd kept her gaze focused at a distance on nothing in particular. Her remark made LaTonya laugh.

"Damn!" LaTonya said. "You a cold bitch, ain't ye?" The laugh lingered as a smile on her lips, showing off perfectly aligned teeth stained a pale yellow from cigarettes. Trudy had moved her eyes to look at LaTonya, but she answered with a shrug. "You think you too good to talk to me?" LaTonya asked.

"Why would you say a thing like that?" Trudy asked.

"Cause you actin' like it, bitch."

"I wish you wouldn't call me that. My name is Trudy."

"Don't take no offense when I calls you a bitch. I calls everbody that. You ain't special."

Trudy looked at her and frowned, again without speaking.

LaTonya pulled a pack of cigarettes from the pocket of her jail jumpsuit and offered a smoke to Trudy. "Just how old are you?" she asked when Trudy declined. She flicked her lighter and lit her cigarette, blowing the smoke toward the ceiling.

"I'll be a hundred and two next month. How old are you?"

LaTonya sputtered out another laugh and picked a piece of tobacco from her tongue. "You full of shit," she said, still laughing. She put her cigarette pack down on the table and stood. "I'm fixin' to get myself a cup of coffee. You want one?"

"Sure," Trudy said. "Sugar, no cream." She watched as the big woman walked toward the coffee machine, wide hips swaying, her body moving with the grace of a cat. When she returned, she placed a paper cup full of coffee in front of Trudy and sat down across from her with her own cup.

"You ain't never been in here before, have you?" LaTonya asked. "I can tell. You got that look."

"My first time." Trudy blew on her coffee, forcing some of the steam away. "How'd you know it was a felony?"

"Harboring a wetback. Word gets around in a place like this."

"She's not a wetback. Don't use that word."

"Don't use what word? Wetback? Shit, that's what they are."

"Don't use it. How do you like it when someone calls you a disrespectful name?"

"Like what?"

Trudy shrugged. "You tell me. What do you hate for people to call you?

LaTonya was silent for a moment. "Nigger," she said, "and Ho Cause I ain't one, and I don't want my kid to hear somebody call me that."

Trudy tried to keep the surprise out of her expression. "I'll remember that," she said, "and you remember not to call Marta a wetback. Because she's not one."

"Shit!" LaTonya stubbed the lit end of her cigarette into the ashtray next to her with a murderous force. She leaned back in her chair, scowling for a moment, then leaned forward to speak to Trudy. "Don't ever admit what you done the way you did with me. You hear that? You plays it dumb, see, like you don't know what they's talkin' about when somebody says you harbored a wetback, or whatever."

Trudy nodded and said solemnly, "Thanks for the tip."

"What'd you do it for, anyway?"

"Do what?"

LaTonya threw her head back with another laugh. "Now you catchin' on, girl." She gulped some of her coffee and leaned toward Trudy again. "So, why'd you do it?"

"She was hiding out in my basement, on her way here to Lubbock to find her daughter. I didn't invite her into my basement; she just showed up there."

LaTonya nodded. "That's what you tell the lawyer and the judge. You got that?"

"Got it."

"So she has a kid, huh?"

"Yes, a daughter. They took her away from her mother."

"Fuck the bastards."

Trudy nodded. "Fuck the bastards."

For no more than a second, LaTonya looked as if she might cry. She looked away and said, "Got a kid of my own. Bastards took him away from me, too."

"I'm sorry."

LaTonya turned her gaze back to Trudy. "Don't be. Shithead boyfriend beat him up. He's better off without me cause I'm still living with the shithead."

After a moment of uncomfortable silence, Trudy asked, "So what are you in here for?"

LaTonya's eyes narrowed. "Nosey bitch, ain't you?"

"So are you."

LaTonya's laugh was a small one this time. "Yeah, I guess so. They got me for murder."

Trudy's breath caught in her throat, and all she could manage to say was, "Oh …"

LaTonya let the word linger between them for a moment before she snickered. "Naw, I was shittin' you. Just wanted to see what you'd do. I'm in for receiving."

"Receiving?"

"Receiving stolen property," LaTonya said as if she was explaining something to a toddler. "Bastard boyfriend brought a F-150 to my house. Nearly new. Told me he'd split the money with me if I sold it. You don't want to know the whole story."

"Oh, okay."

"So, you got a good lawyer?"

"Public defender."

"You're screwed, bitch."

Trudy looked down at her coffee cup, took the last swallow, and stood to toss the cup in the trash. "Yeah," she said. "I'm screwed, bitch."

After leaving the common room, Trudy sat down on the edge of her bunk, trying not to think, except to wish she had access to one of the Ambien pills a doctor had prescribed for her after her husband died. She'd taken only one and felt so hungover the next morning she never took another. The rest of them were in the drawer of her nightstand, since she didn't need them. She'd hardly slept at all since she'd been in jail, though. She'd risk a hangover for a few minutes' sleep. She was still sitting there, not thinking of anything except the pounding in her head, when the red-headed guard approached and unlocked her cell, greeting her with only one word: "Lawyer."

Trudy stood up and walked to the visitor area. She saw a young man seated at the window with a stack of papers in disarray in front of them. He was going through them like an eighth-grader who was unprepared for his book report.

"Oh, Ms. Walters!" he said when Trudy sat down. He sounded as if he might have been expecting someone else. "My name's Toby Adelstone." He ruffled a few more papers before he looked at her again and, smiling, said, "How are you today?"

"Been better," Trudy said.

"Yes, of course," the lawyer said. Hadn't he said his name was Toby something? No one older than twenty-five was named Toby. "Now, let's see," he said, looking at his papers. "Harboring, isn't it?" When Trudy didn't answer, he said, "The penalty can be stiff."

"Thank you for reminding me."

"Certainly." Toby absently brushed back a shock of his unruly dark hair and sounded as if he hadn't heard Trudy's sarcasm. "Not sure that's what it was. Not sure they can prove it, at least." He checked one of the papers in front of him and pointed to a typewritten line with his index finger. Trudy caught only a few of the words he mumbled. "Title eight, code thirteen … subsection A three. Oh! And two also, because you transported …" He kept reading for a while before he looked up at Trudy. "Now, my understanding is that you didn't know who the woman in your basement was or why she was there, and when you found out, you brought her to Lubbock."

Trudy stared at him before she tried to speak. "Uh … brought her to Lubbock? Well, not exactly. You see …"

"I understand," Toby said. "Your intent was to get her back to Mexico."

"Get her back to …? Yes. Yes, of course."

Toby scribbled something on one of the papers. "Where is she now? The alien, I mean."

"The alien? Oh, you mean Marta. She's … I don't know where she is."

Toby appeared alarmed. "You mean she has escaped?"

"Well, maybe. I mean no! What I mean is, I don't know where she is because I've been in jail for two days."

"Oh, yeah. Of course." Toby seemed to have relaxed a little and made a gesture of gathering his papers. "Oh, one more thing. You weren't planning to hire Mrs. Ramondino, were you?"

"Hire her? No. I don't need to hire anybody. I do everything for myself."

"You don't have a gardener?"

"Good Lord, no." Just as Trudy spoke those words, she felt her mouth twitch and a knot form in her stomach. Did Toby know about the lie she'd told the policeman about Amos? How could he possibly know? Unless Adam ... Where was Adam anyway?

"Or a housekeeper?"

"I should be so lucky!"

"Excuse me?"

"I don't have a housekeeper.

Toby nodded absently and tapped his papers on the desk, trying to straighten them. "Thank you, Ms. Walters," he said, standing before he'd put the papers back in his brief case or hung up his receiver. He was about to hang up before he brought the receiver back to his mouth. "I almost forgot to tell you; your hearing is scheduled for Monday. The judge wants to get this one out of his way so he can clear his docket for the big one."

"Monday?" Trudy was alarmed. "That's less than a week. Will you have time to prepare?"

Toby didn't hear her. He had already hung up and was on his way out of the room. One of the papers from the stack he had stuck under his arm freed itself and drifted to the floor. Toby didn't notice and continued his way to the door.

"What big one?" she called. She watched as he disappeared out the door.

Trudy was preparing for another sleepless night on her narrow bed when the red-head stopped by again, this time with another handcuffed woman with her. The woman, a weathered blonde with a netting of wrinkles around her eyes, swayed unsteadily and said nothing. The guard opened the cell and led the woman inside.

"You take the top bunk, Everett. Walters is already settled into the bottom," the guard said as she unfastened the handcuffs.

"Heather," the woman said, slurring her words. "Name's Heather. Don't call me Everett. That's the sombitch that …" Heather never completed her objection. She sat down hard on the floor, then toppled over, using her arm for a pillow, snoring loudly. She stayed there until sometime in the night when she got up to throw up in the toilet. She tried to climb up to the top bunk after that but gave up when she fell from the first ladder rung. She spent the rest of the night on the floor.

Heather's first words when she awoke the next morning were, "I gotta pee." Trudy pointed to the stainless-steel toilet in the corner. When she had finished and flushed the toilet, she went to the sink to wash her hands, then looked at Trudy and shook her head. "I guess I did it again," Heather said with a deep sigh. She went to Trudy's bunk and sat next to her. "Don't bother telling me about AA," she said. "I already know about that."

"I'm sure you do," Trudy said.

Heather rubbed her face with both hands as if she were trying to rub away memories before she turned to look at Trudy again. "What are you in for?"

"Murder," Trudy said, mimicking LaTonya.

Heather stared straight ahead at the wall and seemed not to hear her. "I'll be outta here in a few minutes. They only keep drunks long enough to sober up. They got me for disorderly conduct; otherwise I wouldn't be here." She turned to Trudy again. "You hear them say anything about what I did?"

"Not a word," Trudy assured her.

"Probably hit the son of a bitch," Heather said. She held her head in her hands for a few moments, then spoke through her hands to Trudy. "You ever do any work for hire?"

"I, uh, gave that up," Trudy said, trying not to blush at the thought of working as a prostitute.

Heather shook her head and looked sad. "I just can't catch a break."

"Sorry about that."

"Don't be," Heather said. "We all try to do better. And anyway, I haven't completely made up my mind yet."

"About what?"

"If I want the son of a bitch dead."

"Oh." Trudy leaned her body away from Heather. Heather wasn't talking about prostitution. She wanted to hire a killer!

"Wouldn't even consider it if the son of a bitch didn't beat the shit out of me every chance he gets." Heather breathed another deep sigh. "You don't look like the type that ever got beat up by a man."

"Well, I, uh ..."

"Don't look like the type to be in for murder, either," Heather said, interrupting Trudy's stammer. "You're not fucking with me, are you?"

"I would never do that," Trudy assured her. She was grateful that the red-headed guard showed up at just that moment to tell Heather her husband had paid her bail and she was free to go home.

"You going with him or not?" the guard asked when Heather didn't move from where she was seated on the bunk.

"All right. I'll go," Heather said, rising slowly from the bunk. "Just one more time. Son of a bitch better not hit me again, though." She was still muttering as the guard led her up the hall toward the exit.

"Wait!" Trudy called. "Heather, wait!" Neither Heather nor the guard turned around. "You don't have to put up with it, Heather!"

This time Heather made an effort to respond. "Got no choice."

"You *do* have a choice," Trudy called. "You …" Before Trudy could say more, the guard jerked Heather's arm, led her further down the hall, and pushed her through the exit.

It was the next day before Trudy had another visitor. Hank came to bring her some chicken-fried steak and fried okra from Black Eyed Pea and to tell her Jasmine's bank robbery attempt had been unsuccessful.

"You're telling me she actually tried it?"

"In a manner of speaking. She'd gone to the trouble of stealing your gun and going to the bank."

"Steal my gun? She belongs in a juvie lock-up!"

"I don't think she'll try anything like that again," Hank said.

"You can't be sure about that," Trudy said. "I knew I should never have taken those two in. I don't know what happened to me. Lapse in judgement. That's not like me."

"No, ma'am."

"Hitchhiking, you say? It's a wonder she didn't get herself raped and killed."

"Yes, ma'am."

Trudy brought a fork full of food to her mouth. "This okra can't hold a candle to the way Adam fixes it." She looked at Hank. "Did he ever show up?"

Hank shook his head slowly.

Trudy put her fork down and shoved the food away from her. "You got to find him," she said. "Do whatever you have to, but find that man. You hear?"

Chapter 17

"*Mi hijita!*" Marta said as soon as she saw her daughter standing in the doorway. The girl didn't speak, nor did she move. She simply stared at the woman standing in front of her.

"Who is it, Connie?" a voice from inside the house called.

"*Mamá! Eres tu, Mamá?*" Concepcion said, finding her voice at last.

A woman walked into the entryway. She held a rose and a pair of scissors in her hands. "How many times do I have to tell you that we speak English in this … Hello, can I help you?" she asked when she saw Marta and Adam.

"*Por qué dejaste que me llevaran?*" Concepcion held herself back from Marta.

"*No! No los dejé. Te alejaron de me.*" There were tears in Marta's eyes as she spoke.

"What are you saying?" the woman demanded. "What are you saying to each other?"

"I think Mrs. Ramondino is saying someone took her daughter away from her," Adam said.

The woman looked at him with an alarmed expression, as if she hadn't expected him to be able to speak. "That's not possible," she said. "Her mother was a criminal. In prison! We are in the process of adopting Connie legally." She reached for Concepcion and pulled her close to her.

Concepcion made no attempt to escape the woman's arms, but she pointed to Marta and said in English, "That's my real mama."

"No, I'm your real mama now." The woman's voice broke, and there were tears streaming down her cheeks.

Conception broke free from her and took Marta's hand. *"Tenia miedo. Pensé que me dejastem Mamá.* She was silent a moment before she added, *"Aún me amas?"*

"Siempre mi hijita!" Marta said. This time it was she who took Conception in her arms.

The woman put the rose and scissors she had in her hands on a table next to the door and dabbed at the corner of each eye with the tip of a finger. "Talk English, please," she said, then added, "Come inside. I'll show you the adoption papers. I'm sure we can get this cleared up."

"You may have adoption papers, but that doesn't necessarily make the adoption legal," Adam said. "Concepcion was taken away from her mother illegally when she asked for asylum."

"She was in *jail!*" The woman spit the words at him.

"She was jailed illegally." Adam kept his voice calm. He'd learned the hard way to do that when a white person shouted at him.

"What business is this of yours?" the woman demanded.

"I'm just trying to help Marta. She doesn't speak English."

"So I gathered. But if you are not related, then none of this is any of your business."

"She's my real mama," Concepcion said, still clinging to Marta.

"Oh, Connie!" The woman buried her face in both of her hands, muffling her voice. "We wanted another daughter for so long!"

"You have other children?" Adam asked.

The woman didn't answer, but Concepcion spoke. "They have none."

The woman sobbed as she spoke to Concepcion. "We have you, Connie! You're my daughter now. We're your family. We'll raise you as a Christian child."

"I was always a Christian," Concepcion said.

"She goes to our church now. We're Presbyterian," Barbara said, speaking to Adam, as if for reassurance.

Concepcion pulled away from Marta and said something to her in Spanish, a question that included the word *católico*. Marta answered in Spanish with a soothing voice.

"What are they saying?" the woman asked to no one in particular. "Why are they doing this to me? Speaking in a foreign tongue?"

"I think she's trying to reassure her daughter," Adam said. "Reassure her that it's okay to be Catholic. She's telling her everything is going to be okay."

"But it's not okay!" the woman's voice was high-pitched, bordering on hysteria. "She's trying to take my daughter away from me." She gave Adam a look as if to imply everything was his fault. "She *is* mine. My husband and I legally adopted her. The agency said her parents abandoned her. They said they were probably dead."

Adam shook his head. "I'm sorry, ma'am. I don't know how to solve this."

She ignored him and pulled at Concepcion. "You know we love you, don't you, Connie? And you're happy here. I know you are. You're a Jackson now. You're one of us."

"Yes, ma'am," Concepcion said. "You love me, and you're good to me. You've done everything to make me happy, and I feel safe here, safer than I did in Guatemala."

"See!" Mrs. Jackson said. "She's happy and safe here. I'm her mother now. You can't take her away from me!"

Adam shook his head in a weary fashion. "No," he said. "We can't take her away, not now at least. This is something for the courts to decide."

"The courts? No! I won't put Connie through that."

"I'm sorry, ma'am. No one wants that, but that's what it's come to." Adam pulled his mobile phone from his pocket and started to type. "Excuse me," he said. "I have to do this so I can translate what's happening to Marta." When he'd finished typing, he showed the translation to Marta, then watched as the color drained from her face. When she spoke in a trembling voice, he was able to understand only a few words, enough to know that she was afraid of involving the courts because that would mean she'd be sent out of the country again.

When Adam drove Marta back to the hotel, he had her wait in the parking lot while he went inside to make sure the lobby was clear before he bought her in. The lobby was empty except for the desk clerk, so he made his way to the elevator lobby to make certain that area was clear as well. He was only halfway across the lobby when the desk clerk spoke to him.

"Can I help you, sir?"

Adam stopped and turned around. "I was just on my way up to my room," he said.

"You're with the Walters party?"

"Yes, that's right."

"Yes. I recognized you. I'm afraid they've checked out, sir. Your key would no longer work for any of the rooms rented by Mrs. Walters and her party."

"Checked out?"

"That's correct. If you had any belongings in the room, I assume they took them when they left."

"I see," Adam said, then added a befuddled, "Thank you."

He went back to Trudy's car in the parking lot and was relieved to see that Marta was still there. She must have been too afraid to leave the parking lot. He got into the car and sat for several seconds, trying to decide what to do. Was Trudy still in jail? Should he go there to check? Not a good idea, he decided. Not a good idea to have Marta anywhere near law enforcement. If both Jasmine and Grace were gone, they must have driven back to Anton in Hank's pickup. Where else would they have gone?

With that thought, he started the car and told Marta they were going back to Anton. She nodded slightly as if she understood. At least she must have understood the word "Anton."

Once they reached town, Adam drove to the back of the boarding house where Trudy always parked her car. There was no sign of Hank's pickup. Adam helped Marta out of the car and went to the back door, expecting to find it locked. If it was, he wasn't sure Marta would consent to hiding out in his place. She might consider it improper to stay with a man.

To his surprise, the back door was unlocked, and when he stepped inside behind Marta, he was surprised to see Trudy sitting at the kitchen table with a steaming coffee cup in front of her.

"Well, the car thief shows up," she said. "You come by to burglarize my house?"

"Trudy! What are you doing here?"

"I live here. Remember?"

"I mean, how'd you …?

Before he could ask how she got out of jail, Jasmine showed up in the room and interrupted. "Did you find your daughter, Marta?" She turned to Adam. "Did she?"

Adam almost didn't recognize her because she wasn't dressed in black. She wore regular jeans and a white shirt—not a T-shirt with a band name scrawled across the front, just a plain white shirt. "Yes," he said, "but there's a problem."

"We've all got problems," Trudy said.

Adam pulled a chair out for Marta to sit at the table. "We're going to need a lawyer."

"Don't we all?" Trudy said. Jasmine sank into one of the kitchen chairs, looking forlorn.

"How'd you get out?" Adam asked, turning to Trudy.

"You first," Trudy said. "Tell us about Marta and why you stole my car."

"I didn't steal it."

"Did I hear you say something about needing a lawyer?" The question came from Grace who had entered the room behind Jasmine.

"Yes, for Marta," Adam said. "We found her daughter."

Everyone's attention turned to Marta as she reached for one of the paper napkins in the rooster-shaped holder and used it to dab at her eyes. *"Ella es adoptada,"* she said.

Trudy frowned as she watched Marta. "What did she say?"

"She said her daughter has been adopted," Adam said.

"So she knew what we were talking about," Trudy said. "She understands more than she lets on."

"Except she doesn't understand why Concepcion got adopted," Adam said.

Jasmine responded with her opinion: "Assholes."

"Concepcion was considered abandoned because her mother left the US," Adam explained.

"What a crock of shit!" Jasmine was almost bellowing. "She didn't leave because she wanted to. She was deported, for Christ's sake!"

Adam answered with a shrug as Marta reached for another paper napkin. The first one was wadded into a wet ball in her lap. "Like I said, she needs a lawyer if she wants to get her daughter back," Adam added.

"I can recommend a good lawyer." Grace, who had been silent up until this moment, brought everyone's attention to her. "Trudy's public defender, Mr. Adelstone," she said.

"A public defender?" Adam asked, with more than a little disdain.

"He got Trudy out," Grace said.

"At least for now." Trudy sounded more than a little begrudging.

Grace ignored Trudy's cynicism. "He's good. I was there with him and Trudy when he went before the judge. He got her out on her own recognizance until the hearing. He explained how there was no way Trudy could have known Marta was illegal."

"But it's not the end of it," Trudy said. "It was just enough to get me out of jail, but I have to go back to court and, in the meantime, I can't leave the state."

"He got you out with a lie. Trudy knew who Marta was all along."

"Jasmine! Watch your mouth." Grace's eyes flamed with anger and fear.

"I didn't say I disagreed with that," Jasmine said. "I think it's cool." She turned to Trudy. "But I still say you're going to have to have a top-tier lawyer if you're going to beat the rap."

"You will have nothing to do with whoever her lawyer is, and don't call it a rap." Grace's tone was jagged-edged sharp.

Jasmine lowered her eyes and said nothing. Trudy resisted the urge to tell her that the correct reply to what her mother had said was a contrite, "Yes, ma'am." Rules were different now, she told herself.

"Jail *no mas* for you," Marta said to Trudy, surprising everyone with her three English words.

"*No mas.* That means no more," Jasmine said. "Maybe she's clairvoyant."

"Concepcion. See *no mas.*" Marta didn't bother to reach for a napkin to stop her tears.

"You don't know that!" Jasmine said. "You can't see the future."

Chapter 18

B arbara Jackson could feel a migraine coming on. She wanted desperately to close herself up in the bedroom with the shades drawn, trying not to move her head and praying that she could hold off the vomiting. She wouldn't retreat to the bedroom, though, and leave Connie alone. She would take one of her migraine pills and wait for Connie to ask permission to go to the Bakers' house two doors down where her friend Angela lived.

Barbara had been thrilled when Connie found a friend close to her age. It would help cement her happiness. Connie's happiness and safety were the two most important things in the world for Barbara. Connie was her only daughter, the daughter she had wanted all her adult life. She and her husband had tried for years to conceive a child, and when they finally did, she couldn't carry the pregnancy to term. Sam had been as brokenhearted as Barbara was. Barbara could easily call up the sight of a sketchy form with a beating heart she'd seen on the ultrasound. She had, until recently, had dreams about the beating heart, which had turned into nightmares of a half-formed child walking away from her, refusing to turn around and come back even when Barbara called out her name. She'd awakened Sam many times with her cries of, "Emily! Emily!" Sam had always held her in his arms and cried with her until they either both fell asleep exhausted or got up, staying up and trying to slog through the day, Sam at his insurance agency and Barbara at the school where she taught special-needs children.

They tried again, even after the doctor had told them a full-term pregnancy was not likely because of Barbara's misshapen uterus. When they finally decided to adopt, Barbara was forty and Sam was forty-two. After three years, no baby was found for them. Sam had heard of Christian Rescue from a coworker and approached Barbara with the idea of adopting an older child. "An abandoned child," the counselor at the agency had said. An abandoned illegal alien—Barbara balked at first. She wanted a baby. She wanted to hold it swaddled in blankets and smell the newborn scent she remembered from her sister's two children. She wanted to change its diapers, worry about its diet, watch it grow out of onesies. Sam had persisted, however, and when she finally agreed, it had been only a matter of months before they were introduced to eleven-year-old Concepcion Ramondino. She didn't have the blonde curls Barbara had always envisioned, nor the blue eyes that ran in both her and Sam's families. She was smaller than most eleven-year-olds. Her hair was black and straight. Her eyes were big and golden brown. But she was a perfect little girl, the most beautiful child Barbara thought she had ever seen. She fell in love immediately.

They decided to keep her birth name but call her Connie. It seemed like a way, Barbara thought, of making her their own. It wasn't easy at first. Connie cried for her mother. She wouldn't eat. She seemed to have a constant cold. Nevertheless, Barbara read to her several times a day, played with her with the abundance of toys they bought her, tucked her in every night, let her play in the pool once the weather turned warm enough, and worried more than she ever realized when she was sick.

In time, Connie's tears stopped, and she began to smile, even to laugh. She was eager to go to school. She made friends with Angela, and they spent hours playing with dolls aand more recently, video games. Barbara was ecstatic to at last be able to compare notes with other mothers. She and Sam had agreed to the agency's insistence that she be raised in a Christian home, and even though there had been some reluctance to their Presbyterian choice as a denomination rather than an evangelical church, things had finally been ironed out and the adoption process was advancing.

Now this—a visit from Marta Ramondino had come out of the blue and threatened everything. Sam was on his way home now after the frantic call he'd received from Barbara.

"Don't worry," he had said on the phone. "We'll solve this." Then, he promised to leave his office immediately and come home.

Barbara tried to take comfort in his words, but she couldn't. She was a bright, educated woman. She knew situations like the one they found themselves in now were seldom easily resolved. But how could she live if it wasn't resolved in their favor? How could she give up another heartbeat, a little girl who had learned to kiss her good-night, to say, "I love you, Mommy?" How could she survive more nightmares of a child walking away from her?

She was not foolish or naïve enough to think that Connie didn't remember her previous life, although she no longer spoke Spanish and no longer cried herself to sleep. When, in the early days, she had asked questions about her family, Barbara had told her that her mother had gone back to Guatemala. When Connie asked why, Barbara said simply that the government told her she couldn't stay. She didn't want Connie to think she'd been abandoned, but she did tell her that her mother wanted her to be here where she was safe and where she could be happy. Connie was still young enough to be malleable, and she quickly adapted.

Now this, Barbara said to herself again. Marta Ramondino's visit had upset Connie. As Barbara watched her daughter now through the undulating haze of the migraine, she thought of asking Connie if she'd like to invite Angela over for a while. She wouldn't suggest that Connie go there. She didn't want her out of her sight. It was obvious, however, that Connie was in no mood to play. She didn't seem inclined to even leave the sofa. She lay on her stomach, her head resting on her arms, which were folded on the arm of the sofa as she stared out the big window at the lush yard and blue swimming pool in the back. She didn't seem to be looking at anything in particular, though, and she was clearly ignoring the streaming movie Barbara had turned on for her.

"Connie?"

Without turning to face Barbara, Connie spoke in a voice barely audible. "That was my real mama."

Barbara resisted the urge to cry out that she was her real mama now. Instead, she turned away and went to the bedroom she shared with Sam and closed the door. She sat on the edge of the bed and let the tears stream from her eyes, finally giving way to sobs that left her exhausted.

She had no concept of how long she had been there when the door opened, at first just a little, and finally wide enough that she could see Connie standing in the doorway looking frightened.

• • •

It was several days later when Sam came home with the news that Marta Ramondino had never officially given up custody of her daughter and that meant the adoption couldn't go forward.

"That can't be true!" Barbara insisted. "The agency told us everything was final and we—"

Sam put his arms around her. "I know. They told us that we were free to adopt." He held her for a moment before she pulled away.

"We have to fight this! We can't let them just take our daughter."

"Barb," Sam said, "if we fight it, we could stir up more trouble for all of us."

"What could be worse than losing our daughter?" Barbara's voice was almost a screech. "What's wrong with you? We can't just give up!"

"I'm not giving up," Sam said. "It's just that you have to know the courts are going to give us extra scrutiny because we were foster parents first, and we signed papers agreeing not to adopt."

"But the agency freed us from that agreement!"

"Maybe. But it's not that simple."

"Of course it's that simple. They gave us signed papers that said we were no longer bound by that!"

"Barb, listen to me. She's the daughter of an illegal immigrant who never gave up custody. The agency may be in as much trouble as we are. It could get ugly."

"I don't care how ugly it gets! I'm not giving up my daughter!"

Sam moved toward her again. "Barb …"

"No!" She backed away from his attempt to touch her. "I'm not! I'm not giving up! How could you even think about it?"

"I'm just trying to warn you that it could be a long fight."

"That woman abandoned her daughter." Barbara pointed a finger at Sam as if she were scolding a misbehaving child. "She does not deserve—"

"No." Sam shook his head. "She did not abandon her daughter. Connie was forcibly separated from her."

"Because she's a criminal. She was in jail."

"She was seeking asylum. She may have been jailed illegally."

"You're taking that woman's side against me! I can't believe you're doing that!"

"I'm not taking her side. I just want you to know how it is."

"How it is? How do you *think* it is? You have no idea, do you? No idea what it would be like for me to lose my only daughter." Barbara was sobbing as she spoke, and she turned away toward the hallway that led to their bedroom, leaving Sam alone in the living room.

It was only seconds before Connie peered around the corner of the hallway. She had been in her room and had heard everything.

"Am I going back to my real mama?" she asked, speaking to Sam's back as he stood staring out through the glass doors into the backyard.

Sam turned around suddenly, surprised to hear her voice. "Connie!"

Sam sat on the couch, then slumped over with his elbows on his knees. "I don't know." After a few seconds, he added, "There are some things that are just impossible to know." A few more seconds elapsed before he looked up at Connie, who was sitting in the chair across from him. "Would you like to go back?" he asked.

Connie didn't answer at first. Finally, after a long pause, she whispered, "There are some things that are just impossible to know."

Chapter 19

Concepcion's mama had told her it would be a long trip and that she might get tired and hungry while they traveled. Concepcion knew why they had to leave, but she was secretly a little excited about it. She'd never taken a trip, although she'd heard Miguel talking about the one he made to Guatemala City. Miguel was fourteen, five years older than Concepcion had been at the time.

Miguel had talked about his trip for months and said he could hardly wait to go back. The things he saw! American tourist women in Guatemala City wearing short pants that showed off their legs almost all the way to their private parts. He'd seen pictures of that, of course, but to see it up close was different. He laughed when he described the way they looked to some of the other boys. The men in the village laughed even harder than Miguel and told him he had a lot to learn. Miguel said he couldn't wait to learn whatever it was.

He saw things in the store windows he had a hard time describing. There was food he'd never seen before and diamond jewelry that he'd heard about but could hardly believe when he saw it. He was there with his father to try to find work, and when there was no work to be found, they had to sleep on hard asphalt behind one of the big buildings. It was while they were back there, trying to sleep, that a boy offered to sell them something that he claimed would take away their hunger pains on the journey back home.

"The cost was too much," Miguel said. His father told the boy he had only a few quetzals left and couldn't afford it. The boy, who was thin and sickly looking and could have been hungry himself, finally said he would give the two of them what he called a "line" for whatever money he had. He described how to sniff the powder into their noses and promised they wouldn't have to eat for at least a day. Miguel's father was eager to try the magic powder, so he gave the boy the last of his money for a tiny amount of the white powder. When he saw what a small amount he got, he tried to get his money back from the boy, but the boy hit Miguel's father hard in the face, making his nose bleed, and then he ran away. Miguel tried to chase him down, but he disappeared into the darkness behind one of the other buildings.

When he got back to the alley where he'd left his father, he saw that his face and the front of his shirt were covered with blood, but at least his nose had stopped dripping blood. Later, after he'd sniffed some of the powder, his nose started bleeding again, but he laughed and said he felt the way he did on his wedding night. Miguel sniffed what was left of the powder.

"It made me drunk," he said to Concepcion and the other kids standing near him.

"What was it?" one of them asked.

"*Cremita*," Miguel said. "It's like a powder, and you sniff it into your nose."

"Did you bring some back?

199

"Too expensive," Miguel said. "But as soon as I save enough money, I'm going back and buy some."

Concepcion didn't care much for Miguel's account of his adventures, and she could have easily forgotten about them until the first of the *buchons* showed up. Miguel brought him into the village, but no one seemed to know how he had met the short, stocky man with the big mustache. Concepcion was as curious about him as everyone else in the village because visitors to the remote settlement were rare except when the American missionaries came. She hadn't seen a missionary in more than a year, though, and she soon learned that the new man in town was called a *buchon* because he sold the *cremita* Miguel had discovered in Guatemala City. It wasn't long before other *buchons* started coming in. A few people bought some of the stuff they were selling, but most couldn't afford it. It wasn't long after the *buchons* started showing up now and then that Miguel disappeared. People said he had joined them and was now a *buchon* himself.

Things got bad after that. People were killed, and their bodies were left to be found bloated and covered with flies in the forest. Everyone said they were the ones who couldn't pay what the *buchons* asked or else they had failed to obey orders from them.

Concepcion's family was small. Now that her father and brother were dead, there was only her mother and her grandmother. Marta, Concepcion's mother, walked the short distance to the only store in the area every day to work. It was the store her father once owned. Marta waited on customers and, for a while, sold some of the weavings her own mother made until the old woman's eyesight weakened and she could no longer make the scarves and table coverings men from the bigger towns sometimes bought to take back with them to sell to tourists.

Concepcion knew that her mother talked to some of the other women about leaving the area and trying to make it to Guatemala City where she might be able to find a better job. Concepcion knew she would never go, though, because her *abuela* was nearly blind and frail and could never make the journey.

It was soon after Concepcion had turned eleven that everything changed. Concepcion had made the short walk to the store where her mother worked, hoping to make a few quetzals like she sometimes did by selling passion fruit to the store owner. She was approaching the front of the store with her meager harvest when the men showed up behind her.

"Hey! You're a pretty little bitch!" one of them said to her.

Concepcion tried to ignore them and go inside, but one of the young men stood in front of the door so she couldn't enter.

"You want to go inside?" the one holding the door asked. "Not until I get inside you." He reached between her legs, while another held her from behind.

Marta heard her scream and ran to the door, shouting at them, telling them to leave her alone, while the store owner stood back and shouted to Marta, "Shut up and don't cause trouble for me."

Concepcion would remember those words and the look on her mother's face as she rushed through the doorway and grabbed her, holding her close and shouting at the men who had accosted her.

"Leave her alone! She's a child!" Marta was shielding Concepcion with her body. One of the men hit her hard in the face with the back of his hand, making her stagger back. She didn't let go of Concepcion, though.

The one who had hit Marta laughed, making the others laugh with him—all of them except one. It was only then that Concepcion noticed it was Miguel who was hanging back.

"I can make her grow up fast. She will like it, too. First time's the best," the one who had hit Marta said.

Suddenly Marta pushed Concepcion back through the door of the store. "Go home to *abulita*," she said. She stood in front of the doorway, keeping the men from entering. "Leave her alone!" she said again. "Take me instead!"

Concepcion was hurrying toward the back door. She wanted to run home but not to find her grandmother as her mother had ordered her to do. She would find someone to help her mother. It was obvious no one at the store would help, not Alonzo who was cowering in the back, not Miguel who still showed no sign of coming forward. She ran toward the cluster of houses where the hut she shared with her mother and grandmother sat. She stopped at every house she passed, pleading for help. Several of the houses were empty because the occupants were working in the coffee fields. Others refused to help Marta and Concepcion when they learned who was assaulting her. Concepcion knew their fear. Her father and brother weren't the only ones in the village who had died or disappeared mysteriously when they crossed the *buchons*.

Only *Abulita* and one other old woman in the village, *Abulita's* friend, Inocencia, were willing to help. They left *abulita's* hut armed with wooden clubs, the only weapons available to them. "What have we got to lose except self-respect?" Inocencia said and shouted all the swear words she knew as she passed each house.

They had not yet reached the edge of the settlement when they saw Marta making her way toward them on the path leading from the store. She walked slowly, stumbling frequently. Concepcion ran toward her, fearing she would fall to the ground. Concepcion knew what the group of men had been demanding of her mother because she had seen it happen to her before, but she didn't expect to see her bruised and bleeding. The blood came from her mouth and from somewhere on her head, and it was streaming down her legs.

Concepcion took her mother's arm and screamed for the other women to come help her. The two old women shuffled toward her and helped Concepcion lead her back to *abulita's* house where they helped her out of her bloodied dress and washed her wounds. No one spoke as they ministered to her, and only Concepcion cried softly as she watched. Her mother did not shed a single tear. When Marta was clean and Inocencia had persuaded her to lie down, *abulita* finally spoke.

"They will be back for you. You can't stay here. You must leave."

Marta sat up on the bed. "No," she said.

"How many times does this have to happen to you? You should have left the first time. Now you must! Think of your daughter."

"I can't leave you alone," Marta said. "How could I leave my own mother with no one to buy her food or care for her when she—"

"She will live with me," Inocencia said.

"But your son can barely provide enough food for you and his family. He can't—"

"I will share my food. We are both old. We need very little."

"No!" Marta said again.

"Think of your daughter." *Abulita* was standing as she spoke, and she had somehow managed to appear tall and commanding despite of her small stature. "You know what they will do to her when they come back. They won't be satisfied until she is—"

"I will die before I let them touch her." Those words coming from her mother frightened Concepcion.

A scowl crinkled *abulita's* face. "And what good will you be to any of us if you are dead?"

Marta seemed about to speak, but she said nothing as she stood and left the hut. Concepcion could see her standing alone outside. The stars had punctured the sky with their burning spikes before she slipped into the little bed she shared with Concepcion. The next morning she bundled her belongings with Concepcion's and held *abulita* in a long, silent embrace before they left the village.

Concepcion turned around to see *abulita* one last time, but she had already gone back into the hut. Marta never turned around once.

The journey was long, weeks long, maybe months. Concepcion lost track of time. Sometimes they rode in the back of trucks or in buses when Marta would decide to spend a little of the money she had brought along. Only rarely did they buy food, and they were often hungry. Concepcion learned from others who joined them on the journey how to beg for food or sometimes how to steal it. She stayed close to Marta and learned, as Marta did, how she must ask for asylum and how she must say she would be killed if she went back to her village. That was not a lie. Concepcion knew the *buchons* were ruthless.

Concepcion did not expect the worst to come after she and her mother set foot in the US. She did not expect to be separated from Marta and put behind bars. She had still not turned twelve years old when someone told her she was to be released to a family for foster care. She had no idea what foster care meant. By the time she met the American family, the Jacksons, she had learned a little English, but it was still difficult to communicate.

They were nice enough, although Mrs. Jackson insisted Concepcion call her "Mom," and she was told she would be called "Connie." The house they lived in was beautiful, the food was plentiful, she had her own room, and she was allowed to go to school. Still, Concepcion cried herself to sleep at night wondering where her mother was and if her grandmother was still alive. No one knew the answer, and no one seemed willing to find out.

At first, the kids she met at school avoided her, and that made her hate where she was even more. Finally, she met Josefa who was from Mexico and was also new to the school. She had come to the U.S. the same way Concepcion had. She was the only person who could pronounce Concepcion's name correctly, but after a while, even Josefa began to call her Connie. In time, Concepcion's English became fluent, and she started to say her new name as the Americans did rather than as "Co-nee."

She made other friends, white kids, including Angela, and, on her thirteenth birthday, they all came to her party and brought gifts. By that time, she had met Danny Martinez, an American boy who had never been to Mexico and had never met his family who lived there. Some of the white girls were jealous of the attention he paid to her.

It was not long after the birthday party that she started hearing Mom and Dad talk about adoption. It was possible now, they said, because her mother had abandoned her and was now in prison.

When Concepcion heard that, she stayed in her room for two days and couldn't make herself eat anything.

"I can't bear to see you like this," Mom said as they sat together in the waiting room at the doctor's office. "We'll find out what's wrong, though. Don't worry."

It was clear the woman she now knew as Mom was worried, and that made Concepcion worry, as well. Maybe she did have something wrong. Perhaps she would die soon. If she did, would she see *Abulita*. Who must be dead by now? Concepcion had succeeded in not allowing herself to think about A*bulita* or *Mamá* or her old life in the village until now. The memories made her feel sicker.

The doctor, a nice American woman, checked her heart and her breathing, looked in her mouth and her ears, and asked Connie if she was in pain or if she was afraid or worried about anything. Connie answered "no" to all those questions.

"How are things going for you at school?" the doctor asked. "Are you happy there? Is anyone being unkind to you? Threatening to hurt you? Do you have friends? Are you having trouble with any of them? Are you having trouble with your classes?"

The questions seemed to go on forever, and Connie assured the doctor that school was fine, that she wasn't having trouble of any sort, and that no one was being unkind to her. She had to wait in another room while the doctor talked to Mom, but since the door was not completely closed, Connie could hear phrases like, "Not unusual for teenagers ... Perfectly healthy ... Give it a few days ... Perhaps an antidepressant ..."

The end result was that a bottle of pills was delivered to the house that night. Connie knew they were antidepressants. She'd learned a little about them in health class. She took them for a few days and was feeling a little better when *Mamá* showed up at the door.

That night, Connie flushed the rest of the pills down the toilet.

Chapter 20

Trudy sat in a rusty lawn chair on the skimpy grass in the back of her house, wondering what it would be like to spend the last chapter of her life in prison. She had placed the chair in the shade of one of the ancient trees in the back, and she was facing the alley and Adam's back door. A flock of sparrows pecked at a patch of seeds Adam had spilled in the alley the day before when he was trying to fill his bird feeder. The sparrows sang out occasional notes to a piece still in composition. While she watched, Adam opened his door and stepped outside, carrying a steaming cup and causing the birds to scatter.

"What you doing out here?" he asked when he spied Trudy.

"Getting some sun. Can't get that in jail."

Adam pulled up a chair across from Trudy. "Can't get sun by sitting in the shade, either," he said.

Trudy didn't answer, but she made sure he saw her roll her eyes.

"You had coffee?" he asked.

"More than I should. I'll have to get up and go pee before too long. Grace made coffee as well as breakfast for everybody this morning."

Adam was silent for a moment, watching the birds who had returned to resume their breakfast serenade. Finally he spoke. "We got to do something about Marta and her daughter."

"Yes." Trudy's voice sounded tired.

"The law is going to come looking for her, and this is the first place they'll look. I'm surprised they ain't been here already."

"Haven't, not ain't."

"Good God, Trudy!"

"Sometimes it's easier to worry about grammar than to worry about people's lives."

"You've got to be serious about this. You and Marta both could end up in jail if they come and find her here again."

"Well, hell, I'm probably going to jail for the rest of my life anyway."

"Don't be that way, Trudy."

"Aren't you going to scold me for swearing?"

Adam didn't reply, but when Trudy looked at him, he looked as if he was about to cry.

"You're right about Marta, though. We can't let her go to jail, and we have to help her get her daughter back," Trudy said.

"It's not that simple."

"Nothing is ever simple," Trudy said.

"What I mean is, her daughter may not want to go back to her mama, even if it's possible. She was torn away from her family once. Now it seems like she's settled in, and it's about to happen again. I think it would just about ruin Marta if she loses her daughter for good after all she went through to find her."

Trudy felt even wearier than she had before. She leaned back in the old lawn chair, hearing it creak in response. "You got anything stronger than coffee?"

As they were sipping whiskey from their mismatched coffee cups, Hank's patrol car approached.

Adam sat up straighter in his chair, alarmed. "Where's Marta?"

"In the kitchen last time I saw her."

"Go tell her to stay out of sight," Adam said.

Trudy had just risen from her chair when she heard Hank's voice. "Well, now, don't y'all look comfortable out here in the shade? Morning's hot already, isn't it?"

"Have a seat," Trudy said, standing. "I was just about to go in to use the bathroom. I'll bring you a cup of coffee when I come back."

"Keep your seat, Trudy. It's too hot for coffee." Hank leaned his tall frame against the trunk of the tree and pushed his hat to the back of his head. "I just got a call from the feds. They're looking for Marta again. Don't suppose you know where she is, do you?"

"Haven't seen her," Adam said.

Trudy shook her head. "No, I haven't, either. She's probably still in Lubbock."

"Uh huh," Hank said. "That's what I told 'em." He pulled away from the tree and straightened himself suddenly, looking toward Trudy's house before he said, "Shit!"

Trudy and Adam each turned their heads toward the house in time to see Marta standing there and then disappearing quickly.

Hank shook his head. "Damn it, Trudy, you can't keep on doing stuff like this. What are you thinking?"

"It was my idea to bring her back here," Adam said. "Trudy didn't want to, but I forced—"

"Oh, shut up, Adam. Nobody forces me to do anything I don't want to do. You and Hank both know that."

Hank walked a few paces away from the tree and into the yard before he turned around and faced the two of them again. "You know it's my duty to report this," he said.

"Do what you have to do," Trudy said.

"It was your duty the first time you learned she was here," Adam said.

"It was different then," Hank said. "I could get by with saying I didn't know she was illegal then, but this time ..." He took off his hat and rubbed his arm against his forehead. "Shit!" he said again. He looked at Trudy, pointed a finger, and opened his mouth as if he was about to speak, but he said nothing. He forced his hat down on his head and walked away.

Trudy and Adam watched until he was out of sight before Adam spoke. "You just can't stay out of trouble, can you?"

"Never could," she answered and took a long drink from her coffee cup.

The next morning, Adam was just about to knock on the back door to Trudy's house when Grace came hurrying out of it, almost running into him.

"Woah! Where you off to in such a hurry?" Adam asked.

"Got an interview for a job," she said. "At the sheriff's office."

"Is that right?"

"Quit my other job, but I have to work, you know."

"I was just about to give you some good news," Adam called to her back as she hurried away. "That part I ordered for your car?" he said when she turned to face him. "It's here. I can have your car fixed in a couple of days and you can be on your way to Dallas again."

"Oh. That's … that's good." In spite of her words, Grace looked crestfallen. "Thank you, Adam." She turned away again, walking toward Hank's office.

Adam turned back to Trudy's house and knocked on the back door. When no one answered, he let himself in and called out Trudy's name. She answered with a downward motion of her hand, a signal for him to be quiet as she was speaking on the phone. Adam sat down at the kitchen table, waiting for Trudy to finish her conversation. Her end of the exchange consisted of "yes" and "no" and one question: "That soon?" After a while, she hung up the phone and sat down in one of the chairs opposite Adam.

"I see you invited yourself in and made yourself comfortable," she said.

"I knocked first."

"You're supposed to wait until you're invited in."

"I'll try to remember that." When Trudy didn't come back with a cantankerous reply, Adam asked, "Something wrong?"

"I just got a court date," Trudy said. "Day after tomorrow."

"You ready for this?"

"Doesn't matter whether I am or not. I just hope the lawyer's ready."

"You gotta have faith."

Trudy shot him an irritable look. "Don't give me that bullshit." After a pause, she added, "You're going to have to see after the place for me while I'm in the slammer."

"Trudy, you're not going—"

She cut him off. "Will you?"

"Yeah, okay." There was another pause before he asked, "What about Marta?"

"I don't know." Trudy sounded tired. Adam studied her face again for a moment before he got up and moved toward the door. "Where you going?" Trudy asked.

"I got to think about this," Adam said and let himself out.

When the court date arrived, Adam was the only one to accompany Trudy to Lubbock.

Hank was miserable and apologetic. "I hope you understand why I don't dare show up there with you, Ms. Trudy."

Trudy assured him that she understood, and besides, there was nothing anyone could do anyway. She was grateful that he still had not notified ICE that Marta was still at her house. She wouldn't admit how disappointed she was, however, when he said he thought it best that Grace didn't go either, since she was now employed by the sheriff's office. Jasmine agreed to stay with Marta. No one wanted to admit that Jasmine was, in fact, making sure Marta didn't leave the house and get herself caught by ICE. Trudy didn't even say that it was nobody's business what Marta did as she might have done at another time.

"Place feels like a damn meat freezer," Trudy said when she and Adam walked into the courtroom. Adam didn't have time to remind her not to swear before Mr. Adelstone met them and ushered Trudy to a table at the front of the courtroom and instructed Adam to sit in the public gallery. In less than five minutes, while Mr. Adelstone was still shuffling papers he'd pulled from his briefcase, the judge entered and the bailiff told everyone to stand.

The judge had her blonde hair pulled back in a bun, and her makeup had been artfully applied with just a hint of rouge and lipstick. She looked young to Trudy, surely no more than early fifties. When they were seated, Trudy leaned toward Mr. Adelstone to whisper, "Where's the jury?"

"There won't be a jury," Mr. Adelstone said. "You consented to a bench trial. The judge will perform the duties of the jury."

"I consented?"

"Yes, you signed the paper, remember?"

Trudy knew she had signed papers, and she remembered Mr. Adelstone explaining what she was signing, but she had been too frightened and upset to take in anything he said. "I'm not sure I remember—"

"Shh!" Mr. Adelstone said, cutting her off as the judge began speaking.

The trial lasted all morning, with the government lawyers explaining how Trudy had harbored an illegal immigrant and had unlawfully transported the alien to Lubbock in order to hide her until she could find work. Adelstone had countered that Trudy had not knowingly harbored the illegal alien at first, and when she learned the truth, she transported her to Lubbock to be surrendered to federal authorities.

None of it was true, neither the government's case nor her defense. It left Trudy stunned. When she was questioned, she admitted that she had not known that Marta Ramondino was an illegal alien because the woman didn't speak English, and since Trudy couldn't speak Spanish, they were unable to communicate. She answered that the local sheriff had advised her to bring Mrs. Ramondino to Lubbock and that they had stayed in a hotel when they arrived because the courts were closed. She made no mention of anyone helping Marta find her daughter, and she said she wasn't sure where Mrs. Ramondino was now. That wasn't a lie, she told herself. After all, Marta could be on the road again. The government lawyers confirmed that no one knew of Mrs. Ramondino's whereabouts

When the court took a thirty-minute recess for lunch, Trudy was not allowed out of the courthouse. She was served a cheese sandwich and a cup of tomato soup in a small room off the courtroom.

After Trudy finished her lunch, a court official opened the door to the little room. "Bathroom break," the woman said.

Trudy stood. "Nice of you," she said, not meaning it. The woman waited for Trudy until she came out of the stall and watched her closely as she washed her hands. "You can go if you want to," Trudy said. "It's fairly clean, and I'll stand watch for you." Trudy almost laughed out loud when the woman rolled her eyes and grabbed Trudy's arm to escort her back to the tiny room. She stayed there for what seemed to her to be an eternity, growing restless because there was nothing to read and no television to watch. She tried to sleep by resting her head on her arms at the table but to no avail. She was standing and walking back and forth across the room, trying to ease a pain in her back, when the door opened again, and the same woman appeared.

"Another bathroom break?" Trudy made no attempt to keep the sarcasm out of her voice. "Well, I got nothing to pee out of me, since you left me in here with no water or anything else to drink."

"Back to the courtroom," the woman said.

Trudy swore under her breath but once again followed the woman out of the courtroom. The woman made sure Trudy was walking in front of her as they entered the court. Adelstone was sitting at his table, and the lawyer for the government was ensconced at the other table. Adam was in the visitors' area, and he gave her a nod as she entered. Trudy responded with a weary shake of her head. She was directed to her chair next to Adelstone. He stood when he saw her and held the back of her chair for her. She took a deep breath as she settled into the seat.

"Nervous?" Adelstone asked in his quiet voice.

"You could say that," Trudy answered without looking at him.

"It's going to be okay," Adelstone said.

Trudy turned her head quickly to look at him and was about to ask him how he knew that when the bailiff gave the command: "All rise."

The judge entered and took her seat at the bench. She shuffled a few papers before she looked up, her eyes going first to Trudy. "I've met in my chambers with both lawyers, Mrs. Walters, to further discuss this case, and I've carefully considered all of the evidence. Please rise and approach the bench for sentencing."

A hot shock of fear shot through Trudy almost paralyzing her, but she somehow managed to stand. She was grateful for her lawyer's arm at her elbow as she walked to the front. When the judge raised her eyes to look at her, the heat of fear was replaced with a cold jolt to her heart, which she was certain had stopped beating until it responded with a relentless hammering, sending a rush of blood pounding and throbbing in her ears.

"Mrs. Walters," the judge began, "I am convinced that it is true that you did not know the woman Marta Ramondino was in the country illegally when you discovered her in your basement. Giving a person a place to sleep in your house under those circumstances does not constitute knowingly harboring an alien. When your local sheriff apprised you of the situation, you brought her to Lubbock to turn her over to authorities. That is a questionable act, Mrs. Walters."

Trudy's breathing involuntarily stopped, and for a moment she felt lightheaded.

"You should have notified the authorities here in Lubbock," the judge continued. "You should have allowed them to transport the suspect here. If that had happened, the suspect would have been less likely to escape."

"Yes, ma'am," Trudy managed to say, since the judge's penetrating gaze seemed to demand a response.

"However, it is, I believe, the sheriff's poor judgement that influenced you to take that action. Since I can find no reason to believe you had intent, I cannot find you guilty under Section 1324-a of the Immigration and Nationality Act."

Trudy's lightheadedness returned, and she squinted at the judge as if to make sure she had heard her correctly. The pounding of the gavel on the bench brought Trudy back to her senses. The lawyer took her arm again and turned her around while he whispered, "Congratulations."

"Thank you," she managed to say. "And congratulations to you. Your work's not too shabby."

The lawyer looked at her for a second before he said, "No, it's not, is it?"

Before she could say more, the lawyer left the room with the other attorney. Adam was at her side. In the next moment, Adam was hugging her. Her first reaction was to scold him for doing that in public before she realized that it wasn't really public since there was no one in the room except the court reporter locking up her machine. She hated to admit it, but after what she had been through, a hug was just what she needed.

When they were in the parking lot, she handed the keys to Adam and said, "You drive. I'm too tired."

"Well, you're a free woman now," Adam said after he had helped her into the car and was behind the wheel.

"I don't feel good about it," Trudy said.

"You don't feel good about it? You mean you would rather go to prison? You *ought* to feel good about it."

"It was all a lie. I let her stay in my house even when I knew she wasn't legal, and you know as well as I do that we brought her to Lubbock to find her daughter, not to turn her in."

"No, what I know is, you did the right thing to try to help her. You don't deserve prison."

"Don't give me that sugar-coated stuff. My whole life is a lie, and you know it."

"Trudy ..."

"Don't!"

"You ever hear of civil disobedience?" Adam asked, ignoring her.

Trudy turned her face to stare out the window and didn't respond.

"What you did for Marta was morally right, even if you had to break the law more than once to do it. Thoreau says that government gets its power from the majority, and the majority isn't always right, and he says—"

"Wait a minute! Why are you sounding like some 1960s' hippie? Where did you ever hear of Thoreau anyway?"

"Just because I never went to college doesn't mean I can't read, does it?"

"Well, of course not, but—"

"You ever read Thoreau?"

"Long time ago."

"How long?"

Trudy shrugged. "I don't know; maybe sixty years?"

"Time to read him again."

"Well, I know one thing," Trudy said, "whatever he wrote is not the Bible, so don't try to make me feel better by quoting some long-dead Yankee."

"Never knew you to read the Bible much anyway, Trudy."

She turned her face away again without responding.

Trudy stayed in her dark mood the rest of the way home. Even Jasmine's ebullience when she heard the story wasn't enough to cheer her up.

"Damn! I wish I could have been there," Jasmine said. "That guy is one awesome dude!"

"And we didn't have to pay him all the money in the bank," Adam said.

Jasmine looked at him and shrugged. "Yeah, well …"

"That should teach you not to act so impulsively," Grace said.

"I'm going to law school after college," Jasmine said, sounding as if she hadn't heard her mother. "I want to be a killer lawyer like that guy."

"Where's Marta?" Adam asked.

"Upstairs in her room," Jasmine said.

Adam's forehead creased into a worried frown. "You sure?"

"She's up there," Grace assured him. "I think her depression is making her sick."

A part of Trudy hoped she wasn't still up there. If she ran away, her own troubles could end.

"We have to help her get her daughter back," Grace said. Adam and Jasmine both nodded.

"No we don't!" Trudy said. "We just have to mind our own business and stay out of this. "We can't just keep breaking the rules until we get caught."

Chapter 21

Trudy's despondence was still with her the next morning, and it worsened when Hank showed up at the front door in an equal state of depression.

"Where's Grace?" Trudy asked when she had poured Hank a mug full of coffee and sat down across from him at the kitchen table with her own mug. "Did you just leave her to hold down the fort by herself?"

"I trust her. She can handle anything that comes up."

"Like nosey inquiries from ICE?"

"I told her to call me if they call. She has my mobile number."

Trudy studied Hank's face. "You expect them to call?"

"Oh, hell yes." He was staring at the contents of his coffee mug as if he might find an answer to his own unspoken question in the dark liquid.

"Something wrong?" Trudy asked.

Hank glanced up at her. "You could say that. I think I just got us in a shitload of trouble by breaking the law when I didn't turn Marta in. Excuse me. I shouldna said shitload."

"Wasn't you that caused the shitload," Trudy said. "It was me, and you know it."

"I shoulda turned her in."

"Yeah, well, you didn't do that, did you?"

"I broke the law, and it's worse because I'm a lawman, and I'm still not turning her in."

"Adam calls it civil disobedience."

"That don't make it right."

"That's what I said." Trudy took a sip of her coffee, then pushed the mug aside. "We both ought to be in a shitload of trouble. I beat the rap because I had a lying lawyer."

Hank looked at her with a sad expression on his face before he looked down again, staring into the depths of his coffee. He and Trudy both sat in a gloomy silence until Adam burst through the back door without knocking. He was holding his mobile phone away from his body as if it were a pot of boiling water.

"Hey, y'all gotta hear this," he said, handing the phone to Trudy. "Here, talk to her."

"Talk to who?" Trudy asked, taking the phone.

"Just talk!" Adam said.

Trudy frowned and put the phone to her ear. "Hello?" she said as if she was questioning who was on the line. "Who?" She frowned again.

"This is Barbara Jackson," the voice on the other end said.

"Oh!" Trudy said and looked at Adam.

"I'm calling to ask you to put Mrs. Ramondino on the phone. Connie wants to talk to her."

"Who's Connie?"

"You may know her as Concepcion. She wants to speak to Mrs. Ramondino."

"What makes you think I know where Mrs. Ramondino is or even who she is?"

Trudy turned to Jasmine and mouthed, "Go get Marta out of the house."

"Don't bring her down here!" Hank said. "Not while I'm here!"

"Then leave!" Trudy said. "No! Don't leave," she added. "You're in this as deep as any of us. Now's not the time to chicken out on us." Trudy turned her attention back to the phone. "No, not you. I was talking to someone else." She looked at Adam again. "Are you sure this isn't some kind of trap to get me—"

"It's not a trap," Adam said. "Tell her to put the girl on the phone."

"It's not a trap," Barbara said. She had obviously heard the exchange between Trudy and Adam. "I'm not going to turn you in to law enforcement. I wouldn't do anything to hurt Connie. She's been distraught ever since Adam brought Mrs. Ramondino here. She insists she wants to talk to her again. I tried to tell her it wouldn't be good for either one of them, but she won't listen. She cries all the time. She won't eat. I thought maybe if they just spoke to each other for a moment, she would calm down."

"Uh huh," Trudy said, still skeptical.

"I told Connie we could work something out so she could talk to Mrs. Ramondino occasionally, even if she's deported again."

"Deported?" Trudy said.

"Well, you know it's coming."

"No, I don't know that, and I don't know where she is."

"Don't lie to me. That man, Mr. Bailey, he knows. He talked to Connie."

"Oh he did, did he? Well, I can tell you Mr. Bailey doesn't know what the hell he's talking about." She looked at Adam as she spoke, directing all her anger and fear toward him.

"Please, I beg of you. Just put her on the phone. I'm not going to report you, and I'm not going to report Mrs. Ramondino. I told you I won't do anything to hurt Connie, but she's going to make herself sick if you don't …"

There was a brief pause and then a younger voice spoke. "If my mama is there, let me talk to her." The voice was young, and hoarse, as if she'd been crying, but enunciating in unaccented English. "Mr. Bailey brought her to me once, and … and when I called him just now, he said my mama can talk to me."

Marta and Jasmine were standing in front of Trudy, Jasmine's expression questioning, Marta's frightened. Trudy felt stunned as she handed the phone to Marta. "Your daughter wants to talk to you," she said.

Jasmine's eyes widened. "Really?" She turned to Marta and translated. "*Su hija.*"

Marta looked as if she might faint, but Hank moved a chair behind her and she collapsed into it. She accepted the phone with trembling hands. "Concepcion?" she asked. She listened as tears flowed down her cheeks. She spoke intermittently in rapid Spanish that Jasmine couldn't translate. Marta was still talking and crying as Trudy ushered everyone out of the room and into the parlor.

"She needs privacy for this," Trudy said.

"We don't know what she's saying anyway," Jasmine said. She was the only one who made no move toward the parlor.

"She needs privacy." Hank's voice was stern as he took Jasmine's arm. Jasmine didn't pull back. Instead, she gave Hank a surprised look and let him lead her to the parlor.

Trudy spoke, standing in the middle of the parlor before everyone was seated. "All right, let me get this straight, *Mr. Bailey*," she said, emphasizing the name Barbara Jackson had used. "Concepcion called you, so that means you left your phone number with those people."

"Yep," Adam said.

"Why on earth would you do that?" She made no attempt to hide her irritation.

"It's my phone," Adam said. "I reckon I can give my number to anybody I want to."

"And then you led them straight to me."

"You woulda done the same thing," Adam said.

Trudy's irritation rose to the level of anger. "No! No, I would not have. I am not so thickheaded that I wouldn't know telling people that Marta is here could get me thrown in jail again!"

Hank shifted uneasily on the velvet sofa, but he didn't speak. Jasmine watched and listened with her eyes wide, moving back and forth from Trudy to Adam.

"You woulda done the same thing if you heard that little girl pleading to talk to her mama. You're not anywhere near as mean and hard-hearted as you try to make everybody think you are."

"What's mean and hard-hearted about trying to stay out of jail?" Trudy tried to keep her anger from boiling.

"You had Jasmine go get Marta so she could talk to Concepcion. You didn't have to do that, and it didn't do anything to help keep yourself out of jail."

"Still …" Trudy felt her lips tremble as she tried to continue.

"Besides that," Adam said before she could say more, "Mrs. Jackson told me that Concepcion had tried to run away once to find her mother."

Jasmine sat up straighter. "Cool!" she said.

Trudy sat down wearily in the chair across from her and said nothing. She was acutely aware of Adam looking at her, but she refused to meet his eyes.

"This isn't going to turn out good for any of us," Hank said.

There was a long gloomy silence that lasted for several minutes before the back door opened and Grace called out, "Hey! Where is everyone?"

"In the parlor, Mom," Jasmine answered.

Grace entered the parlor and looked around the room at each of them. "Did somebody die or something?" she asked.

Trudy stood up suddenly. "Is Marta still in the kitchen?"

"She's washing the coffee pot." Grace still wore a puzzled look on her face. "What's going on?"

"You're not going to believe this, but it's kinda good news," Jasmine said. "Concepcion called and—"

"I better get back to the office," Hank said, standing and giving Grace an accusatory look.

"No, you don't," Grace said. "You close the office at five o'clock every day. It's almost six now. I closed up for you."

"You stayed late," Hank said.

"Well, we got a phone call. I had to take down all of the information," Grace said. Her face was pale, and she had to lean against the banister to steady herself.

Hank frowned. "Phone call from who?"

"ICE. They say they believe there's an illegal alien somewhere in our area. A woman, they say."

It was less than half an hour before the phone rang, and Barbara Jackson reported that Connie had run away again, and that she was probably trying to get to Anton.

Chapter 22

"We have to get Marta out of here," Adam said.

"How?" Trudy asked. "We can't just take her someplace and leave her to fend for herself."

Adam didn't answer her. He was rubbing his hands together in a nervous gesture.

"If Concepcion , uh, tries to make her way here again, we can't move Marta until they're together," Jasmine said.

"We don't know where Concepcion is," Grace said.

"She's on her way here," Jasmine said. "She'll be here before dark."

"You don't know that," Adam said. His worried frown had deepened.

"Yes, I do know that. Bobby is bringing her."

Grace turned to her daughter. "Who?"

"Bobby Lightner, the same guy who brought me here when I was hitchhiking."

"How could that be?" Trudy looked suspicious.

"I called him," Jasmine said. "After I talked to Concepcion, I called him and told him what was going on. I told him where Concepcion is, and he's going to pick her up and bring her here."

"Why would he do that?" Trudy asked.

Jasmine shrugged. "'Cause he owes me a favor."

Grace suddenly sat up straighter. "What kind of a favor? What did you do for him?"

"I'll tell you later."

"You'll tell me now!" Grace said.

"I lied for him, to the cops."

Hank let out a whoosh of breath. "Oh my God!"

Grace stood up and looked down at Jasmine. Her expression was deadly. "Jasmine …"

"It was no big deal," Jasmine said. "He needed some help, so I helped him out."

"We are going upstairs, and you are going to tell me everything." Grace was having a difficult time keeping her voice from shaking.

Jasmine frowned. "What? Go upstairs?" Her frowned dissolved into a disgusted expression. "Oh, I get it. You think I did something like, immoral or something. For God's sake, Mom, is that what you think of me? I lied about his weed, that's all."

"His weed?" Now it was Grace who was frowning.

"Yeah, he had some in his glove compartment," Jasmine said. "When a cop stopped us for speeding, he found it. I convinced the cop it was mine, that's all."

"You lied to a cop?" Hank said.

Jasmine shrugged. "It was the least I could do."

"You shouldn't—" Hank began.

"Look, the guy needed help," Jasmine said, interrupting Hank. "If he got caught with even a fraction of an ounce—and that's all it was, less than half an ounce—he could get fired, so I told the cop I hid it in there. It was like, he kind of expected it to be mine anyway, so he took it, and I got by with a warning. No harm done, see?"

Hank breathed out a puff of air and rolled his eyes before he spoke. "So, you called him up and asked him to repay the favor and bring Concepcion here."

"Yeah. You catch on fast."

"Don't be impertinent," Grace said.

"I'm not," Jasmine said and smiled at Hank.

"So now I'm going to have a runaway staying with me." Trudy's voice was a mixture of anger and weary resignation.

Hank stood up. "Listen, I can't let this go. I have to—"

"No, you don't!" This time it was Grace who interrupted him. "You do not have to take her into custody. As soon as she arrives, we'll call Mrs. Jackson and let her know that Concepcion is here, safe with us. Then we'll go from there."

"Go from there? Hell, yes, we'll go from there. It's my duty to return her to her legal home."

"Not if she has permission to stay here, which I intend to get when we talk to Mrs. Jackson," Grace said.

"Way to go, Mom!"

"We? What do you mean we will talk to her?" Hank said.

"Come on, we'll call Mrs. Jackson now," Grace said as she headed for the telephone in the kitchen and motioned for Hank to follow her. "It will be a comfort to her to hear your voice and know you have things under control. Just tell her Concepcion is on her way here, and in case she's already called the cops in Lubbock, you can tell her you will take charge and notify them."

"I don't know how I ever did my job without you," Hank said.

The two of them barely had time to reach the telephone when it rang. Everyone in the parlor could hear Grace's voice when she answered with a brisk, "Hello," after the first ring.

"I hope that's not the Lubbock cops," Adam said.

"I would be grateful if it was," Trudy said. "I've had enough of—"

"You're being grumpy, Trudy," Jasmine said.

Adam snorted attempting to stifle his laugh. In the same moment, someone knocked on the front door, causing everyone in the parlor to look at each other with wide-eyed alarm.

Trudy got up from her chair and opened the door to Concepcion, looking frightened and with a tear-streaked face. Bobby stood directly behind her.

"Where is Mamá?" Concepcion asked as her eyes swept the room.

"In the kitchen," Trudy said. She'd hardly spoken the words when Marta appeared in the doorway to the dining hall. She spoke Concepcion's name and rushed toward her to take her in her arms. Concepcion responded by burying her face in Marta's shoulder and crying softly.

"Hey, thanks," Jasmine said and gave Bobby a fist bump.

"Listen, I know nothing about this," Bobby said.

"You got it," Jasmine said. Adam gave him a nod, and Trudy stood silently by the door, aware of all the eyes in the room on her.

Trudy looked away for a moment before she spoke. "Yeah, okay," she said finally.

"How about you?" Bobby asked, directing his gaze toward Hank. "You cool?"

"I…I got nothing on you at the moment," Hank said.

Bobby gave him a worried look before he said, "I gotta go."

"Can we pay you for your trouble?" Adam asked.

"Nah, don't need anything," Bobby said. "That poor kid told me her story about what her and her mama ran away from and all the trouble they been through, so, well, no decent human being wouldn't want to help." He turned and was all the way out the door before he turned back. "Say, listen, y'all, I heard on the radio that they got ICE out looking for an illegal immigrant in the area." He glanced toward Marta and Concepcion. "Y'all be careful, hear?"

Grace came back into the room. "I just talked to Mrs. Jackson," she said. "She'll be here in a few hours. She's greatly relieved."

"Had she called the police?" Hank asked.

"Yes, but she said she'd call them back. Everything's under control."

"Ha!" Trudy said.

"Mom is coming here?" Concepcion sounded alarmed. "She's going to take me back?"

"Over my dead body," Jasmine said.

Grace put a hand on her daughter's shoulder. "Leave this to the grown-ups."

Jasmine responded with an angry look before she turned to Concepcion who was speaking to Marta in Spanish. "You just told her what's going on, didn't you?"

"Yes," Concepcion said. "She's scared out of her mind, and so am I."

"Don't be," Grace said. "I'm sure we can work something out."

"Ha!" Trudy said again.

"You're being grumpy," Adam said.

The entire household, as well as Adam and Hank, were seated at the kitchen table while Trudy served everyone a supper of warmed-over pot roast when someone knocked on the door.

"Mrs. Jackson?" Grace said.

"Or ICE," Hank added.

His suggestion left everyone in stunned silence for a moment before Trudy pushed back from the table and started walking toward the front door.

"I'll go with you," Hank said.

"Stay there. I'll take care of this," Trudy said over her shoulder.

"Can I help you?" Trudy asked when she saw a well-dressed woman standing in front of her when she opened the door.

"I'm Connie's mother," the woman said, "Barbara Jackson."

"I see," Trudy said, resisting a momentary urge to tell her the girl's name was Concepcion and her mother was Marta. "Well," she added, "come in. Have a seat." She motioned toward the sofa. "I'll get Concepcion."

The woman smiled weakly and sat down on the edge of the seat to wait.

When Trudy returned to the kitchen, everyone around the table eyed her with either questioning or frightened looks. "It's Mrs. Jackson," Trudy said, looking at Concepcion. "She wants to see you." Trudy's gaze shifted to Marta, who sat stone-faced, showing no emotion.

Concepcion pushed away from the table and walked toward the parlor without a word or even a glance at her mother.

Barbara stood when Concepcion entered the parlor, but she made no move toward the girl she'd come to think of as her daughter. When Concepcion saw the tears in Barbara's eyes, she hurried toward her and embraced her.

"I'm so sorry, Mom."

Barbara responded by tightening her own embrace of Concepcion. "I was terribly worried," Barbara said. "And I'm so glad you're safe. I was imagining all sorts of things that could have—"

"Don't," Concepcion whispered. "I shouldn't have done it. Or at least, I should have told you I was going to. I just … I don't know; I'm confused or something …"

Barbara gently pushed Concepcion's hair away from her eyes. "Of course, you are. We all are."

"I didn't know Mama was … They told me she went back to Guatemala, and I …" Concepcion was unable to say more, and she tried to fight back the tears that threatened to pour from her eyes.

"I know. I know," Barbara said, pulling her close again. "None of this should have ever happened."

Concepcion pulled away from Barbara and turned her back to her so she wouldn't see that she was losing her battle with her tears.

"You must know, Connie, that I couldn't love you more if I'd given birth to you myself. And your daddy loves you, too."

Concepcion turned back to Barbara. She went to her and kissed her tenderly on the cheek. "I love you and Daddy too." Just as she spoke, she sensed Barbara stiffen and turned to see why she was staring at something behind Concepcion. She saw Marta in the doorway to the dining room. She didn't speak.

"Oh," Barbara said, "I …"

Before she could say more, Concepcion turned away and fled up the stairs. Barbara was about to follow her when a voice stopped her.

"Leave her be!"

Trudy was now standing next to Marta. Barbara sensed that Trudy had been somewhere just out of sight and that she had heard everything. Trudy's next words confirmed her suspicion.

"You heard her say she's confused. She needs time to figure this out. Come on back to the kitchen with me." Trudy took them by their arms and marched them back to the kitchen.

"What happened?" Jasmine asked as they entered. "Mom wouldn't let me go with you, Trudy, so you have to tell us ... Where's Concepcion?"

"She's upstairs," Trudy said. "She needs some time alone." Her words were hardly spoken when another knock at the front door once again startled everyone.

"ICE!" Hank said.

"Who?" Barbara asked.

"We have to get Marta out of here," Hank said. He turned to Jasmine. "Take her out through the back."

Barbara looked frightened. "What's going on? Why do you have to—"

"Go!" Hank commanded, but Jasmine was already on her way out with her arm around Marta. He turned to Barbara. "They'll send her back to Guatemala. May even try to send Concepcion with her."

"We have to get Concepcion down the back stairs!" Trudy called to Grace just as they all heard a louder, more frantic knock at the front.

"I'll take care of this," Hank said as he moved toward the parlor.

"No!" Trudy said. "This is my house. I'll take care of this."

"Who's there?" she called through the closed door as she reached the front.

"ICE, Agent Foster," the man said. "I hear you got a visitor."

"As a matter of fact, I have several. We were just sitting down to supper, but why is that any of your business?"

"I have a warrant for one of them," the ICE voice said.

"Show it to me."

"You have to open the door for me to do that."

"Slide it under the door," Trudy said.

Within a few seconds, a slip of paper slid under the door by Trudy's feet, and she heard a voice behind her. "Let me have a look at that." Hank reached for the slip. He examined it carefully before he handed it back to Trudy and spoke to her in a low voice. "It's a true warrant, signed by a court official. He wants Marta, and the warrant is to search you house."

"What do I do?" Trudy asked.

"We have to talk to him."

"Make sure Marta is out of the house," Trudy whispered.

"You know I can't do that." Hank looked troubled.

"Well, then you can talk to the bastard," Trudy said and hurried toward the kitchen.

"Trudy, come back here!" Hank called. "The guy has a warrant for Marta's arrest as well as to search your house."

Trudy turned around in time to see Hank open the door. There were two men standing there. Hank spoke to them through the screen." I'm Officer Richardson," Hank said. "Can I help you?"

"Officer Foster," the man standing in front, nearest the door, said with a note of sarcasm. "Local sheriff, I suppose." Without giving

Hank a chance to reply, he continued, "You saw the warrant. We're going to search the house."

"Do you want to start by searching downstairs?" Trudy asked, hoping Marta and Jasmine had time to slip out the back door.

"I'll take the upstairs. Nelson will search downstairs."

Trudy felt a void in her chest. Had there been time for Concepcion and Jasmine to leave? She glanced at Hank who responded with a blank expression. With a sigh, Trudy led the way to the dining room. Hank followed Agent Foster upstairs.

"There are four rooms down here: the dining room that we seldom use, the kitchen, an extension off of the kitchen, and my bedroom," Trudy said. "Oh, and the bathroom. Do you need to go?"

Agent Nelson looked embarrassed for a moment. "No, thank you," he said while a wicked smile played at Trudy's lips. He passed through the dining room slowly, bending to look under the table, trying to peek behind an old oak cabinet that still held the stoneware dishes Trudy's great-grandmother had used to feed her boarders and shining the beam of his flashlight into every crevice. "Who's in there?" he asked when he heard noises coming from the kitchen.

Trudy felt her heart trouncing against her chest. "My guests," she said. "We were eating supper until we got interrupted." She stepped into the kitchen with Nelson behind her. She glanced at the table first and saw that all of the plates except hers and Adam's had been cleared away. Marta and Concepcion were nowhere in sight. Neither were Jasmine, Grace, nor Barbara. Only Adam remained at the table eating slowly. He glanced at Nelson when he entered.

Nelson studied the table for several seconds. "Somebody else eating with you?" he asked and pointed to the two plates still half full of food.

"Hank and I were eating with the others until we got inter-rupted," Trudy said, hoping she sounded as grumpy as she'd been accused of earlier, but thankful that Adam had been so astute. "There's a little bit left if you're hungry," she added. "Probably cold by now with the fat kinda congealed around the edges, but you're welcome to it." She made a point not to look at the table as she spoke, lest her little twitch of a smile turn into a full-blown grin.

Nelson didn't respond but methodically searched the kitchen. Trudy held her breath, hoping Adam hadn't left Marta's and Grace's full plates in the sink. It was clear of dishes. Nelson continued his search, even opening cupboard doors and stepping all the way into the pantry.

"Bedroom's there," Trudy said, pointing to her room. She fol-lowed the agent as he went in to inspect, opening drawers and closet doors, even searching under the bed. She felt her chest tighten again when she thought of Hank leading the other agent, the one called Foster, around upstairs. He had such a compulsion for honesty that it worried her he might divulge something about the room Marta had been occupying. Still, she forced herself to keep up her charade of innocence. "Want to look in the cellar?" she asked when they returned to the kitchen. "Keys are on that hook there by the door."

Nelson moved to the door and lifted the keys from the hook. Trudy called to him again as he walked out the door. "Watch out for mouse traps. Got a problem with the little devils. I've been thinking of getting a cat."

Nelson didn't respond as he exited. Hank and Agent Foster entered just as he left.

"Who's staying in all those rooms up there?" Foster asked. "Three of them are occupied."

"My guests," Trudy said. "My niece and her daughter are visiting. They've gone to Lubbock to shop." Below them, they could hear Nelson shuffling around in the basement.

Nelson's hand went to grip the gun at his side. "What's that?"

"Just your partner," Trudy said. "Went down to search the basement." She glanced at Adam as if to ask if that was where Marta and Grace were hiding. Adam answered with a near-imperceptible shake of his head.

"All of you stay here," Foster said. He switched on his flashlight and went to the door. When he was gone, Hank gestured with a finger to his lips that no one was to speak. Everyone, including Trudy, obeyed, although Trudy wanted desperately to know where Marta and Grace and Jasmine and Concepcion had gone. She glanced at Adam and, with a nod of her head toward his house, raised her eyebrows as if to ask if they were there. Adam once again read her signal and responded with another slight nod of his head.

What was only a few minutes seemed like hours to Trudy before the two men reentered her back door.

"That little white house back there on your property?" Foster asked Trudy.

"No," Trudy said, hoping that, if she spoke only one word, her voice wouldn't tremble.

"That's my house," Adam said at the same time as Trudy's short answer.

"We want to have a look inside," Foster said.

"You got a warrant?" Adam asked.

"All you have to do, boy, is open the door. Won't take us long to look."

Trudy felt her breath catch in her throat at the word "boy." The room thrummed with tension emanating from Hank.

"All you have to do is show me a warrant, and I'll be glad to." Adam's voice was calm and his face expressionless.

Foster mumbled something incomprehensible before he turned to Nelson. "Come on; let's go." Looking at Adam, he said, "We'll be back, boy."

Trudy didn't move to see them out, and no one spoke until they all heard the front door open and close again.

When Adam started to stand, Hank cautioned him. "Stay where you are. They're probably out there waiting to see what you'll do."

"This going to cause you a heap of trouble, Hank," Adam said.

"Don't worry about it," Hank said, but the look on his face belied his remark.

When he left through the back door, Trudy watched him through the window. He walked all around Adam's house and up the alley, then back to the street that ran in front of Adam's house. Finally, he showed up at the back door with Grace and Jasmine.

"Where are the others? Trudy asked.

"Still in Adam's house," Grace said. "We thought it would be okay if we came back. They probably know we're you guests."

"Looks clear outside," Hank said as he entered. He glanced at Adam. "Go back to your house and see if everything's okay. I couldn't get in to see inside since the door was locked."

"They're okay," Jasmine said. "We told them to stay inside, and Mom and I would go see how things were going."

"I'll escort them back here, if you think it's safe, Hank," Adam said.

"I think it's okay for now," Hank said. "Those two will be back with a warrant for your place."

Once again everyone watched at the window as Adam went to his house and let himself in. It was only a few minutes before he reappeared. He was alone as he hurried toward Trudy's back door.

"They're gone!" he said. "Even Mrs. Jackson is gone."

"Gone? No, they can't be!" Grace said.

"We have to look for them," Jasmine said.

"No!" Hank held up his hand as a caution. "I'll look for them. The rest of you stay here."

"I'm going with you!" Grace said.

"No, you're not!"

Ignoring Hank's words, Grace followed him out and got into the car beside him while Trudy, Jasmine, and Adam stood silently for a few seconds in the kitchen.

"No point in any of us going to bed," Trudy said. "Turn on the TV. It'll help pass the time."

Adam started clearing the table and ran water in the sink to wash the dishes. Trudy and even Jasmine joined him. The task was finished too quickly, and they made their way to the sitting area off the kitchen. Jasmine turned on the television. Trudy found it hard to concentrate on the cop drama Jasmine had chosen. There was too much real-life drama going on all around her.

An hour later, Jasmine was sprawled on the sofa asleep, while Adam snored softly in the reclining chair. Trudy had long since switched off the television and alternated between trying to read a novel and walking to the parlor to see if Grace and Hank had returned. Trudy was thinking once again that this was not the quiet, uneventful life she had envisioned when she sold her Dallas home to live here.

She'd planned to move away from people and events. She would live in the old house she'd always loved with a garden to keep her busy in the spring and summer and books to occupy her mind in winter. Her plan to close all the bedrooms upstairs had also gone astray as well. Now four of the six rooms were occupied, since Jasmine had moved back to the room she'd originally occupied, claiming she needed her privacy and deciding to ignore the ghost across the hall. Five of the rooms were occupied if you counted the ghost Trudy had invented, and the sixth was crammed full of old furniture.

She was standing in the kitchen watching Adam's chest rise and fall as he slept in her chair and wondering where she had gone wrong when Hank and Grace came in the back door. Both were grim faced.

"You didn't find them," Trudy said.

"We found them," Hank said. "At least we found Marta and Concepcion. I don't know where Mrs. Jackson went. I told Marta and Concepcion to wait in the car until I made sure the coast is clear."

"You found them!" Jasmine sounded elated despite her sleep-hoarsened voice.

Adam got out of the recliner and was walking toward Trudy as she spoke. "You don't look too happy about finding them," she said. "What's wrong?"

"There's been another murder," Grace said, sounding choked.

"A murder?" Adam spoke as he reached Trudy's side.

"Who?" Trudy asked.

"Both of the ICE agents who were here." Grace sunk into one of the chairs around the table.

"Oh my Lord!" Adam said. Trudy found she couldn't speak, and even Jasmine was stunned into silence.

"But that's not all," Grace said, but she seemed unable to say more.

"What?" Trudy asked.

Grace still didn't speak. She glanced at Hank, as if begging him to answer for her.

"Border Patrol and ICE say the evidence points to Marta and her daughter," Hank said.

Chapter 23

"What are we going to do about all of this?" Grace asked to no one in particular when Marta and Concepcion were in their room upstairs. She, Jasmine, Hank, Trudy, and Adam were once again around the kitchen table with coffee cups and, in Jasmine's case, a can of Pepsi.

"We're not going to do anything until we talk to a lawyer," Trudy said.

"What lawyer?" Grace asked. "You said we couldn't afford one."

"Mr. Adelstone, the public defender," Trudy said. "The one who helped me before."

"You can't hire a public defender," Hank said. "He has to be assigned by the court."

"Then I'll get the court to assign him," Trudy said.

Hank shook his head. "Oh Trudy, you can't just tell the court what to do."

"Maybe I can't, but then again, maybe I can."

Jasmine gave Trudy a big smile. "Cool!"

While Hank and Grace exchanged knowing looks, Adam leaned forward and spoke. "ICE is bound to come back here looking for them. We need to get them out of the house again. How about we put them back in my house for now? They don't have a warrant to search my place yet."

"That doesn't mean they can't get one," Hank said.

"What else can we do?" Adam asked.

"I don't know. I guess it's worth a try. We'll just have to keep an eye out for them," Hank said. "We can hide 'em in your house for now, but we've got to think of something better."

"We've got to worry about Mrs. Jackson too," Grace said. "Will she be likely to turn them in?"

Trudy shook her head. "She wouldn't do anything that could harm Concepcion."

"Still, we ought to find her," Grace said. "I'm going to call her." She was already on her way to the telephone.

Trudy sighed, letting everyone know she was tired of all of it. "All right, you do that. Maybe she'll take both of them. What an unholy mess! I never wanted any of this."

"You're being crabby again," Jasmine said.

"None of us wanted this, Trudy." Adam's voice was scolding. "And if Concepcion doesn't want to go back with that woman, I'll take her in, and her mama with her. We're not going to just throw them to the wolves."

Trudy turned her back to everyone so no one could see how chastened she felt. She made her way to the stairs to bring Marta and Concepcion down. She didn't like the idea of leaving anyone for the wolves, but she hadn't let go of her dream of a quiet small-town life. Having four extra people in her house was not conducive to that. But

Adam had said he would take them in. Adam had a big heart. His house was small, however, barely big enough for one and certainly not big enough for three, while she had more space than she could ever use. She'd never felt more miserable in her life.

When Trudy knocked on the door to the room Marta and Concepcion shared, a frightened Concepcion came to the door.

"Come with me. Now!" Trudy said. "I have to get you out of the house. I don't want those people from ICE to find you here when they come back."

"I heard what they told Hank." Concepcion's voice was shaking. "They think we killed those people. We didn't do it. How could we?"

"Of course you didn't," Trudy said. "But that doesn't mean you can't be charged." She glanced at Marta who was seated on the bed. Her face was pale and her eyes wide with fear. "Come along now," Trudy said. "We have to get you out of here."

"Where are we going?" Concepcion asked.

"Adam's house again, for now at least." Trudy stepped all the way into the room and helped Marta to her feet and led her toward the door.

"Where's Mom?" Concepcion asked. "Mrs. Jackson, I mean."

"No one knows. Grace is trying to call her now," Trudy said. "Strange how she just disappeared. Everyone thought she was following Grace and Hank when they left."

Concepcion nodded, but she seemed unable to speak at first. "I'm afraid for her," she whispered.

"Be more afraid for Marta and yourself," Trudy said.

When they reached the kitchen, Trudy noticed that Hank was missing.

"Where's Hank?" she asked.

"Had to leave," Adam said. "Said he had to help find who killed those two men."

"I wish I could have gone with him," Jasmine said.

Adam reached out to Marta and Concepcion. "Come on," he said. "We're going back to my house." Just as he spoke, Grace put down the phone and walked toward the group.

"No one answers at Barbara's house," she said.

"Call Daddy's phone." Concepcion sounded frantic. "He's in the investment department at First National." She recited the number to Grace.

"Hurry! Come with me," Adam said.

"No," Grace said. "You stay here with Trudy. "Jasmine and I will go with Marta and Concepcion. They need us. No offense, Adam, but I think we will be more comfort to them than a man could be. You stay here with Trudy. I have a feeling she's going to need you."

Trudy growled something incomprehensible, but Adam nodded and stood out of the way so the four could leave.

"Door's not locked," he called to their backs as they left.

Trudy watched them leave. "That's just bullshit," she said. "I don't need anybody to stay with me. I can take care of myself."

"You got any of that pie left that we had for supper last night?" Adam asked, ignoring her tirade.

"On the counter. It's that dish that's covered with foil."

"Okay," Adam said. He opened a drawer and pulled out a knife to cut the pie, then pulled a plate from the cupboard.

"Well, help yourself to some pie, Mr. Bailey." Trudy made no attempt to hide the sarcasm in her voice.

"Why, thank you, Mrs. Walters," he said. He kept his back to Trudy so she couldn't see that he was chuckling. "Want a piece?"

Trudy's reply was a sharp "No. And I told you, I'm not Mrs. Walters. I'm Ms. Bailey."

"Worried about your figure?" Adam asked and slid a bite into his mouth.

"Why should I worry about my figure? You worried about it?"

"Can't say that I am," Adam said, cutting off another bite with the edge of his fork. He had not connected the morsel to his mouth when they both heard a knock at the front door.

"It's them," Trudy said. She didn't move from her chair.

Adam nodded and said nothing until there was another knock at the door. "I'll go," he said and stood up from the table.

"No. It won't look right. I have to do it." She started toward the front. Adam followed her, carrying his dish of pie. When they reached the parlor, Adam sat on the sofa and resumed eating his pie as Trudy approached the door.

"Who is it?" she called, just as she had before.

"ICE," came the answer. "We're going to search your house again."

"Why would you want to search my house?"

"We believe you may be hiding fugitives. We have another warrant."

"Slide it under the door," she said. How quickly she had learned the routine. When the paper appeared on the floor from beneath the door, she picked it up, examined it, and opened the door. This time it was a heavy-set man accompanied by a female with a blonde pony-tail protruding from the back of her blue ICE cap.

"What fugitive?"

"No need to play innocent," the young woman said. "You know who we're talking about."

"What's the name of this fugitive you're talking about?" Trudy said.

"Marta Ramondino," the chubby officer said.

"She's not here."

The woman glanced over Trudy's shoulder at Adam. "Who's that?"

"Name's Adam Bailey." His fork made a scraping sound as he cut off another bite of pie.

"You live here?" the woman asked.

Adam spoke around the morsel in his mouth. "Just visiting. I like the pie."

"Bailey," the woman said and turned to her partner. "Didn't know he was black, did you?"

Her partner shook his head and remained silent, but Trudy spoke up. "How does that make a difference?"

The woman ignored her question and spoke to Adam. "We have a warrant to search your premises too."

"Not until I see it," Adam said.

The woman stepped inside the house, followed by her partner.

"I didn't invite you in," Trudy said.

The woman's answer was a sharp, cutting sound. "Don't need an invite. We got a warrant." She walked to the sofa where Adam was seated and handed him the other warrant. "Not only do we believe the two of you are harboring an illegal alien, but you are harboring a murderer."

"Who are you accusing of murder?" Trudy sounded indignant.

"You know who," the woman said without looking at Trudy. "You've seen it on TV by now. That alien you've been harboring is accused of killing an ICE agent."

"No murderers in this house," Trudy said.

The woman spoke to her partner and ignored Trudy. "I'll take this house. You take the one in the back." She had already started for the stairs.

"Wait!" Trudy said. "You people sure like sniffing around my house, don't you? But you're right. Marta lives with me, and she couldn't have killed anybody yesterday. She was here with me all day, so she didn't murder anybody."

"Uh huh," the woman said on her way up the stairs. "That might be hard to prove."

"She was here, cleaning my house."

The woman turned around. "You hired an illegal alien. That's a criminal offense."

"I didn't hire her. She just cleaned it."

"Why would she do that?"

"Because it was dirty."

The woman made a scoffing sound and started up the stairs again.

"Don't trouble yourself," Adam called to her. "She's at my place with her daughter and some friends."

The woman stopped her climb and turned around slowly. With a confused look on her face, she glanced at her partner. Trudy felt unable to breathe as she turned her gaze to Adam. Before she could collect her thoughts enough to say anything at all, Adam was leading the agents out the door and, presumably, to his own door where he would turn Marta over to them. Her plan had been to stall them with double talk about Marta needing work. She'd make it up as she went. She felt too stunned to follow Adam now and could do nothing more than slump into one of the chairs next to the bricked-up fireplace.

Trudy had no sense of time or of how long the three of them had been gone when she heard a noise at her back door and, within a few seconds, heard footsteps she knew to be Adam's. He made his way to the parlor and sat down in the chair across from her on the opposite side of the fireplace. Trudy refused to look at him at first. They sat in an awkward silence for several minutes until Trudy said in a voice choked with anger, "They took her."

"Yes."

"Where's Concepcion?"

"With Grace and Jasmine. She's pretty upset."

Trudy was quiet and still filled with anger until finally she said, "You son of a bitch."

"Yeah, I know," Adam said, "but they were going to take her anyway. Maybe it will go easier for her this way. Grace is already on the phone trying to get hold of the ACLU."

Trudy didn't respond. She stood and walked away from Adam, going toward the kitchen.

"That was brave of you to lie for her," he said to her back, "to tell them she was with you when the murder happened."

Trudy paused for a few seconds with her back to Adam before she made her way to the kitchen.

Chapter 24

Adam didn't show up at Trudy's back door the next day or the next. Jasmine and Concepcion had become fast friends, it seemed, and they stayed upstairs together in one or the other's room. Trudy knew Concepcion also spent a good part of her time on her phone talking to the woman she called Mom. By overhearing half of the conversation, Trudy surmised that Barbara Jackson told Concecpion that she had left Adam's house to go home. She felt it was the best thing for both of them for the time being. Concepcion had refused to go with her. Trudy told herself she wouldn't eavesdrop, but she convinced herself that she did, after all, have to go upstairs occasionally to change the sheets or sweep the floors even if Concepcion and Jasmine had offered to do it for her. It was on those occasions that she heard Concepcion crying and telling Barbara she didn't know what to do, and yes she might be home soon, but she had to stay in Anton for now so she could learn Marta's fate from Hank and Grace.

Hank was often out of town working on the murder case, while Grace held down the office. She left early and came home late and tired, hardly taking time to eat before she went upstairs to bed when she wasn't on the telephone talking to the ACLU lawyer she wanted to take Marta's case.

Trudy didn't want to admit that she was lonely. After all, wasn't solitude what she came here for? She did see Adam working in his garden from time to time, and he always greeted her with a smile and a wave and an occasional "Good morning" or "Hot today, isn't it?" It occurred to her that she could invite him in for a glass of ice tea or bring one out to him with an invitation to join her in the chairs under the tree. She didn't do that, though. It still felt awkward and strained to be around him. She'd called him a son of a bitch, and that was what drove the wedge between them. Maybe she should apologize.

No, she told herself, he should be the one to apologize for sending Marta off to jail. He had offered to take Concepcion to see Marta, but Marta had sent word through Hank and an interpreter that she didn't want Concepcion anywhere near the jail.

The result was that Marta languished in the lockup, Concepcion cried herself to sleep every night, Adam worked in his garden, Hank was gone all the time, Grace worked all the time, and Trudy dragged herself through each day trying not to admit how lonely she was or how worried she was for Marta and Concepcion.

Trudy's personal hell lasted for almost two weeks until Grace came home early one evening, rushing through the back door and into the kitchen, crying, "Good news! It finally happened. Wait until you hear … Where's Concepcion? And Adam? They're both going to want to hear this." She hurried to the foot of the stairs and called up to the girls. "Jasmine, Concepcion. Get down here. I have news— good news!"

Back in the kitchen, Trudy pressed her for answers. "What good news? Tell me!"

"I want everyone to hear it. Wait until the girls come …" She turned quickly and went to the back door to open the screen and call out to Adam. "You've got to come in here, Adam. Hurry! I have something to tell you."

The girls came downstairs, Jasmine looking at her phone and Concepcion with red and swollen eyes, just as Adam entered still with a small garden spade in his gloved hand.

"She's free!" Grace said, her eyes dancing with excitement.

"Free? You mean Marta?" Trudy asked.

"Yes!" Grace said. "Well, not free actually, but she's not going to be charged with murder."

"Glory be!" Adam said while Concepcion grabbed the back of a chair to steady herself. Jasmine hurried to her mother and encircled her in a big hug.

"Explain." Trudy sounded calm, but she felt as if seltzer water was rushing through her veins.

"Hank found the killers. He's on his way with the Feds to take them to the federal lockup in Lubbock."

"Good Lord, Grace, don't make us drag the details out of you like that," Trudy said. "You said killers. How many? How did he catch them?"

"Okay," Grace said, collapsing into a chair and looking as if her excitement had been exhausted. "It's like this. The Feds were out doing their investigation, and they didn't want any interference from Hank because he's, you know, just a local sheriff, so he was on his way back to the office. That's when he noticed something out in the Yellow House Canyon. You know where that is?"

"Sure," Trudy said. "Just south of town. Little bit of green in this desolate stretch of Texas. People go there just to get a change of scenery."

"These two guys that Hank arrested got a change of scenery all right. They drove their car off one of those cliffs. Hank saw it down at the bottom and recognized it, an old Ford Falcon."

"I know the car!" Jasmine said. "Two guys in it driving crazy, like they were drunk."

Concepcion nodded. "They passed us on the highway when Mr. Hank was driving me and Mamá away. I remember he said he ought to go after them and arrest them, but he didn't want to take the time. He wanted to get us to safety."

"You actually saw them!" Grace said.

"They looked like foreigners, like me and Mamá." Concepcion's eyes shone with excitement. "The ICE officers must have been chasing them. We saw the officers' car speeding after them. Mr. Hank thought they were after us, so he drove off the road and parked behind an old barn. He left me and Mamá in the car, while he walked back to the highway to see what was going on. That's when Mamá got out of the car and made me get out with her so we could run away. Mamá said if we didn't go then, the ICE people would come back, and we would both go to jail. So, we got out and hid in another one of the old rundown buildings close to the old barn. Mr. Hank never found us because Mamá knowa how to hide. She's had plenty of practice."

"Well, I guess the ICE people caught up with the two guys. Turns out they were illegals, just like you and Marta," Grace said. "Apparently the two guys shot and killed the officers. Hank found the gun that fired the bullets in the car, along with the two guys who were pretty beat up. He had to take them to a hospital after he radioed the feds in Lubbock."

"That means Marta can get out of jail," Adam said.

Grace shook her head and glanced at Concepcion. "I don't know. They may keep her. They will claim she's illegal if we can't prove she was seeking amnesty."

Concepcion looked at the floor and said nothing. Jasmine put her arm around her.

Trudy stood and moved toward the phone. "I have to get her some help," Trudy said in a voice that sounded as if she was speaking to herself rather than those in the kitchen with her. Her back was to Adam so that she didn't see him nodding and smiling.

It had been three weeks since Hank had taken the two immigrants into custody. He had since learned that they were wanted in their native state of Chihuahua, Mexico, for a number of crimes ranging from attempted murder to drug offenses. They had confessed to the murders of the ICE agents and drug runners. Hank said they confessed in the hope of not being sent back to Mexico where they felt their fate would be worse than if they were convicted here. Marta was out on bail and allowed to stay in Anton while the slow wheels of justice turned to determine her fate.

Concepcion had spent the three weeks with her foster parents in Lubbock, but Barbara and Sam brought her back to Anton.

"She hardly eats at all, and I don't think she sleeps much," Barbara said to Grace and Trudy. "Everything has been so hard for her. I know she loves us, and we love her, but I can't bear to see her so unhappy. She cries and talks about Marta. We had to give in and bring her here. I feel so awful, like everything is my fault."

"It's not your fault," Grace said. Trudy watched as she put her arms around Barbara and then Sam. She stayed in the parlor talking to the Jacksons, while Concepcion sat with Marta on the glider under the trees in the back, clinging to each other.

It was several months later that Grace came home and once again announced that she had good news. This time she was accompanied by Hank who seemed unusually quiet.

"Look!" Grace said, thrusting her left hand forward. A small diamond sparkled on her finger."

"Mom!" Jasmine screeched. "Are you sure about this?"

"I couldn't be more certain," Grace said, smiling at Hank.

"It will be all right," Hank said, looking at Jasmine. "It will work out. We love each other."

"Love? Really?" Jasmine seemed unable to say more. She looked silently from Grace to Hank.

"Oh, I feel happy!" Marta exclaimed in English before she lapsed into Spanish. "*Ustedes dos están hechos el uno para el otro!*"

Concepcion smiled at her mother. "She says you are meant for each other." She turned to Jasmine. "I am happy for you too, Lobo. It means you will stay here, and we will go to school together."

Jasmine rolled her eyes. "Yeah, sure. But what about the Jacksons? Don't they want you back?"

Concepcion's expression turned somber. "I love them both, but I belong with Mamá. I will see them as much as I can. I'm going to school here in the fall. It'll be fun," she added. "Hey, you know that guy, the one we saw at the drug store, the cute tall dude?"

"Yeah?"

"He's the same age you are. He'll be in your class."

"Oh," Jasmine said.

"I think he likes you. Did you see the way he looked at you?"

"Well…" Jasmine left her response hanging and went toward Hank and her mother. "Congratulations." It came out sounding awkward. Nevertheless, Grace reached out and embraced her daughter.

Grace was still clinging to Jasmine when she spoke to Marta. "There's more news. I found a job for you. The lawyer said it could help speed your way to gain permanent residence. And just like I told you, he says you won't be considered an illegal if you seek amnesty." Concepcion translated the news to her mother.

"Good Lord," Adam said. "This is just too much to take in all at once."

"Don't even try," Trudy said. "Come on to the kitchen. I'll warm up some leftovers for supper."

"Leftovers?" Jasmine said, sounding disgusted. She followed along anyway.

"Grace is a good person," Trudy said to Adam later after they had all had supper. "The world needs more people like her."

Adam took a sip of tea and set his glass down. "You're a good person, too, Trudy."

She sent him a surprised look from across the table.

"You are," he said. "You've given all these people a place to stay. You contacted the lawyer for Marta. You even lied for her."

Trudy was not used to being complimented about her generosity. She was more accustomed to being labeled grumpy or crabby. Now she found she didn't know how to reply. Finally, she spoke. "Josephine told me that Hank lost his lease on that place he's living in on account of the owner moving in himself. I wonder if that means he'll move in here. I don't know where I'm going to put all these people. Grace has the room on the end. Jasmine has gone back to her old room. The third room has no bed, the fourth is still full of stuff I can't find a place to put, and the fifth room where Marta and Concepcion have been staying has sprung a leak, so I moved them to the sixth room. Can't get a contractor out here for two more weeks."

"I can put Marta and Concepcion up at my house," Adam said.

Trudy gave him a questioning look. "Where would you stay?"

Adam shrugged. "Guess I could sleep in the room that sprung a leak."

"No, you cannot!"

Adam shot her a look that said he was surprised at how forceful she was. "Why not?" he asked.

"Because the leak is worse than you think. I think the entire ceiling is about to collapse."

"Can't be that bad."

"It *is* that bad," she snapped at him.

Adam frowned, and neither of them spoke for several seconds. Finally, Trudy said, "You're a good man, Adam. No, you're a special man, a special kind of good."

Adam frowned again. "Something wrong with you, Trudy?"

"I'm sorry I called you a son of a bitch. You did the right thing for Marta. You always do the right thing."

Adam smiled and reached across the table for her hand. "There is definitely something wrong with you."

Trudy took a deep breath and let it out slowly. "Will you marry me, Adam?"

"What?" Adam looked as if he might fall out of his chair.

"I just proposed to you. Can't you give me the courtesy of giving me an answer?"

"You just proposed to me."

"Well, I'm not going to have a man living in my house with me unless I'm married to him."

Adam nodded. "Oh. Of course not. We can't have that." He was silent for a few seconds before he added, "You always said you wished you could be a Bailey again. You could have just gone to court and had your name changed, you know. Make it legal, instead of going to all this trouble."

Trudy squinted at him, considering what he'd just said. "Well, I'll swear I never thought of that." She shook her head, still considering it. "No, I'd rather do it the old-fashioned way." She waited a moment. "Well, are you going to accept my proposal or not?"

He stood up and walked around the table, pulled Trudy to her feet, and took her in his arms before he spoke. "I could never say no to you, Trudy. You know that."